How Can I Help?

First published 2020

Cover by Arcane Book Covers

Paperback ISBN 9798562341549

Queries and Feedback: howcanihelpnovel@gmail.com

To Elin and Nora,

The other two sides of the triangle.

Chapter 1

"Just to let you know," rasped a hoarse and possibly inebriated Scottish woman at the other end of the phone line, "John Lennon is not dead."

"He's not?" asked Justin through a yawn.

"No, he's not. He was never really assassinated. His demise was faked by the CIA, who took him for interrogation and research. They thought his pacifist beliefs could start a war. They also wanted to know if his songwriting ability was the result of alien abduction and experimentation. However, as they were flying him to a secret location, he jumped out of the helicopter somewhere over the Pacific, and after surviving the fall, he was swallowed by a giant tuna fish."

Justin snapped to full attention at this unexpected turn of events. "Really?"

"Really. And after several years, the giant tuna fish, through the natural flow of the ocean's currents, made its way to Fiji, where a master angler finally brought it to shore after a three day battle of wills. John Lennon was then regurgitated and after a period of hibernation, settled on Ono-i-Lau, where he has been working ever since as a designer of grass skirts."

"His music days are over, then?"

"Yes, he sees a much better future in the grass skirt industry. Anyway, you'll pass that along for me then? Thanks now."

The line went silent and the countdown started. Justin had ninety seconds to summarise and categorise the call before the line cleared and the next one came in. He didn't need that long to sum

1

up Miss Peal's latest episode of craziness. She was a regular caller and always insisted that the information she provided was passed on, but she never specified to where or whom. He had no idea why she called this number or who she thought she was speaking to, but her madness was an oasis in the desert of shitty calls. 'Inappropriate call' and 'No action required' would cover that one. Seventy-seven seconds left.

He let the time tick down and looked around the room. It was a dreary sight he'd seen hundreds of times. There were dozens of cubicles, many still empty and some others occupied by people in headsets swallowing their pride and getting on with their jobs. Next to him, Chip and Tanya were both taking calls. All along the walls were posters of supposed motivational advice to those who worked in the call centre, such as 'Be Positive', 'Listen Respectfully' and his personal favourite, 'Talk With A Smile In Your Voice'. He wondered what this was supposed to mean, exactly. He had discussed it many times with Chip during the quiet hours of the day, but they had yet to reach a satisfactory conclusion.

On the wall at one end of the room was a big electronic board with the number of calls in the queue and how long the callers were having to wait. Justin wasn't sure exactly whose benefit this was for; he didn't give a shit how long they had to wait. The team leaders had the same statistics on their computers, so if they needed the phone monkeys to speed up their calls, they could just tell them. It seemed so pointless. Fourteen callers were waiting an average of two minutes and forty-one seconds. It was busy this morning, more so than normal, and it had barely gone eight o'clock.

Usually at this time on a Monday morning, the team would be drinking coffee and having a briefing. This was supposed to be a chance to talk about any issues that had arisen and what was expected to drive the calls in the coming days, but that generally took a couple of minutes, and then they would spend the next fifteen minutes discussing what they'd done over the weekend. But there was a new team leader coming in for training today and in order to set a good example, the usual team leader Linda had asked them to be on the phones at eight o'clock sharp. No one minded though; she'd let them have an extra smoke break later to make up for starting when they were supposed to.

Click. Justin's ninety seconds were up and another call came in. "Tech support. How can I help?"

"Hello, young man. Before we start, may I just ask where you're based?" said a posh, middle-aged man.

"May I ask why? We're not supposed to give out personal information."

"I'm not asking for personal information, I just want to know where your call centre is."

"It's in Nottingham."

"Nottingham, England?"

"Yes."

"Jolly good. I often call one of these numbers and end up speaking to someone in India. Now, I'm not a racist but I can't understand those people and they can't understand me. Much better to talk to a real Englishman."

"What can I help you with today?" asked Justin.

"Ah yes, well, my phone isn't working."

"What exactly is wrong with it?"

"The screen is frozen and nothing happens when I touch it. I can still receive calls but I can't make any or do anything else. I'm calling you from the office now."

"Has this happened before?"

"Yes, it has. Twice."

"And did you call tech support for help then too?"

"Yes, but I got through to India, so I hung up again. I just let the battery die, then I recharged the phone and it was fine."

"Can you open the phone and take out the battery now, please?"

"Yes, I'm just doing that now. It's done, now what?"

"Leave it for about ten seconds then put the battery back in again."

"Certainly."

"Turn the phone on and wait for it to boot up."

"Yes, that's done. It seems to be working. Yes, yes, that's it.

It's working perfectly. Great job, young man."

"For future reference, this should be the first thing you try any time there's a problem with your phone. Taking out the battery, or like you did before, draining it, reboots the phone and solves seventy percent of problems."

"Really? Well, thank you very much. That is magnificent service. Not only have you solved the problem, but you've given me some insider advice too. Excellent. That's the English touch, you see. I'm sure the Indians wouldn't have given me customer service like that."

"I'm sure they would. We all get the same training, no matter where we're based."

"Well, training is training, but it's the rapport, the personal touch you get from a true Brit that makes all the difference."

"Is there anything else?"

"No, that's great, thanks."

"Okay, bye then."

Although Justin had only taken two calls, he felt drained already and his belly had started to rumble. He was beginning to regret trading breakfast for an extra ten minutes in bed. Monday mornings were always a struggle and this one felt worse than normal. He was mentally tired as well as physically. The thought of forty-five hours of this shit in the coming week filled him with dread. Then Jolene arrived.

It was ten past eight, a little late even by her standards. Justin finished the wrap-up notes on his previous call in time to watch her walk in. He loved seeing her for the first time each day. Apart from finishing time, it was his favourite part of the shift. Her hair was tied back, but he knew it would only stay in place until she took her first difficult call. She took off her coat and Justin saw she was wearing her Coldplay t-shirt again. Shame. Still, she had a pair of tight jeans on that hugged her arse. At least she'd be sitting so he couldn't stare too much. When she wore a skirt, he spent the whole shift sneaking glances at her legs and couldn't concentrate on his conversations with Chip.

She gave him a little smile as she sat down and started up her computer. Like the others, she looked tired. Her eyes were only half open.

Linda turned to the team and motioned for them to wrap up the calls they were on. Justin was relieved. His countdown had four seconds left and he was grateful to hit the 'Not Ready' button while he sat watching Jolene and waited for the others to finish up.

Chip hung up and turned around. He nodded at Justin, who nodded back. They'd get a chance for a chat in a little while. Justin loved Chip. He was intelligent and witty and liked to talk about jam.

"We're still waiting for Tanya to finish," said Linda. "We've got a few things to get through today."

Tanya heard this and wrapped up her call quickly. She was a conscientious worker and didn't want the team to lose work time waiting for her. Everyone else really wanted to lose work time waiting for her, but it never seemed to happen. Justin shook his head as she hung up. Chip tutted loudly.

"Chip?" asked Linda. He shrugged. "Okay," she continued, "first up, as you know, I have only two weeks left and you'll be getting a new team leader." She looked at her watch. "I was expecting him at eight sharp, so I wanted you to be on the phones when he arrived, but he hasn't turned up yet and we need to get on with this briefing. I'll introduce him when he gets here, but have any of you heard who it is?" Tanya nodded, but didn't say anything. She looked miserable. More miserable than usual anyway. The others shook their heads.

"Well, it's Jim Jefferson. He's coming over from the Robin Hood team. I'm sure you all know him, or of him, at least."

"Who's Jim Jefferson?" asked Jolene. "I don't know him."

"You might know him better as Ford," said Linda.

"Ford? *Ford* is our new team leader? Oh my God."

"Give him a chance. I'm sure he'll work out fine. Management seem very impressed with him, so just see how it goes. In fact, here he comes now."

Justin looked at the man walking, almost strutting, from the manager's office onto the main call floor and towards their team section. He was wearing, not quite a suit, but an assortment of clothing that would generally make up a suit. The grey trousers were about an inch too short and although his socks were both black, they weren't exactly a match. One was plain black and the other looked as if it had a pigeon, or some other type of diseased bird, on it. His jacket may once have been black and his tie was bright blue against a white shirt. For someone who usually wore ripped jeans and a Nottingham Forest top to work, this was a definite step up.

"Guys, I'd like to introduce you to Jim," Linda said as he arrived and sat down. "He'll be your new team leader when I leave. He's going to be shadowing me for the next couple of weeks to get him up to speed, so if you could all be patient with him and help him out, that would be great. I'll introduce you all first, then Jim will probably want to say a few words."

"These are the boys, Justin and Chip." They both gave a little nod. "And the girls, Jolene and Tanya." Justin noticed Ford's eyes light up as they lingered a little too long on Jolene. He disliked this Ford already.

"Okay, well, as Linda said, I'm Jim, but everyone calls me Ford, so you can too."

"Why?" asked Chip.

"Why what?"

"Why does everyone call you Ford?"

"Well... Chip, if that is your real name, that's a story for another time. There's work to be done now. I'd just like to say that I'm looking forward to working with you all, I'm sure we'll make a great team. It's a real honour for me personally to have been trusted with the position of team leader and I'll do everything in my power to live up to that responsibility. But I'm just the captain of the ship and you are my crew. We are a team now and if we all pull together, we'll move in the same direction. Remember, there's no 'i' in team." No, but there's a 'twat' in piss-taking twat, thought Justin. "I'll be working closely with Linda during the handover," continued Ford, "so I'll trust you to get on with things in the meantime. We'll have plenty of time to get to know each other better in the days to come. So, I'll hand you back to Linda now. Thank you."

He remained standing for a moment and looked at his new

team expectantly before sitting down again quickly. "Er, Linda, are you doing the briefing?" he asked. She nodded.

These briefings usually lasted about fifteen minutes and could be stretched out for up to half an hour, but with Ford here, Justin was worried that it would be, in fact, brief. With Linda seemingly intent on showing Ford how a team leader was supposed to do their job, it had all the makings of a very long day.

Linda handed a sheet of paper to everyone. This held information on technical issues and other problems that had arisen recently and the appropriate responses to give to the callers. More often than not, these were out-and-out lies.

"There shouldn't be too much to worry about today," said Linda. "Although it does seem to be quite busy this morning, so I don't know if there are any issues that have come up unexpectedly. If you look at the briefing sheet, you'll see that there's a new software update due to be rolled out later in the week. Maybe they're testing it early and that's why it's busy this morning, but if they are, no one has told me. You know what it's like, if there's a technical issue, tech support is always the last to know."

"The guy that I just spoke to had some sort of operating system glitch," said Tanya. "Maybe it was something to do with this?"

"Could be. Let me know if you get any more calls like that. Next up, there's a new policy on repairs and replacements. If a customer has a damaged handset, you have to ask them if they did it themselves. Except you can't actually ask them."

"What?" asked Chip.

"You can't ask them straight out if they damaged their phone, because that implies blame. You have to say things like 'has the phone been dropped recently?' or 'has the phone been in contact with water?'"

"Has the phone been baked in a cherry pie?" said Chip.

"Has the device been inserted into a rectal passage?" said Justin.

"Has the..."

"Guys, that's enough," said Linda. Her eyes darted to Ford, who looked on impassively. "Now, we'll still fix or replace the phone if it's within its warranty period, but there's been a lot of returns lately and management wants to see if there's a problem with the manufacturing or if the customers are breaking the phones themselves. Of course, most of them will probably lie about it, but you have to ask them anyway."

"Okay, is there anything else we need to know about?" asked Tanya.

"Not just now. I'll let you know if anything else comes up. Time to get back on the phones."

Ford stood up. "Good luck with the calls today. Like Linda said, there are no major issues that should give you any problems, but you never know what the day can bring. And, er, Jolene, just before you start, I'd like a quick word." He took her to one side and handed her a piece of paper. "I'd like you to fill this in please."

"What is it?" asked Jolene.

"It's a late form."

"A what? Do we have those?"

"Yes, we do. I was sitting in the office and saw you come in at eleven minutes past eight and you were supposed to start at eight."

"Isn't that just like, a guideline?"

"It's no guideline. You were late, you'll have to fill in one of these forms. Two more and that's an official warning."

Jolene had been working here for almost two years and she'd only ever been on time in the first few weeks, and *now* she was getting a late form? And from *Ford*? Linda shrugged and smiled apologetically at her. The others were getting ready to take calls, but were watching from the corners of their eyes and listening intently. Justin shook his head and snorted, then put on his headset.

Click. "How can I help?"

Chapter 2

The first hour had flown in and now some of the nine o'clock starts were shuffling in like zombies. The queue was down to four, waiting an average of thirty-three seconds. It was time for a smoke break. Justin finished helping a caller download a paranormal activity tracker app and looked around. Linda had gone into the office and Ford was nowhere to be seen. He'd probably gone with her. The timing was perfect. He didn't want to have to explain himself to Ford, and wasn't particularly keen to smoke with him either. He turned to Chip.

Chip knew that look well, they'd rehearsed it many times and both had a sixth sense that flared up when there were no supervisors in the room. He motioned to Justin that he'd finish up his call.

"I'm afraid I'm going to have to leave it there, sir. Your point has been well noted and I'll pass it on to the phone's designers," said Chip. "Goodbye, sir."

Click. Shit. Just as Chip finished up his call, Justin's countdown had expired and another call came through.

"Tech support."

"Hello tech support. I'm afraid I have a bit of a problem charging my phone."

"Take out the battery, leave it for ten seconds, put it back in and restart the phone. Call back if that doesn't work."

"But, the phone's working fine, it's that charger that's..."

"Try the battery thing first. We need to know that the battery's working before we proceed."

"But..."

Justin hung up and pulled his headset off, took a quick glance around and pressed the 'Personal Time' button. This was intended for toilet breaks and for cooling down after a particularly tough call. It had to be used sparingly to avoid raising any flags with management, but Linda usually didn't care as long as they didn't go over fifteen minutes a day. He got up and headed for the door with Chip following closely behind.

"So, how's it going then? Busy this morning," said Chip as soon as they were out the door.

"Yeah, I haven't even had a coffee yet. Strange morning. And Ford..."

"I know, I thought Tanya was a sure thing for the job. She's practically been doing it these last few months since Linda mentally checked out."

"Like she'd be any better. Fucking jobsworth."

Chip opened the back door to his and Justin's secret smoking place. It was a small space underneath the fire escape and no one ever went there, as it was on the other side of the building from the official smoking area. Nevertheless, he took a quick glance around to satisfy himself and waved to Justin that the coast was clear.

"All right, lads?" someone said as soon as they set foot around the corner. It was Ford. Where the fuck did he come from?

"Er, yeah," stammered Chip. "Just having a quick puff."

"I didn't realise it was break time already," said Ford.

"No, we're er... just..."

"Just having a crafty one, eh?"

"No, er..."

"Don't worry mate, I'm having a sneaky one myself. Of course, I don't have calls to take anymore, but never mind. It'll be good to have a chat away from the office for a few minutes, a bit less formal."

Justin lit up his cigarette and stood back, happy to let Chip do the talking.

"So," began Ford, "I've never worked with you lads before, but I've seen you on the call floor."

"Yeah, and we've heard you," said Justin under his breath.

No one in the call centre could have failed to hear Ford on some of his calls. He practically screamed at the callers when he didn't like what they were saying. Now this twat would be their team leader?

"What was that?"

"Oh, nothing, just we've seen you too, on the other side of the room."

"Well, we'll be on the same side of the room from now on. I'll be taking over formally in a couple of weeks, after the training and all. It's quite a small team, right?"

"Yeah," said Chip. "There's six of us call agents, but Nicola's on holiday for a few weeks and Alex is off on the sick. Depression. So, it's just four of us plus Linda at the moment. And you too now, I suppose."

"Tight team, is it?"

"Yeah, we get on well."

"Anything I should know about? Neither of you is shagging that Jolene, are you? She's fucking gorgeous. I tell you, if I was with her, that girl would get cocked more times than Davy Crockett's rifle."

Justin went bright red and nearly choked on a mouthful of smoke. He knew he wasn't the only guy to fancy the hottest girl in the call centre, but he wasn't expecting this level of fowardness.

"You okay there, Justin?" asked Ford.

"Yeah, just took some smoke down the wrong tube. I'm fine."

"Good, you need to take care of your throat, you've still got a lot more calls to take today. So, Jolene, then. Neither of you two is doing her. Do you know if she's seeing anyone?"

"Why don't you ask her yourself?" said Chip.

"I might just do that. Should probably give her a bit of the old Ford charm first though, eh? Anyway lads, I'm going to pop back in. We'll talk a bit more later, maybe at lunch time. Remember though, if there's anything you need, just ask. I'm new as team leader, but don't forget I've been a call agent myself." He stubbed out his cigarette and walked to the door, then turned around. "Don't be too long, there are calls in the queue."

Chip held up both thumbs and nodded.

"Fucking twat," said Justin.

"Yeah, he is, but he's your boss now."

"He's not my boss, he's a supervisor in a call centre."

"He's still your boss."

"He's nothing to me."

#

"I'd like to make a complaint," said a voice Justin recognised instantly. It was the dreaded Mr. Abbott. His first call back after his smoke break and it was Abbott. He really didn't need this shit. What had he done to deserve this?

"What would you like to complain about, Mr. Abbott?"

"How do you know who this is? I didn't tell you my name. You're tracking my number aren't you? How dare you!"

"I just recognise your voice, I've spoken to you before," said Justin. "Many times." They were also tracking his number, but he didn't mention this. The callers' numbers flashed up on the screen whenever a call came in, along with their name if they'd given it previously. Justin cursed himself for not checking this, but he hadn't been paying attention. It might not have made any difference though, Abbott was clever. He changed his number often in an effort to avoid getting flagged. Certain persistent callers were monitored by management and anyone who was designated as a nuisance had their number flagged. This didn't mean much; they still had to be treated with the same courtesy as every other caller, but it acted like an advance warning system and let the agent know that the customer had a colourful call history. Abbott was most certainly a nuisance caller. Often, Justin would hang up immediately when he saw a call like this coming through and pretend the line had dropped, but now he'd have to just get on with it.

"Oh, well, that's all right then. Who is this?"

"It's Justin."

"Justin? Ah, yes, we have indeed spoken before. That's good. You understand, don't you? You understand why I have to keep calling to complain about the problems with your phones.

Someone has to hold these corporate beasts to account. You're not a company apologist, are you?"

"I wouldn't say that, but if you're not happy with our devices, other brands are available."

"Please. The others are even worse. Your software might be terrible, but at least I get good battery life."

"Talking about batteries, have you tried taking yours out for ten seconds? That might solve the problem."

"I never told you what the problem is."

"No, but taking out the battery can fix up to seventy percent of problems before you even need to call us. Anyway, what is the issue this time?"

"Last evening, I downloaded a fuel efficiency app to my phone, which started to glitch immediately afterwards. A small flicker along the top of the screen. I intended to call directly, but I was so incandescent with fury that it took my wife several hours to calm me down. I had to have two glasses of brandy and milk before I could even sleep."

"Brandy and...?"

"Brandy and milk. Wonderful for the nerves. Warm, preferably. The milk, that is, not the brandy. My wife heated it up for me whilst I was doing my breathing exercises in the den. I digress, shall we get back to the matter at hand?"

"Please do," said Justin, bemused. What the fuck was a den? Somewhere that animals live?

"As I was saying, the poor technology in this phone caused the app to glitch straight away. What do you have to say about that?"

Justin flicked through the papers on his desk, looking for last week's briefing sheet. He remembered ignoring something about this app while he and Chip discussed the physics of using an umbrella as a parachute like in the old cartoons. It would never work, they'd concluded with tangible disappointment. He found the paper and quickly read through it while Abbott continued to rant.

"The official line here," Justin said, "is that this app is not sanctioned or supported by our company, so we can't be held responsible for any glitches it causes to your phone." Of all the apps in the world, the one that causes the phone to play up had to be downloaded by this fucker. "To ensure that your device works as intended, you'll need to remove the app."

"I'll do no such thing! I've been looking for an accurate fuel price tracker app for many months, Justin, and now that I've found one, I will most certainly not be removing it."

"But it's the app that causes the glitch."

"And it's your technology. I paid a lot of money for this phone and I expect technical support to be able to deal with my issues. If you can't resolve this and the phone doesn't work properly, I shall be demanding compensation." So this was what the bastard had been angling after all along.

"Mr. Abbott, I'm sure we've told you before that we can't give compensation. We're tech support for the device itself. We don't deal with any form of monetary issues. Any compensation that may be due needs to be taken up with the phone company that provides your network service."

"So you're admitting that compensation is due, then?"

"I didn't say that."

"No, but my phone company did. I have already spoken to them, and they told me that the glitch was caused by the technical side, so it's you who need to compensate me for my trouble."

"We can't do that."

"You can. You've done it before. Why, just last week, I received a twenty pound voucher that can be applied towards a new phone or any accessories made by your company." Shit. Was he bluffing? Most people in the call centre knew better than to give him even the time of day, but what if one of the new starts didn't know? Or worse, someone who was on the way out decided to leave a proverbial floater? Fuck. If someone had actually given him a voucher for something, they'd never hear the end of it. He'd be pulling the precedence card until the end of religion.

"Well, that's not our usual policy and, as I mentioned, the problem is with the app and not the phone, so I won't be able to help you this time, Mr. Abbott."

"I am not having this at all. I want to speak to your supervisor on this matter. Right now, if you please."

"My supervisor wouldn't be able to help you either, she'll just tell you the same thing I've told you." This was often the way with this type of call. The supervisor would tell the caller exactly the same thing as they'd just been told. For this reason, the agents were discouraged from escalating calls. Either that, or the supervisors just couldn't be arsed dealing with them.

"Supervisor. Now."

Justin rolled his eyes and put Abbott on hold. He turned to Linda, who was hunched over her computer browsing an online shoe store. She seemed to be having difficulty deciding what to buy. Justin knew from experience that she was never sure about ordering shoes online in case the size wasn't right or they looked different in reality. Returns were a nightmare, apparently.

"Linda, I have a caller here who would like a word with you."

"Who is it?" she asked.

"A certain Mr. Abbott."

"No way am I speaking to him," she said. "Just fob him off, tell him I'm not available or something."

"He'll wait. He always does."

"Let him wait."

Justin was happy enough to do that and let Abbott stay on hold for a while.

"Actually, Justin," Linda said after a few minutes, "I'm not the only supervisor you have now." She smiled and her eyes moved towards the man at the next desk.

"Ford? Are you busy?" Justin asked.

"I'm always busy, but I can spare a moment for my new team members."

"I have a caller here who is demanding to speak to my supervisor. I suppose that's you now, and you'll probably have to take quite a few of these calls, so it might be good for you to get the first one out of the way. Should I put him through to you?"

"I don't know, I haven't had any training in taking escalated calls yet."

"Yeah, I know, sorry. It's just that Linda's really busy at the moment."

"Well, I've only been here for an hour!"

"Yeah, but you're good at dealing with awkward callers, right?"

"Right. Okay, I'll take it, I suppose. What's it about?"

"That app glitch thing from last week."

"Did you give him the official answer from the briefing sheet?"

"Yeah, but he won't accept that. He doesn't want to remove the app and he thinks we should take care of it for him."

"What's his name?"

"Erm, I didn't get his name, sorry."

"Okay then, pass him through. Extension 155."

Justin pressed the transfer button and fought hard to keep from grinning as he did so. Ford had worked here for quite a long time and was no doubt familiar with Mr. Abbott. This could be fun. It could turn nasty. He pressed 'Not Ready' and sat back to enjoy the fireworks.

"Hello, sir. My name is James and I'm Justin's supervisor. You'll be dealing directly with me now. I believe you're having trouble with an app."

Ford was quiet for the next few minutes as Abbott ranted at him. Justin could hear him shouting, but couldn't make out exactly what he was saying. Ford was silently mouthing an impressive string of swear words, shaking his head and wringing his hands. He was clearly suffering and desperate to unload.

"Please listen, sir," he said eventually. "You've already been told that the problem is with the app and not with the phone. We do not endorse this app and if you remove it, the phone will function normally again. Sir... Sir."

Ford was silent again for a time, but now his voice was rising and he was visibly starting to lose his temper. "Listen to me, Mr. Abbott. I've done all I can for you. I can't say it any clearer. Remove the app. There will be no compensation because this is not our fault. That's my final word on the matter. Good day."

He hung up, ripped his headset off and glared at Justin.

That was fucking stupid, thought Justin. He'd played his hand too early. He would have to be very careful from now on in escalating this type of call. If Ford suspected he was deliberately not dealing with customers properly so he could pass on difficult or annoying calls, there would be retribution, he had no doubt of that. He could see it in Ford's eyes, already plotting revenge across the partition. Justin had been comfortable, perhaps too comfortable, with the status quo for a long time and now there was a new faction, new politics. Or maybe he was giving Ford too much credit; maybe he was just the irresponsible piss-head he'd heard about. He looked over at Ford again, who nodded at him and gave a crafty smile. No, that bastard was out to get him.

"Justin," said Ford.

"Yeah?"

"You're not taking any calls and there are a few in the queue. I can see you're sitting on 'Not Ready'. Why?"

"Er, because I'm... not ready?"

"Well, hurry it up."

He had forgotten to make himself available again. This was a schoolboy error. He was normally a master of the 'Not Ready' button, coordinating it skilfully with the call wrap-up countdown to ensure he was available for the least possible amount of time per day without arousing suspicion. He had genuinely forgotten to press it. Ford was watching him and he had played right into his hands, and so soon. He cursed himself silently.

He was already pissed off with Ford for giving Jolene a late form and now he'd handed him a loaded gun. And they weren't even two hours into the day yet. Justin still couldn't wrap his head around the fact that Ford had been promoted to team leader. His reputation preceded him. He was rude and impatient with the callers, often argued with management and prior to this morning, hadn't been seen or heard from in over a week. Justin wasn't the only one to think this; the others seemed baffled too. No one was quite sure how he'd got the job.

Chapter 3

Ford wasn't quite sure how he'd got the job. He'd filled in the application form in the pub after a few pints and a spliff. It had been a bit of a joke, really, something to do while he was drinking. He had been moderately drunk at the interview too. In fact, he'd been drunk for the last week, had turned off his phone and not turned up to work at all. He had been trying to get sacked; he couldn't claim benefits for months if he simply left a job, that was out of the question. When he finally switched his phone on again on Friday, it was no surprise that he had several missed calls from Phil, the big boss of the call centre. What was surprising, shocking even, was that Phil was calling to offer him the promotion. After profuse apologies about being so ill he couldn't even get out of bed, never mind call in sick, he promised to be back at work on Monday to take up his new position. He definitely didn't want to get sacked anymore. No, this would do nicely. No more taking calls, a significant salary increase and all the stationary products he could steal.

But now he was team leader and things would have to change. That would happen in two ways. First, he would be firm. He'd already given Jolene a late form, though he'd been somewhat reluctant to do this. His own punctuality record was patchy to say the least and Jolene was hotter than Satan's arsehole after a vindaloo, but he felt it was important to stamp his authority early on.

The second way things were going to change was that from now on, he was only going to bring half a bottle of vodka to work. Well, he'd start that from tomorrow.

18

Ford looked across at his new team, trying to size them up. They were all busy on calls and not looking in his direction at all. They hadn't seemed overly impressed with his introduction speech, despite it coming across exactly as he'd practised. Maybe he'd laid it on a bit thick? No, it was a good speech and he felt it was a little rude that they hadn't given him a round of applause.

Then there was that fucking Justin. He'd have to keep his eye on him. He'd deliberately escalated that call to an inexperienced team leader and pretended he didn't get the man's name. Little bastard. So, that was how it worked in the Brian Clough team, eh? Now that he was warned, Ford was determined not to be caught out again. Thank God it was only Abbott and was easily brushed off. If that had been a legitimate caller with a proper complaint, it could have been a lot worse, untrained as he was.

He had expected to at least have proper training before he started to take escalated calls, but they'd thrown him in at the deep end straight away! Apparently Linda was too busy to take the call, but she didn't seem busy to him. She hadn't been much use with the training at all so far. All she had shown him was how to access call waiting statistics on the computer and those were displayed on the board on the wall anyway.

He'd always loved that display board, as previously, it had served as a perfect skiving guide. Too many calls in the queue and he would stretch each one out as long as possible before spending the full ninety seconds on wrap-up. Few or no calls and it was smoke or drink break. He was reasonably sure he wasn't the only one who had figured this out, so he'd probably ask management to take it down now that he was off the phones.

He looked over at Linda again. She still didn't seem busy but did look a bit stressed out over something. He decided not to bother her. He could do with a break anyway. They had two weeks for training and anything he didn't pick up in that time, he could just wing. He looked down the call floor to where his old team was based. Most of them were there, but his mate Vik hadn't turned up yet. That was a shame, he'd have to pop out on his own and would have no one to tell what he got up to over the weekend. He briefly considered asking Chip, but then decided it was a bit too soon for that.

#

Tanya was fuming and trying to avoid looking anywhere near Ford. That was supposed to be her job. She'd spent two and a half years keeping her nose clean and grinding away day after day waiting for a team leader job to become available and when it finally does they give it to *Ford*? She had already been learning the ropes from Linda and covering for her whenever she took time off. There was no justice. She'd been told on Friday that she hadn't got the job. Management had decided to 'go in a different direction' and the position had gone to Ford because they were impressed with his ability for 'independent thinking'. From what she'd heard of him, it was alcohol and his penis that did his thinking for him, usually in cahoots.

She watched him disappear for the second time already today and shook her head in disgust. If she'd got the job, she would have been so busy she wouldn't have taken a break at all and would probably have worked through lunch. She really wanted a smoke, but there were calls in the queue and her break was still half an hour away, so she'd have to wait. Her phone clicked and a call came through. Shit, she'd been preoccupied and still hadn't finished wrapping up her last call.

"Hello, I have a complaint to make."

"Certainly, sir," she said. "You're speaking to Tanya. How may I help you today?"

"It's this new phone. I've been having problems with it from day one. It just won't hold a charge."

"Well, that is a problem indeed. One of our main selling points is that our phones have excellent battery life and if that isn't the case here, we'll need to look into it."

"It's already been looked into. That's what I want to complaint about. I've sent you my mobile twice to be repaired and both times it's come back and nothing has been done to it. It's a fucking disgrace."

"Language please, sir."

20

"Sorry, love, but I'm just pissed off. It's all a big fucking joke to you lot."

"Sir, I've asked you once already, and I have to ask again, please refrain from using foul and abusive language."

"I wasn't using foul and abusive language."

"Sir, you were swearing."

"I was, yes. But I wasn't using foul and abusive language. It was foul, I'll give you that, but it wasn't abusive. Did I abuse you or anyone else?"

"Well, no, but I will have to ask that, for the duration of this call, that you do refrain from using foul and abusive language."

"Are you reading from a book, or a manual or something?"

"No. Why do you ask?"

"Well, you've just asked me twice to stop using foul and abusive language, even though I've explained that my language was simply foul but not abusive. Just because I'm a working class lad from Newcastle doesn't mean I haven't had an education. It sounds like you're reading your lines from a book."

Tanya was mortified. Reading from a book, indeed. She didn't need to read from a book. She'd memorised it in her first week.

"Tell me what you'd like us to do for you, sir."

"Nothing, really. I'm taking the phone back to the shop I bought it from and asking for a refund. I'm done with you lot. I'm trying to run a business and I need to be contactable at all times. It's hard enough running a business in the current economic climate without this nonsense. I just wanted to complain about your engineers. They're a useless shower of bastards. Is that abusive enough for you now?" Click.

Tanya sighed and started to write up the call summary. It didn't take long, there wasn't much she could write. The caller had a genuine complaint but hadn't left his name or any other details so she couldn't move forward with it. He just wanted to ventilate, really. She looked at the call board on the wall. Nine callers were waiting an average of one minute and forty-two seconds. She had fifty seconds left on her countdown and moved to press the 'Available' button. She liked to keep her wrap-up time as short as possible in order to keep her total contact time down. Her finger paused. Fuck it. She'd let the timer run down, take a little breather. Just this once.

#

Linda took a quick look at Tanya to check if she was all right. She wasn't talking or typing, which was unusual. She looked all right though and it had been an unusual day so far. Ford had come across a lot better than she expected when he met the team. His speech was maybe a bit much, but she'd actually been drawn into it. She'd thought about leading a round of applause, but decided against it. He was, however, supposed to be shadowing her for training, but he was proving very hard to pin down. She'd only been able to keep hold of him long enough to show him how to access the call waiting statistics. She wasn't too upset about this; she'd been allocated two weeks to train him, but in reality it would only take two or three days at the most. This depressed her a little. The full extent of the job she'd spent five years doing could be summed up in a couple of days.

This was it then. Not long to go now. She had been so excited when she heard she'd got the airline sales executive job, but now the nerves were kicking in. Despite how desperate she'd been to leave the call centre, she realised now that she was going to miss the place. But, onwards and upwards. She needed to get these shoes ordered soon so they'd arrive in time for her first day in the new job.

It was really busy for mid-morning, generally a time when the team would be able to have a bit of a gossip. She hoped it didn't get any busier, as team leaders were expected to help out on the phones if there were more than twenty people in the queue. The shoes weren't going to order themselves and if she had to take calls, she'd lose valuable decision-making time. In fact, she was hoping to avoid talking to any customers for the next two weeks. She'd already fobbed off a supervisor call to Ford and was hoping for more opportunities to do the same. That one had extended her streak of avoiding escalated calls to an impressive twenty-six. The record was thirty-one, set by Davey Jones, a veteran team leader with eight years experience of dodging responsibility. She was desperate to break that record before she left, but with only two weeks to go, it wouldn't be easy. Just one nasty caller could snap the whole streak and destroy her legacy.

And she still couldn't decide whether to go for the strappy heels or the sensible flats. She sighed.

#

Ford bounced back upstairs, buoyed by his first drink of the day. That would take the edge off and now he could get back to training with Linda. He was a little disconcerted though. Justin and Chip had somehow found his secret smoking area underneath the fire escape where no one usually went. He may have to stop going there entirely. He had contingency plans however, and had two more concealed spots lined up in case that one was ever discovered. He'd have to pop back later though and remove that bottle of gin he'd hidden in the overgrown bushes.

He pulled the door open and saw his old teammate and long-term drinking buddy Vik had just arrived and was making his way to his desk. "Ah, Vik, how's it going, mate? I was looking for you just now."

Vik puffed. "I'm running a bit late today. Big night last night. Two air hostesses. Ryanair."

"Keeping it classy, mate."

"Do you want to head down and get a quick gulp and I'll tell you all about it? I'm late already, doesn't make any difference now."

"I'd better not, mate, I'm just on my way back up."

"And?"

"Things are a bit different now. I got the team leader job, just found out on Friday. Kind of have to make a good impression. I've already given a speech."

"Fuck off. Lying bastard. I was there when you applied for the job. You were as high as a fucking kite. Didn't you write something about pushing the envelope to see the bigger picture or some shit?"

"It was moving the goalposts, but yes. Seems to have worked."

"You're serious, aren't you? You really did get the job. Fuck sake mate. Well done. I'm amazed, but well done. Listen, I might just pop down for a swig anyway, just to take the edge off. That bottle of gin still there?"

"About that. There's a couple of boys in my new team, they know about the fire escape. Caught the bastards down there earlier. You might need to move the bottle, it's in the bushes."

"That's all right, I don't mind, I've been going into bushes for years."

"See you later, mate," said Ford. He shook his head. That fucking Vik. Two air hostesses? That beat his weekend's activities hands down and he didn't want to listen to Vik's gloating, especially considering Vik was late and had had plenty of time to work on the finer details of his story. Suddenly he'd had enough of the cunt. Maybe he was moving on. He shouldn't be mixing with the likes of Vik any more, not with his new position of responsibility. He considered giving the fucker a late form.

Linda beckoned Ford over when she saw him coming in. He walked over and sat down beside her. He hoped the breath mints and the deodorant would cover any lingering smells.

"You ready for a bit more training, Jim? I really think we should do some work on you taking escalated calls. That's very important. You've already taken one and I'd like you to start taking more of them going forward," she said.

"I prefer to be called Ford," he replied, "and there's no point starting now, is there? It's nearly lunch time."

"It's twenty past ten."

"Yeah, well, I was thinking of taking lunch a bit early today. I'm starving. I haven't eaten anything yet. Nerves, you know. I was so worried about starting today that I hardly slept." He had hardly slept because he was drinking until three in the morning, but kept this to himself.

"Okay then, just make sure you take care of yourself. Get something to eat and get your strength up, we've a lot to get through today."

"I will, thanks Linda."

He walked around to his side of the desk and unlocked his computer. He swayed a little for show as he sat down, but he really was hungry. It had probably been about twenty-four hours since he'd eaten and that drink had gone to his head quicker than he'd like to admit. He stared at the screen for a while, trying to look busy, then checked the football scores from the weekend. He'd been too busy on the lash to bother about the game. Fucking Forest lost again! Jesus, another shitty season this had turned out to be. To hell with this, he was going for lunch now.

The rest of the team were taking calls, so he waited a few moments until most of them were finished. "Can I have your attention for a minute please everyone?" he said.

Tanya was still on a call but the others were glad of the excuse to press their 'Not Ready' buttons.

"Thanks guys," Ford began. "I just wanted to say that you're all doing a great job. I've been monitoring your progress this morning and I'm very pleased with how you're working. It's been busy, but no one's had to wait too long. So, good stuff and keep it up." He thought about adding something about teamwork, but didn't want to push his luck. This was a tough, cynical crowd, as he discovered earlier, and it would take him a while to figure out how far he could go with them.

Tanya finished her call and looked at Ford incredulously. She'd only caught a little of what he'd said. "Er, what?" she said.

"Just letting you know how well you're doing, Tanya. I'll be looking for a similar performance from you all this afternoon. See you after lunch."

He turned and walked out, stumbling a little theatrically on the way. Tanya stared after him and shook her head in disbelief. She looked at the time. It was 10.27.

Chapter 4

"The Queen Mother isn't dead either?"

"No, she decided to retire from public life at the age of a hundred and one, so she faked her own death and went to live in the jungles of Borneo with a tribe of monkeys practised in the art of kung fu. The monkeys were trained by a group of Chinese monks from Shaolin, who were on a pilgrimage when their plane crashed on Borneo. Now, these monkeys see the Queen Mother as a form of deity and worship her according to ancient primate rituals. It's the royal blood, you see."

"She must be very old by now."

"That woman will live forever. Pass that on for me. Thanks now."

Justin's stomach was rumbling again. That cheese sandwich he ate for lunch hadn't filled him up and he wished he'd taken an extra minute this morning to put a slice of ham into it. Some butter would have been nice too. His energy levels were low and even Miss Peal's craziness couldn't perk him up. There were still a lot of calls in the queue and everyone was busy. Even Ford was sitting with Linda and looked as if he was doing something.

He turned to Jolene. Her hair was around her shoulders now and shone in the beam of the overhead tube lighting. She had her back to Justin and was talking to a customer. He only heard one side of the conversation, but it sounded like she was trying to help someone upgrade their operating system, without much success. It was almost exclusively idiots who called this number. Anyone with any sort of competence could usually solve their own problems or at least do a web search and take it from there. The exception was when the phone was broken, in which case tech support just served as a buffer to the engineers who would repair or replace it. There was no way to directly contact the engineers under any circumstances; they were obviously far too important to be dealing with routine queries about their own technology that they could answer in seconds. That was left to the plebs on the call floor who had to learn from a manual and two weeks' training. Bill the trainer was a burnt-out former school teacher who traded disrespect from fourteen-year olds for indifference from adults. He spent most of the training sessions sweating and ogling both the girls and the boys. It hadn't been the most extensive of programmes.

Jolene was now practically begging the caller to listen to her. Justin hadn't had a chance to speak to her all day and it didn't seem like that was going to change any time soon. She was stuck on her call and Justin had another on the way.

"Hi, I had an outstanding bill and my account was frozen. I've just paid the bill and wanted to check if my phone is working again."

"This is tech support. I'm afraid we don't deal with anything related to billing."

"Well, I paid the bill online, so I have no way to tell if my phone is working again. Isn't that a technical issue? To make sure the bloody thing works properly?"

"Did you use it to call me?"

"Yes."

"It's working."

Almost exclusively idiots.

Jolene now had her head leaned back on top of her chair and was staring at the ceiling. She kicked the floor and spun around. Justin knew she loved it when management decided to splash out on wireless headsets for the staff, as previously she often got tangled in the cable when she spun in her seat. She caught him staring mid-spin. By the time she came back around, the chair had lost its momentum and she stopped and looked back at Justin. She smiled and held up her arm and made the mouth-opening-and-closing gesture with her hand. He laughed and rolled his eyes. She then pointed a finger at her head and moved it around in circles. He stuck his tongue out and pretended to wilt. She did the same then crossed her eyes. Click. God damn it.

"Tech support."

Justin spent the next half hour on a call that required technical expertise he simply didn't have. Something about dual SIMs conflicting and overlapping. He'd flicked through the manual desperately and finally got lucky just as the caller was losing patience.

He glanced over at Jolene again, but she wasn't there. She must have gone for her afternoon break. Was it that time already? They never seemed to have their break at the same time. He could take another extra break of course, but he'd already ran up a lot of personal time today and didn't want to risk taking any more with Ford on the prowl. According to the break schedule, he was next up, on his own. No one had their breaks together today on account of the heavy call load, so he wouldn't have a chance to talk to Chip either. God damn it.

#

"It's time for word of the day," said Linda during a rare quiet moment after everyone had returned from their breaks. "What have we got?"

"There have been a few good ones," replied Justin. "I've had incandescent, incoercible and paranymph, which is apparently like an ancient Greek best man at a wedding."

"Ooh, that'll be hard to beat. How did that come up in conversation?"

"The caller was quoting 17th Century Mediterranean literature. She was trying to compare the plight of a widow of a Cretan warrior to her frustration at the dodgy wi-fi in her local Costa."

"Haha. Moving on. Chip?"

"Slow day for me. Just ballistic and effervescent."

"Can't see either of those two posing a challenge. What about you, Jolene?"

"I've only had goose-stepping and philanderer."

"Philanderer isn't bad, but I think it's got to be Justin."

"Ramshackle."

"Huh?"

"Ramshackle," repeated Tanya. This was a surprise, she didn't normally play this game.

"In what context?" asked Linda.

"As in 'this mobile is a ramshackle piece of shit'."

"Oh, that is good," replied Linda. She really preferred paranymph but Tanya was making an effort. She'd throw her a bone. "We have a winner then. Ramshackle it is."

"What are the running totals, by the way?" asked Jolene.

"Let's see," said Linda and opened a file. "Chip is well in the lead with 153. Jolene and Justin are neck and neck with 114 and 112. Alex has 97, but I don't think he'll be back any time soon to add to that. Nicola's still off too, but has 57 points, and trailing a bit, but off the mark, is Tanya, with 1."

#

Chip had been firing through one call after another all afternoon. He didn't mind too much. Days like this were good to build up towards the monthly call target and would allow a little leeway later in the week for pissing about when things were quieter. He did feel like he deserved a beer after all this effort though. After several failed attempts at timing his after-call wrap-up with Justin's so he could ask him in person, he just fired off a quick email asking 'pub after work?' He got an immediate reply saying 'Pope Catholic?' Nice. That was the pub sorted then.

"Tech support. How can I help?"

"The screen on my mobile is cracked."

She probably dropped it. "Was the device dropped?"

"Erm, what should I say here? No? If it was dropped, theoretically, of course, would I be liable to pay for the repair?"

"Is it still in warranty?"

"I'm not sure, but I assume so, I've only had it for about six months."

"Then it's still in warranty, so even if it was dropped, theoretically, of course, we would repair it at no charge to yourself."

"Well, in that case, I'm afraid I did drop it. From a rather great height. What should I do now?"

"Package it up, send it to us and we'll fix it within ten working days. You can print a label with the returns address from our website."

"Yes, I'm on the website now. I'll do that. Thanks for your help."

"Is there anything else I can help with?"

"No, that's all. Bye."

He started to wrap up the call and began to have doubts about going to the pub after all. He had a Guild Wars 2 session scheduled for eight o'clock and didn't want to miss that. The gaming group he played with were very strict on attendance. They operated a three strikes and you're out policy. He had one strike against him already from a few months back when he opted to go on a date instead. The date had been a disaster and he hadn't been on one since. It was his own fault really, he knew he shouldn't have relaxed his stance on going out with girls who hadn't seen Star Wars. There were more of them out there than he'd ever thought possible. Anyway, a couple of quick pints and he'd still be home and in front of the computer by eight, even if he did have to skip dinner.

"Tech support. Chip speaking."

"Chip? Is that your real name?" She sounded hot.

"That's what people call me."

"Nice. I've never met a Chip before. Cool name."

"Thanks. What can I help you with today?"

"Well, Chip, it's this dating app I've been using. It crashes my mobile every so often and I was wondering if the software is incompatible with my phone."

"What's the app?"

"Well, hehe, I'm not sure I should say over the phone. It's a bit naughty."

"I can handle naughty."

"I bet you can, Chip, I bet you can. It's called Lovin' Leather."

"Leather?" gulped Chip.

"Yes, it's for leather lovers to meet like-minded people. And, I have to confess, I do like a bit of leather!"

"You do?"

"Yeah, I love the way it feels against my skin and I love how my skin feels after I take it off. Or someone else does..."

"So, about this app."

"Oh, the app. I'd almost forgotten about that! Hehe! Yeah, can you check if it works with your software?"

"It's not on the list of incompatible apps, so maybe it's something else."

"Maybe you should download the app yourself and test it? You can check out my profile while you're at it. My username is foxxxyfelicia138."

"Foxy?"

"Yeah, with three x's. And can you guess why it's 138?"

"Well, that's 69 twice, isn't it?"

"Yeah, because once is never enough!"

"And Felicia?"

"Well, that's my name. It's not my real name, I chose it because it sounds like one of my favourite things to do. Can you guess what that is?"

"I think I can."

"Do you like it?"

"It's a nice name."

"I didn't mean the name! Hehe."

"Mmm."

"So, where do you live, Chip?"

"I'm not supposed to give out any personal details, Felicia."

"You can tell me. I'm discreet. Very discreet."

"Nottingham."

"All the way up there? I'm down in Portsmouth."

"That's quite far away."

"Unfortunately it is, Chip. You sound lovely. It's a shame you're not closer to me. But, you know, trains and stuff. Anyway, maybe I'll just use the Lovin' Leather website instead of the app. I don't like it when my phone crashes. Thanks for the help, Chip. Remember, foxxxyfelicia138. Take care, you. Bye for now."

Fuck sake. Why couldn't he meet a woman like this in Nottingham? He probably could actually. Sultry-voiced women with leather fetishes weren't exclusive to the South Coast, although people were a bit wilder down there. Portsmouth wasn't that far away, a few hours by train. Ah, who was he kidding? One call from an unknown woman with a sexy voice and his imagination was running wild. Time to get back to the real world. There were still calls in the queue and the next one was coming in nineteen seconds.

#

The only good thing about busy days was that they flew in and now it was almost finishing time. With fifteen minutes to go, Justin had to be careful that his next call wouldn't run past five thirty. It was a balancing act, trying to time that last call to finish within ninety seconds of the end of the shift, so he could see out the day on wrap-up without having to take another. This meant that the last call of the day was either dealt with in an extremely abrupt manner or was stretched out with small talk about the weather and stuff. Every agent's worse case scenario was to take a call with two minutes of the shift left and have that call drag out, as they would finish late and not get paid either. They really should get overtime for that. Fucking disgraceful, liberty-taking fuckers in management. Sitting on 'Not Ready' wasn't usually an option either, as supervisors were especially vigilant at this time. Even Linda, who normally was pretty lenient, insisted that everyone was available, as the big boss Phil had pulled her up on this on at least two occasions that Justin was aware of. The supervisors however, whilst checking everyone else's status, always did so with their coats on and as soon as their finishing time arrived, they were straight out the door, leaving the unlucky agents who got stuck on a call to fend for themselves.

At twenty past five, Ford stood up and indicated to the

team that they should go on 'Not Ready' once they had finished their current calls.

"Okay, everyone," he said when they were all done, "I'd just like to say thank you for being so good to me on my first day. I've learned a lot already, thanks Linda, and I'm looking forward to learning more tomorrow. You've all been real troupers today and let's hope tomorrow is a bit quieter and we can start to get to know each other better. Keep up the great work!"

What the fuck was this Ford character playing at? This was his third motivational speech of the day. That was three more than Justin had had in the last three years.

"I'm off now," continued Ford, "and I'll see you tomorrow. There's five minutes left, so if you all go back to 'Available' now until the end of the shift, that'll be great." Was this twat serious? He'd screwed them all, making them available for calls at 5.25, and he knew it too. If he really wanted to motivate them, he could've saved that speech for a few minutes and let it run to the end of the shift. No, he'd done this on purpose, the evil bastard. Well, fuck him. Justin pressed his 'Not Ready' button and was prepared to face any consequences that might have.

Luckily, he made it to 5.30 without anyone mentioning anything, then logged off. Chip was logging off too; he'd made it through safely as well. Jolene hadn't been so fortunate and was on a call. Justin caught her attention and she rolled her eyes to the ceiling. He mouthed 'see you tomorrow'. She nodded and smiled. Justin smiled back and ran to catch up with Chip, who was already on his way out.

Chapter 5

Justin and Chip walked into the pub and went straight to the bar. They ordered a pint of lager each. Justin carefully watched the barman pour his drink, as he'd been given several pints with massive heads in this pub in the past. He'd sworn never to come back after the last time, but it was close to work, so the boycott didn't last long. Every time it happened, he felt like he should say something, but he never did. He just took his drink and moaned about it to Chip.

While they were waiting, a man who'd clearly been in the pub for some time came to the bar and stood beside them. He signalled to the barman for service, then turned to the boys. He looked them up and down before attempting to focus on Chip.

"Fuck, you're small," he said. Chip nodded. He'd heard this many times before. "What's the air like down there?"

"A bit cold, but quite refreshing," replied Chip, his standard response to this witty remark. He was short, he'd peaked at a disappointing five foot four, but he tried not to let it bother him. They picked up their drinks and scanned the pub before opting for a table in the back corner.

"I can only stay for a couple," said Chip. "I've got a game at eight."

"No problem, I don't want to drink too much either. I've hardly eaten today."

"Yeah, what a fucking day, eh?"

"The busiest Monday I can remember."

"Well, there was that Monday they updated the operating system to the 3.33. That was busier."

"I still have nightmares about that day. I'll probably have nightmares about this one. That fucking Ford. Do you know him at all? I mean, he's been slinking around the call centre the whole time I've been there but I don't think I've ever spoken to him."

"Nah, not really. I've seen him at a few parties and leaving do's but I've never really spoken to him either. Might have played beer pong with him once. Always thought he came cross as a bit of a prick."

"Right? And now he's the fucking team leader. How the fuck?"

"I have no idea, but there's not much we can do about it."

"We can fucking leave," said Justin. "I can't wait to get out of that place."

"Yeah, I suppose. Anyway, what the fuck was with all those speeches?"

"I think he loves the sound of his own voice."

"Seems that way."

"Enough about that twat. Did you speak to Jolene today?" asked Justin.

"No, didn't get a chance," replied Chip.

"Me neither. But did she seem okay to you?"

"Yeah, maybe a little tired, but I think we all were. Why?"

"I don't know, just, you know."

They didn't really talk about Jolene even though Justin sometimes wanted to. It might be good for him to talk to Chip about her, but Justin didn't want to bore him. He much preferred it when they just talked shit about hats and the callers and stuff. He could be a right boring bastard when he got too serious. At least, that's what his brother told him.

"How was your weekend?" asked Chip. "Sorry I didn't make it out on Saturday night. I fell asleep on the sofa and didn't wake up until after midnight. Then I just went to bed."

"No problem. I just had a few quiet ones with Tony."

"How is he? Is he still on for D&D on Friday?"

"He's good and yeah, I think so. He said he'd let me know. I'll call in and see him on the way home."

"Did you do anything else?"

"I started watching Lost again. You?"

"Again? There are plenty of other shows, you know. I just played some stuff. Well, I stayed up most of Friday night playing, that's why I was so tired on Saturday."

"What were you playing?"

"World of Warcraft."

"You still play that?"

"Sometimes. I go back when there are new expansions and patches and things. You should give it another chance."

"There are plenty of other games, you know."

"Well, it's, ah for fuck sake, look who just walked in."

"Oh, fucking Ford and that mate of his. Have they always came here? I don't remember seeing them in here before."

"Probably, I mean it is close to work. Maybe we just never noticed them before."

"Well, move up there, we don't want them to see us. Shit, it's too late, they're on their way over."

Ford sauntered over with a pint which he set down on the table and then pulled up a chair.

"All right, lads? Don't often see you two in here."

"Are you often in here?" asked Chip.

"Not really, actually. Now and again. It's fine for a quick drink but there's never much fanny in the place."

"Yeah, it's a bit of a sausage fest," said Vik, who had also pulled up a chair and sat down.

"Do you know Vik? Vik, this is Chip and Justin, they're in my new team."

The three of them gave each other a brief nod. Justin took a swig of his pint. He didn't really have anything to say to either of these pricks. He fumbled in his pockets, looking for his cigarettes, before remembering that Ford smoked too and if he was to pop out now, the bastard would probably come out too. He'd stay where he was for now, but he wasn't about to initiate the conversation.

"Busy day today, lads," said Ford. "I mean, I wasn't on the phones but I saw how busy everyone else was. There were nineteen in the queue at one point, and I thought I might have to go on. Managed to stay off them all day though. Apart from that one fucking escalated call, right, Justin? From Abbott."

"Er, yeah, about that, I really didn't know who it was."

"So, you're trying to tell me that you've worked here for years and you didn't recognise his voice?"

"I haven't spoken to him that often actually. And I wasn't really fully awake to be honest. Sorry about that."

"Okay, well, I'll give you the benefit of the doubt this time, but in the future, just be aware of these persistent callers and don't be indulging them. We flag them for a reason, you know."

"Yeah, I'll be careful next time."

"Good. It's not that I mind taking calls when they ask for a supervisor, but those persistent callers shouldn't get escalated."

"I know, Ford."

"Yeah, okay then. Anything else interesting come up today?"

"Not really. Just a variety of different things. There was no major issue, so it was surprising how busy it was."

"Yeah, just the usual mix of nutjobs, idiots and angry bastards," said Chip.

The four of them indulged in some small talk about work for a while. Well, Ford and Vik did anyway. Chip nodded along occasionally and Justin's thoughts drifted to Jolene, travel and surprisingly, aardvarks. After several minutes, he snapped out of his daydreams.

"Enough about work," said Ford. "We've only been working together for a day and we'll be talking about work often enough when we're there. We should get to know each other a bit better."

"So," said Vik, "what do you lads do for fun? Do you like to rock and roll at the weekend? I had some weekend. Two air h..." Justin noticed Ford nudging Vik and giving him a quick shake of the head.

"Do you follow the game at all?" asked Ford instead.

"What game?" asked Justin.

"*The* game. The football."

"Not really. Used to be a big Forest fan, but I haven't followed them so much lately."

"You're one of those type of fans, eh?"

"What type of fan?"

"The type that only follows the team when they're in the Premier League, but loses interest when they have to slum it at Grimsby on a wet Tuesday night in the lower leagues."

"No, it's not that. I've just lost interest in football in general recently. All those spoilt fuckers cheating and rolling around like they've been shot. Surrounding the referees for every little offence. And the sponsors practically run the game now too. It's all money and corruption and I've just had enough of it. So, no, it's nothing to do with Forest at all."

"That's fair enough, mate, but don't hold it against our lads for what the big boys get up to. What about you, Chip, do you like football?"

"Nah, I'm more of an indoor person."

"Me too. I especially love being in the bedroom, if you know what I mean."

"I love the bedroom too," Vik chimed in. "I can sleep for hours."

"I like video games," said Chip.

"I thought you might," said Ford.

"What's that supposed to mean?"

"Nothing."

"No, what do you mean? Are you saying that you think I'm a nerd?"

"Yeah, but don't take any offence. It's not the insult it used to be. I'm not going to steal your lunch money or anything."

"Okay then."

"I'm betting you know your shit though, so tell me, who was that actor that played the bad guy in that latest Marvel movie? You know the one I mean, he turns up in everything, but no one actually knows who he is. But every time you see him, you're like 'oh, it's that guy'."

"I know the guy you mean, but I don't know his name. I'm more of a gaming nerd."

"Google it then."

"I can't."

"What?"

"I don't have a phone to google it on."

"You don't have a phone?" asked Ford.

"No."

"But you work for the tech help for a mobile phone company."

"Yep. But I don't have a phone. I fucking hate the things. I love the internet and use it a lot, but at home or at work. I don't need to be online all the time. All I see everywhere I go is people staring at these fucking devices, flicking back and forward. No one can have a conversation anymore. You go out for a meal and people set the fucking thing beside their plate. Kids in McDonald's will sit and text each other while they're at the same table. People crossing the road don't look where they're fucking going. I keep hoping some of the bastards will get run over. People are so reliant on these fucking devices to do their thinking for them, they can't do anything for themselves anymore. Ask a kid to add twelve and twenty-two and they won't have a fucking clue, they'll pull out their phones. General knowledge is fucked, people don't try to remember anything, out come the phones and they google everything. The cunts have ruined pub quizzes forever. I used to love a pub quiz. Can't fucking go to the cinema anymore either, arseholes have their phones out. People are totally reliant on these things at the expense of their own brains. We've already peaked as a species and we're on the fucking decline. It's sad, it's only 2016 and we're finished. Fuckers are all self-obsessed, posing for pictures and posting them on social media. Don't get me started on that: anti-social media it should be called. It's a toxic cesspool of idiots, racists and show-offs, plus inspirational quotes that have the opposite effect and actually deflate me. Fucking phones. No one can sit still and just relax for a few minutes without pulling them out. If aliens come down to invade, they'll catch humanity with its pants round its ankles and shaft the planet up the arse while people are lining up rows of fucking sweets. It's the end of days, I tell you."

"You done?"

"For now, yes."

"You want another pint?"

"Love one, thanks."

Ford went to the bar to get the drinks in, leaving Chip and Justin with Vik.

"Thirty-four," said Vik.

"What?" asked Chip.

"Twelve plus twenty-two. It's thirty-four. I didn't use my phone."

Justin stood up straight away and announced he was going for a smoke.

"I'll join you," said Chip.

Justin didn't want to ask Vik. He didn't want him to come and someone needed to mind the table anyway. But it would be rude not to, and Vik would probably bitch about him to Ford if he didn't ask.

"What about you, Vik? Want to come?"

"No, I don't smoke. Not tobacco anyway," said Vik with a grin and a wink.

Chip and Justin headed out for a smoke. On the way, they noticed Ford at the bar involved in an animated conversation with the man they had spoken to earlier. Justin couldn't hear the conversation, but he saw Ford holding his hands to his eyes like a pair of binoculars, then jumping up and down while imitating a gorilla. Best not to know. The boys took their time over their cigarettes, although they remained ready to suck them down quickly if Ford came out. He didn't and when they went back in, he was at the table with Vik and the two of them were laughing wildly. Vik stood up and fake humped the table while Ford pretended to slap his arse. Justin considered turning straight around and heading home, but he had a full pint waiting for him on the table.

"I would've come out for a smoke with you if you'd waited," said Ford when they sat down.

"Oh right," said Chip. "I would've asked, but you looked to be having fun at the bar."

"Yeah, that's Old Tibby. He's never out of this place. I have a word with him occasionally whenever I'm in here. He's a total alky like, but he's harmless. He knows my old man. Thinks I'm called Dodge."

"Well, you are a bit dodgy. On that note, are you going to tell us why you're called Ford, then?"

"Are you going to tell me why you're called Chip?"

"No, I don't think so."

"Why not?"

"I don't really know you yet, I think it's too soon to share that." Justin thought it was more likely that Chip needed some extra time to think up a good story. He knew that it was because Chip had ordered a plate of chips for lunch on his first day at secondary school. Some kid noticed and called him Chip and it stuck. He'd had the name ever since. His real name was confined to the history books; even his mum called him Chip these days.

"Well, I'll keep my story for another day too then," said Ford. "It's not much of a story anyway, I have to say, so don't get your hopes up." Justin suspected that he needed some extra time too.

The bar was starting to get a bit busier now as people filed in from the nearby office buildings for a quick drink after work. A group of four women in smart work clothes walked in. They looked to be in their late twenties or early thirties. Ford's eyes snapped to them as soon as they walked through the door. He nudged Vik, who turned around to leer. He rubbed his hands together.

"Minge!"

"Keep your voice down," said Chip.

"I don't care if they hear me," said Vik.

"Well, I do," said Chip. "I think one of them is a friend of my sister."

"You have a sister?" asked Ford. "Is she hot?"

"Like I'm going to answer that."

"Is she hot, Justin?"

"Erm." Justin turned to Chip, who raised an eyebrow at him. "There really is no good answer to that question."

"Well, I'll ask you again when Chip's not around."

"Four of them and four of us! The gods are smiling on us

today, lads," Vik said. "Let's get over there."

"I don't know, I'm not really into older women," said Justin.

"Older! They're not really older. How old are you?"

"Twenty-four."

"Well, they're only about thirty. Dirty thirty! Teach you a thing or two. But if you don't want them, it's all the more for me. Ford, should we dive in there before some other dirty bastards beat us to it. That's the best display of fanny this pub has seen in years."

"Wait a bit, Vik," Ford said, "let them have a couple of drinks first, get them loosened up."

"Then you'll go for it?" asked Chip.

"Well, I'm not here to fuck spiders."

"I don't know what that means," said Justin.

"It means we like to go spelunking in raspberry caverns. As often as possible!" said Vik.

"Steady on, Vik," said Ford. "But yeah, I do like the ladies, I have to admit. I'm looking forward to getting to know that Jolene. That tight little arse of hers and those tits, eh? Am I right, Justin?"

Justin felt his face going bright red and he took a big gulp from his pint in an unsuccessful effort to cool down. "Yeah, she's a good-looking girl."

"I'd bend that over and give it a right good seeing to," added Vik. "She seems like a right stuck-up cow, though."

"What makes you say that?"

"Well, any time I try to talk to her, she just ignores me. She needs a proper shafting, that would get rid of that attitude."

"Yeah, mate, she needs a good, deep dicking to put her feet on the ground. Fit birds are often stuck up, but it's nothing a good lengthing doesn't sort out," said Ford.

"She's not stuck up at all, maybe she just isn't interested in you two," said Justin.

"Doubt that, mate. But tell us then, what is she like?"

"She's lovely, she's friendly and smart. Maybe a bit quiet sometimes, but that doesn't mean she's stuck up."

"Well, she is the best-looking bird at work. And like I said, it's the hot ones who think they're God's gift and better than the rest of us," said Ford.

"What about that Donna from HR?" said Vik.

"Oh, yeah. She's fucking amazing too, like. Shame she sits down in that office of hers most of the time. I'd love to see her up on the call floor more often. But I imagine her down in her office on her own, skirt hiked up, flicking the bean all day."

"What about those two together? Donna and Jolene. Fucking hell!" said Vik.

"Fuck me, the two of them, licking each others' tits and flaps while I watch. Then, when they're juiced up to fuck, I step in and see to the both of them. Fuck me, I'll be dreaming about that tonight!"

Justin couldn't take any more of this. He finished his pint in a few quick gulps. "Right, that's me, I'm off," he said.

"I'm going to go too," said Chip.

"It's only seven o'clock, lads," said Ford.

"I need to go though," said Justin.

"What about you, Chip? You'll stay for one more?"

"I can't. I've got something on at eight."

"Oh, a date?"

"Not the type you're thinking of."

"You're not a crafty butcher, are you?"

"A what?"

"A crafty butcher. Takes the beef in the back door. Not that there's anything wrong with it, if that's your thing. I'd give it a shot. Try anything twice."

"No, no. I've just got an appointment, that's all. I'll get you that pint back next time."

"Don't worry about it. My treat to my new team members."

"Right then, see you tomorrow."

Justin and Chip left the pub and both lit up a cigarette as soon as they got outside.

"Fucking twats," said Justin.

"Yes, they certainly are. We can talk about it tomorrow, I should shoot on here. I've got to get something to eat and get online."

"Well, have a good game and I'll see you tomorrow."

"See you."

They shook hands and walked off in opposite directions to their respective flats. Justin finished his cigarette and lit up another one straight away. He had no idea what he was going to do when he got home. Another night of TV, probably. And another microwave dinner. He liked living alone and not having to answer to anyone else, but sometimes it could get lonely. It had been a while since he'd had someone in his life and there were times when he wished he had someone waiting for him when he got back. Someone like Jolene. Just to hold and talk to. Not necessarily for any sexual reasons, and certainly not for a filthy threesome with Donna from HR, as incredible as that would be. Fucking hell, he shouldn't be thinking like that. Fucking Ford getting in his head. No, just someone to share things with. Like Donna from HR, they could share her. God damn it!

On his way home, he passed the Tesco Metro in the Victoria Centre where his friend Tony worked. He really hoped he was on tonight because he couldn't be arsed calling him later. He'd had enough of phones for one day. Tony wasn't on the counter, it was a girl he'd seen in here a few times before. She was quite fit, but she wasn't Jolene. "Excuse me," he asked her. "Is Tony here?"

"Yeah, he's up at the back stacking the shelves."

Justin walked to the back of the shop where he saw Tony on his knees surrounded by loaves of bread. He had one in his hands and was pushing and pulling at the plastic.

"What are you doing?" asked Justin.

"Justin, hey," he replied, "I'm de-squeezing the bread."

"What?"

"We get all these old ladies coming in and a full loaf is too much for them to eat by themselves in a couple of days. They always try to find the freshest loaf, so they squeeze them to test the freshness. They don't trust the best-before date. It means the bread is always squashed, so I have to de-squeeze it every day. Pain in the arse, really."

"Sounds like it. But I get it, sometimes I buy a loaf of bread and I just can't get through it all before the expiry date and end up chucking half of it out. It's ridiculous that the loaves are so big. They're designed for families and couples and happy people. These bread companies don't think of single people and should really make smaller loaves. It's the same with loads of stuff, it all comes in packs too big for one person. Discrimination."

"Yeah, I guess so. Anyway, how was work?"

"Shit. How's yours?"

"Shit, but it pays the bills. Barely, but it pays them."

A confused-looking man walked past them, checking the shelves like he'd never been in a shop before. He caught sight of Tony on his knees and approached him. "Excuse me, I'm looking for red wine sauce."

"Good luck," Tony replied.

The customer looked a bit taken aback, then he wandered off dumbstruck and began to search the aisles again.

"Aren't you going to help him?" asked Justin.

"No, I can't. We don't sell red wine sauce."

"You didn't think to tell him that?"

"No, if he thinks he's getting it here, he doesn't deserve help. He'll stumble upon the booze aisle soon enough and realise he'll need to buy a bottle of wine and make his own sauce."

"Fair enough. Listen, I just popped in to see if you're still on for D&D on Friday night."

"Yeah, I'm up for it. It's been a couple of weeks already. We still have to finish off that necromancer and rescue the tavern wenches from his tower."

"Yoho. We'll get that sorted."

"We should play at my place again. It's the biggest and Mark won't be home, so we'll have the place to ourselves."

"Will the dog be there?"

"The dog? He has a name, you know."

"I know."

"Call him by his name, then."

"Will Sergeant Shinynose be there?"

"The sergeant is always there."

"Maybe we should play at my place then. That fucking dog bit me the last time I was at yours."

"Well, you did sit on his tail. And, in all fairness, he was a bit drunk at the time."

"Okay, if you can promise that beast will be secured, we'll play at yours. I'll let Chip know. Can you get in touch with Elliott?"

"Yeah, I'll let him know."

Tony finished de-squeezing the bread and walked down to the counter, with Justin following. He relieved the girl at the till so she could go on her break.

"You should ask Amanda there out," said Tony.

"I don't know."

"You should. She's single and very open-minded. She's talked about three-ways before."

"Really? That's a coincid... Nah, I'm not into that."

"If you say so."

"Two girls or two guys?"

"Girls."

"Oh. I... No, not interested."

"Are you still pining over that girl at work?"

"I'm not pining. I don't even know what that means, pining."

A customer came to the checkout with a basket full of groceries, saving Justin. She handed Tony a coupon. He scanned it and it bleeped. He pressed a button and continued.

"You didn't put my coupon through," said the customer angrily.

"Sorry about that, but it's not working when I bleep it."

"You need to enter the code on the back."

"It's not your first coupon then?"

"It is not. It is yours? How have you not done this before? How long have you been working here?"

"Since three o'clock," replied Tony. He then input the code on the coupon and the price updated accordingly. "There you go, madam, a seventeen pence saving!"

"Are you trying to be funny?"

"Is it working?"

"Excuse me? I don't like your attitude. I think I might like a word with your manager."

"Why?"

"Why? I just told you, because of your rude behaviour, that's why."

"I didn't realise I was being rude. If it came across that way, I'm sorry. I was just trying to be friendly and comment on your purchase. I won't do it again."

"Well, I won't be in here again, so you won't have a chance. I don't have time to speak to your boss, so you're lucky this time, but if you continue to behave like this, I'm sure it's only a matter of time before someone else does."

"Thank you for your custom. Next please."

Tony served a couple more customers before the shop emptied and he turned to Justin. "Some people."

"I know, it's the same in my job. I hate dealing with the public."

"Quit then."

"Yeah, I'm going to, but I need to save some money first."

"You have plenty saved. You don't spend anything, all you do is watch TV and have the odd pint. You must be loaded."

"I'm certainly not loaded."

"Well, you do smoke a lot. That's where all your money goes."

"I need to smoke. Talking to all those twats at work all day drives me to it. Plus, it's a good excuse to take a break."

"You need a permanent break."

"Can't argue with that."

"You should have a little fun with your callers, you know, a bit of casual piss-taking. Keep it subtle so they don't even realise you're doing it."

"Easier said than done."

"Nah, I do it all the time, and it's easier for you, you don't even have to see them face to face."

"The calls are recorded though. I mean, no one listens to them, but knowing my luck the one time I would be rude to a caller would be the time that someone did."

"You just have to be careful, Justin. And clever. Always have a reason so you can say there was a misunderstanding if things go wrong."

"I'll keep that in mind."

"Do. Anyway, I shouldn't be talking to you too much while I'm working, got to serve these arseholes, but I'll see you on Friday for the D&D."

"Yeah, see you then."

Justin paid Tony for a microwave pie that would probably be as soggy as fuck after he'd blitzed it, but he was starving and needed to eat something and could never be arsed cooking for just himself. He left the shop and walked home. He reached his door, took out his key and put it into the lock. He turned the key and walked into the darkness.

Chapter 6

Ford was nursing a savage hangover and finding it hard to focus. He and Vik had gone back to one of those business women's houses last night after leaving the pub at closing time. Ford had gone to the toilet then passed out on a single bed in the spare room on his way back before he had the chance to make his move. He desperately hoped that Vik hadn't got anywhere either. He'd never hear the end of it otherwise. It was a bad idea to stay out; he hadn't had a good eight hours sleep in weeks and he needed it more than ever now that he was team leader. That fucking Vik. It was his fault Ford was suffering today. He knew he shouldn't have agreed to a 'quick pint' after work. It was all right for Vik to roll in late, he didn't have any responsibilities at work. It really was time to be cutting ties with that waster.

"Ford," said a voice in the distance. What was going on? "Ford!" It was Jolene. "Are you even listening?" He turned and looked at her. Fuck, she was hot. "Ford, I've been calling you for ages. I have a caller here asking to speak to my supervisor."

"What? Can't Linda take it?"

"She said that you should do it. You need to get some practice."

He looked over at Linda. She looked smug, smugger than usual, like she was trying to keep a straight face. "Linda?"

"Yes, Jim?"

"I'm not sure I should be taking these calls yet."

"We trained on this yesterday, Jim. You should be ready to go now. It's good to get stuck in and tackle them straight away. If you leave it too long, you'll build up a stigma about it. Besides, you took one yesterday already."

"That was just Abbott, but this is different. This is a real caller."

"Ford!?" Jolene again.

"Okay, okay. I'll take it. What's it about, Jolene?"

"The caller's phone keeps cutting out. It sounds like it's a problem with the network rather than the device and I've asked her to check with her provider, but she's not listening. She insists it's our fault and wants to speak to a supervisor."

"Did you get her name?"

"Mrs. Heath."

"All right. Extension 155."

"Hello, Mrs. Heath. My name is James and I'll be dealing with your call now. Jolene has explained the problem and it does sound like it's a network issue."

"It's your phone, it's your issue." God, her voice was shrill. She sounded like a canary with a stick up its arse.

"Well, madam, we are going to diagnose the problem, and if it is indeed our fault, we will happily take care of it."

"How?" she shrieked.

"Well, if your mobile cutting out is our fault, we'll take the phone in and fix it for you."

"What will I do in the meantime?" Her voice reverberated around his head, scratching the back of his eyeballs. "Do you supply a replacement phone?"

"No, madam, you would have to use an old handset. Just put your SIM into an old phone."

"What if I don't have an old phone?"

"Don't you?"

"Well, yes, but what if I didn't? What would you do then?" asked the banshee.

"Let's diagnose the problem, madam. First, take the battery out of the phone."

"I've done all this already with that useless girl I spoke to."

"There's no need to refer to our staff in that manner. She was doing her best to help you."

"Her best wasn't good enough." Fucking hell, this bitch.

"Madam, that's because the problem isn't our fault." His voice was rising now and he had to get rid of this woman. He couldn't let this call drag on any longer. "The network is cutting out on you. Get in touch with them. If they can't solve your problem, then call back here. But you simply have to try them first."

"But, it's the phone."

"Doesn't sound like it. Call the network. Good day."

He hung up before she could screech anything more at him. He really hoped that it was in fact a problem with the network and not the phone, he couldn't bear having to speak to her again later, especially after fobbing her off like that.

That fucking Jolene. Well, it wasn't her fault really, but still. He was beginning to regret not giving her another late form today. She arrived at 8.08, which was a little earlier than yesterday, but not much. He thought that two late forms in two days was probably too much, and there was a hormonal element in play that prevented him from being too harsh on her. There was only so far authority could go before a different approach was required.

In fact, this entire authority lark was already getting him down. He was wondering what he'd got himself into with this job. He'd expected to be off the phones, surfing the internet and lording it over the others with a few well-told anecdotes he'd been working on, but an hour into his second day and he was already dealing with escalated calls and discipline issues. It was too early to sneak off for a drink as well.

He hadn't clicked with his new team as well as he had hoped to. Despite having a pint together last night, Justin was very stand-offish and didn't seem to want to open up. Jolene was obviously annoyed about that late form. He wasn't sure what Tanya's problem was, but she was glaring at him nonetheless. Chip was the only one who seemed okay with him, but even he came across a little prickly. Anyway, Chip was the one he could get on side first. He'd start with him then work around to the others. Chip and Justin were as thick as thieves, so he had to get them apart first. Divide and conquer. That was a sound strategy. Efficient. It was because of independent thinking like this that he'd made team leader. He'd talked about things like this at the interview and he could tell they had been impressed.

Linda's approach to the job seemed to work well. The team did whatever she asked of them and they did seem to respect her. She was only a couple of years older than the rest of them and had got the job because she'd been there the longest and knew the place inside out. She had a quiet authority that came from her knowledge and her indulgence of the team. It seemed that she let them do whatever they wanted, as long as they still got the job done at least reasonably competently. She gave them a lot of leeway, so they didn't feel choked, but she pulled the rope when she needed to. This was what Ford would do.

He should also probably lay off the motivational speeches. He felt like that third one yesterday was overkill and might even have looked like he was taking the piss. No one seemed to appreciate it and he admitted to himself that he'd got that one wrong. Today there would be no speeches at all. He wasn't going to rule them out in the future though; it was always good to have a speech in reserve.

He checked the statistics. It wasn't too busy today, steady but nothing like the bombardment they'd taken yesterday. Everyone was taking calls, except Tanya, who was on wrap-up. Ford looked over at her. She wasn't typing and just appeared to be sitting there.

"Tanya?"

"Yeah?"

"You still wrapping your last call?"

"Yes."

"Maybe you can hurry it up a bit?"

"Yes, sir, fearless leader!" she said, then saluted. Saluted!? What the fuck? It was too soon for that. Someday, he hoped he would inspire that type of admiration from his team, but this early on and it came across like piss-taking. What the fuck was her problem? Whatever. She wasn't at the top of his priority list for this team. She wasn't bad looking, but not in the same league as Jolene, so he wasn't going to make as much effort with her. Actually, maybe he should make an effort; a good, deep dicking was probably what she needed.

This fucking headache wasn't going away though. He popped a few pills and waited half an hour for them to kick in, but it still wasn't happening. He was thinking about slipping out for a cure when Vik walked in. Perfect timing. The bastard was wearing the same clothes as yesterday, not a good sign. Although to be fair, Ford was also wearing the same clothes as yesterday. He didn't wear the tie or the jacket today though and had rolled up his shirt sleeves in an attempt to look different. It seemed to be working, no one had mentioned anything.

"Vik," he called as he walked over to him. "What time were you supposed to start?"

"Ten o'clock."

"Really? So you're early then? It's only quarter to."

"Time for a quick drink then!"

They walked downstairs and around to the fire escape. No one was there today. Ford retrieved the bottle of gin and took a swig, before passing it to Vik. Then he lit up a cigarette.

"I can't believe you made it on time," said Ford.

"Yeah, I woke up at that house and just came straight to work. It's closer than my place, so I got here quicker."

"What did you get up to?"

Vik paused and Ford studied his face. He looked as if he was trying to concoct a story.

"Nothing, mate," Vik said at last. "I'm embarrassed to say it, but I passed out. Shouldn't have skipped dinner like that. I woke up in my clothes on the sofa. What about you?"

"Riding all night, mate. The one with the glasses. Not the best face, but a tidy body on her!"

"Lucky bastard."

"Yeah, mate. You just got to know how to handle your drink, that's all."

"Yeah. Listen, I should head up. Get started on time for a change."

"I'm coming too."

Ford was feeling much better now. The combination of alcohol, nicotine, ibuprofen and fresh air had helped a little and getting one up on Vik had finished the job. He took a quick peak at the call board on his way back in and saw that there were no calls in the queue at all. His team were all facing each other and laughing.

"So he picked up the snail and threw it as far as he could," Chip was saying, "and a year later, there was a knock on the door. Exact same snail. It said 'Oi pal, what the fuck was all that about?'"

"I've got one," said Justin. "A snail is walking down the street and sees a slug hanging around on the corner. Slug turns and says 'Big Issue, mate?'"

"What was the snail doing on the motorway?" asked Jolene. The others shook their heads. "About two miles a week."

"What are you guys doing?" asked Ford.

"Telling snail jokes," said Chip.

"Why?"

"Slow day."

Everyone laughed and Ford struggled to contain himself; it wouldn't be appropriate for the new team leader to indulge in this nonsense. He let them enjoy themselves for a minute before clearing his throat.

"Okay, enough of this," he said, satisfied with the authoritative tone in his voice. "There are a few calls coming in now, time to get back on the phones." Yes, that was it. A little indulgence followed by a pinch of authority. The perfect recipe.

#

"Tech support. Chip speaking."

"Hello there. Listen, I'm having problems connecting my smartphone to the internet. It works fine at home, but when I go out, I have no connection."

"That's because it auto-connects to your home wi-fi. When you're somewhere else, you'll need to set up a new connection, unless you're using your contract data."

"Whoa. Slow down there. Never mind data. What do you mean, I have to set up a new connection? Why won't it connect automatically like it does at home?"

"Because you're out of range of your home connection. But don't worry, setting up a new connection is easy. I'll walk you through it."

"Okay then. What do I do first?"

"First go to Menu, then Settings."

"Listen buddy, don't you start getting technical with me. I don't know how these things work. You'll need to talk me through it step by step."

"Do you see a house?"

"Yes."

"Press it."

"Okay."

"Do you see a cog?"

"What's a cog? I told you to keep it simple."

"Do you see a wheel with bits sticking out of it?"

"Yes."

"Press it."

"Okay."

"Do you see where it says wi-fi?"

"Yes."

"Press it."

"Okay."

"Where are you?"

"What? Starbucks. Why?"

"Do you see Starbucks wi-fi?"

"Yes."

"Press it."

"Okay. I've done that. It's asking for a password. You never said there would be a password. What do I do now?"

"Ask the Starbucks staff for the password, then type it in. And you can do this anywhere you go that has wi-fi, sir. Just press the name of the wi-fi you want and enter the password. It's that simple."

"That is very simple. You must think I'm a bit of an idiot."

"Of course not, sir."

"Are you sure? You sound like you're being sarcastic."

"No, sir. Never. Is there anything else I can help you with?"

"No thanks. That's all."

It was coming up on break time, so Chip checked the schedule. Nice. He had his official break at the same time as Justin. He logged out and they popped downstairs for a smoke.

"Did you see that Ford's wearing the same clothes as yesterday?" asked Justin. "He's taken off his tie and rolled up his sleeves and he thinks he's fooling us. Twat."

"Yeah, I wonder what he got up to? He looked as rough as a badger this morning. Probably stayed out all night."

"Probably. How was your game, by the way?"

"Fuck sake, I missed it. Now I'm on two strikes with the guild. I'm going to have to be extra careful from now on or I'm back to scraping round the servers looking for randoms to join up with."

"I don't really know what you're talking about, sorry. Anyway, I thought your game was at eight. You should have been home in plenty of time."

"Yeah, I got a bit side-tracked. I was checking out this dating website."

"You're using online dating sites? I know it's been a while, but I didn't think it was that bad."

"No, it was just for research purposes."

"If you say so. How was it?"

"It was all right. Lot of leather."

They finished their smokes and headed back upstairs. As they walked back in, Ford motioned to Chip.

"All right, mate? You want to pop down for a quick smoke?" asked Ford.

"I'm just back actually. Break's nearly over."

"Just take it as personal time. I'll make sure it's okay."

"All right then."

Chip walked straight back downstairs again as Justin looked at him and shrugged. Chip just shrugged back. When they got to the smoking area, Ford opened his packet of cigarettes and offered one to Chip, which he gladly accepted.

"How's it going today, then?" asked Ford.

"Yeah, not bad. It's not too busy today."

"It was nice to see you boys in the pub last night. Shame you had to leave so early. I didn't say anything to piss you off, did I?"

"Nah, no no, nothing." said Chip. Well, he had been a little snarky, but it wasn't too serious. Chip would let him off with it this time; he didn't really know him so didn't know what he could and couldn't say.

"Good. We'll have to have a drink again sometime. By the way, which one of those girls last night was your sister's friend? It wasn't the one with the glasses, was it?"

"No, it was the blonde one," said Chip. Ford looked relieved.

"That's good. The things I got up to last night, it would have been a bit embarrassing if you knew the girl."

"What sort of things?"

"You know what I mean."

"I suppose so."

"Riding all night, mate."

"Right."

"I started chatting them up not long after you and Justin left. We had a right laugh. Two of them had to leave early cause they were married and boring, but the other two stayed out and the cocktails were flowing. Me and Vik ended up back at one of their places. Vik was wrecked, he couldn't even stand. The wanker passed out in his clothes on the sofa. I thought, great, I get a run at both of them, but one of them faded too. That was okay though, it was me and the bird with the glasses. The glasses were all she was wearing when I was done with her!"

"That's great. You're a lucky bastard."

"Luck has nothing to do with it, mate. It's all about the chat. Stick with me and I'll teach you everything I know. And I know a lot. I've been with a lot of women."

"Really?"

"Yeah. A lot."

"How many?"

"Counting whores, or...?"

"What?"

"Never mind. A lot, though."

Chip nodded. This guy was full of shit, but he did have the chat. He'd give him that.

#

Jolene pulled her hairband out. She shook her head and let her hair fall around her shoulders. This fuckwit didn't seem to understand plain English.

"Sir, you just have to find the name of the Internet Service Provider that you subscribe to and press on the name."

"What should I press? There are no buttons to press."

"That's because it's a touchscreen phone. You don't need buttons. Just touch the name of the ISP."

"What's an ISP?"

"Internet Service Provider."

"I think I've done that. It says to enter the password."

"The password is written on the router."

"Oh, come on!"

"What?"

"How am I supposed to find that?"

"Well, just go to your router and look at it. The password is usually written on the side or the bottom. Then enter it into your phone."

"How can I do that? There are no buttons!"

"You can bring up a keypad or one will automatically pop up when you press on the box to enter the password."

"No."

"No?"

"No. I can't do this. I'm seventy-two years old, you know. I'm going to have to get my son to come over and do it for me. You're useless, you are. Tech support indeed."

"Hopefully it's not too complicated for your son either."

Fucking hell. That wasn't the first time she'd been called useless today. It wasn't even her fault. It was these callers who were useless, not her. She didn't need this on top of everything else. It had been another terrible date at the weekend and she had actually felt a little useless for a couple of days. She was just starting to come around and now she had to deal with these callers. Another guy who just wanted to get into her knickers and wasn't really interested in anything she had to say. She had a degree in Ethical Studies and French, which she thought was pretty damn interesting! You don't get one of those by being stupid either. Did she just give out fuck me vibes or what?

She turned to talk to the others, but there was no one there. Linda had taken Ford into the office a little while ago for some more training. This meant that Justin and Chip had likely fucked off for an extra smoke break like they usually did when there where no supervisors around. Where was Tanya though? Had she gone with them? Fucking hell, this was ridiculous, there were calls in the queue. Jolene considered taking up smoking, and not for the first time. No, it was a bit disgusting, really. She just wanted an extra break. Well, they weren't the only ones who could play this game.

She was on another call when they came back, stinking of smoke. She finished it quickly and turned to Justin.

"Justin, can you do me a favour?"

"Of course. Anything. What do you want?"

"Well, I have to leave early today, but I don't want to lose any pay. I'm going to go on 'Personal Time' at a quarter past five. Can you log me out at half past? Please?"

"Sure, I can do that."

"Thanks, Justin. You're the best."

The rest of the afternoon was steady, with calls coming in regularly, but there was still some time in between them to chill out. The time passed quickly and it was almost time to go. One more call and that would do her for the day.

"Tech support. How can I help?"

"Well, I watched this documentary last night and I wasn't happy about it at all."

"Okay, what was the problem?"

"Well, it was nothing short of a whitewash. I'm a Conservative Party voter and this programme simply ripped our man apart. Some nonsense about his expenses. It even went into detail about what he spends on light bulbs. Light bulbs!"

"What has this got to do with us, madam?"

"Well, I watched it on my phone, on the iPlayer."

"And was there a problem with the video stream, the resolution or something?"

"No, it was fine. The problem was this disgraceful programme!"

"Well, I can't do anything about the show, madam. Maybe you should call the BBC and complain to them?"

"I'm complaining to you!"

"I can't do anything about that. I have to go now. Goodbye, madam." Perfect, that took her up to 5.15 on the dot. She hit the 'Personal Time' button, put on her jacket, picked up her bag and walked out. See you later, losers!

Chapter 7

"Can you come into the office for a moment, Jolene?" asked Ford. Fucking hell, what was this about? That personal time she took yesterday? She really hoped not; it was one thing running a little late, she could talk her way around that, but there really was nothing she could say about leaving early. He was looking pretty fresh today, like he'd had a good night's sleep and brushed his teeth. He was too perky and it was strange. He'd changed his clothes too.

"Do you know what this is about?" he asked.

"No."

"Are you sure?"

"Yes."

"Listen, Jolene, you should have been here at eight o'clock."

"Why? What happened at eight o'clock?"

"What? Nothing. I mean, it was your start time."

"Yeah, sorry about that. I'm a bit late again, aren't I?"

"Yes. Ten minutes. That's the third day in a row." That's what he thought. It was more like the three hundred and third day in a row. "I don't want to have to give you another late form, Jolene, but you need to work on your punctuality."

"I'll try."

"Please do. I know what it's like, I've been late a few times myself. Just not every day, eh?"

Jolene felt like she was entitled to come in late. All the others took extra smoke breaks, why should she have to suffer for actually taking care of her health? It wasn't fair. "Okay, Ford. I should get started now."

"Well, you don't have to start straight away. I'll take care of it. You can stay here for a few more minutes and we can have a chat. Get to know each other a bit better." Fucking hell. What was this fuckwit up to?

"I should really get started," she said. "I'm already late, like you said."

"Well, okay then."

She practically ran out of that office. It wasn't a big room anyway, but it felt like the smallest room in the world when she was in there with Ford. Justin waved at her as she took off her jacket. She smiled and waved back, then sat down and booted up her computer. It didn't take long for the calls to start rolling in. Same shit every day. No wi-fi, broken screens, battery trouble, yawn, yawn, yawn. Then.

"Tech support. Jolene speaking."

"Jolene? Yes, you're the one with the same genetic fingerprint as Zsa Zsa Gabor." Miss Peal! Yes!

"That's right, Miss Peal. That's me!"

"As you know, I have the same genetic fingerprint as Michael Bublé."

"I didn't know that."

"You did. I've told you before."

"But you're a woman."

"Yes, but I have a male genetic fingerprint. It's a shame I don't have Michael's voice though. Christmas in my house would be less stressful and much more melodic."

"Well, how can I help you, Miss Peal? Or should I call you Miss Bublé?"

"No, you should not! I just wanted to let you know that X-Factor's Louis Walsh was pictured yesterday with a half-eaten cucumber sandwich. In fact, this was no cucumber sandwich, but a mind control device disguised as a cucumber sandwich. He's controlling Simon Cowell and is the real evil genius behind the homogenisation and domination of the UK charts. Pass that on for me. Thanks. Bye."

Jolene laughed and spun on her chair. She noticed Justin

looking at her.

"Miss Peal?" he said.

"Yeah. Talking about mind control and genetic fingerprints, whatever they are!"

"I don't know what she's on about. But she told me that I have the same one as Pope Gregory."

"Which Gregory? There have been a lot."

"That's what I asked. She just said 'you know which one'. Haha."

"Oh, Justin. Thanks for yesterday, by the way, logging me out."

"No problem. You were just right, getting out of here. This fucking place."

"I know. It does my head in sometimes."

"Mine too. The sooner I get out of here the better. You know I'm leaving, right?"

"Yeah, I know," replied Jolene. He'd been saying this for months, but still hadn't done anything about it.

Click. Another call. She pointed at her headset, mouthed 'sorry' to Justin and turned back to her screen. Unfortunately, it wasn't Miss Peal again. It was some boring guy talking about the problems he had receiving a radio signal on his phone. She ran through the diagnosis manual and it actually worked! They managed to boost the signal. Unbelievable.

More boring calls came in one after the other. More broken screens, poor wi-fi signals and non-charging batteries, then all of a sudden it was break time. She went to the break room and made herself a cup of black tea. She left the teabag in the cup, so it would keep getting stronger as she drank, just the way she liked it. This week's copy of Hello! was on the table, so she sat down and started flicking through it. Fuck off Kardashians, bored with Beyoncé, oh, hello Emily Deschanel. While she was reading, that mate of Ford's slinked in looking rough as always. What was his name? Rick? Nick? Vik? Yeah, that was it, Vik. He looked over from the coffee machine and smiled at her. Jolene turned back to the magazine, she didn't want to give this guy any encouragement, but look at that, here he was anyway, sitting down opposite her.

"Hey," he said.

"Hello," she replied.

"So how's it going?"

My face is up here, arsehole. "Fine."

"What's happening in the celebrity world, then?"

"Oh, did you want to read the magazine?"

"No, I was just..."

"Take it. I was just leaving." She stood up, took her tea and walked away. She felt Vik's gaze follow her out of the room. Eyes up a bit, fuckwit.

Justin and Chip were deep in conversation when she got back. She really liked those boys, but they tended to get into a funny mood around this time of the day, especially if they'd had energy drinks when they were out smoking.

"Are you two talking about jam again?" she asked.

"Yeah," said Chip.

She rolled her eyes and tutted. After a brief pause, she asked, "what kind?"

"Lingonberry."

"What's that?"

"It's Swedish. You know, that stuff you get with meatballs in Ikea," said Chip.

"Oh, yeah, I like that. Can you get lingonberries in Tesco? I've never seen them."

"I don't even know what they look like," said Justin.

"We'll just have to forget it then," said Chip. "Thwarted."

"Chip?"

"Yes, Jolene?"

"Do you even know to make jam?"

"Well, not exactly, no, but there's the internet."

"So, what's the difference between jam and marmalade then?" Tanya asked after finishing with a call.

"Well," said Chip, "I think marmalade is made from citrus fruits, such as lemon or orange, whereas a jam can be made from any fruit."

"Or berry," added Justin.

"Or berry," said Chip, "and I also think that a marmalade

usually contains some of the rind of the fruit too."

"Okay, that makes sense," said Tanya. "But then what's a chutney?"

"Chutney?" said Chip. "I don't know, I don't really go in for chutneys. I don't like that word. Chutney. Chut-ney. It doesn't sound appetising at all."

"They taste good though," said Tanya.

"I wouldn't know."

"You're missing out."

"I'm fine with that."

"Your loss."

Jolene's break was over before they could get to the bottom of the situation. She really wanted to know what a chutney was. She'd never tried one either and Chip had a point. Chutney. It did sound disgusting. Who would want to eat something called chutney? She thought to google it but got distracted by a caller with a broken mobile. He was clearly lying about how he'd broken it. There was no way a seagull could carry a phone in its beak for that long. But she couldn't call him out on it and they would repair the phone anyway.

She took some more boring calls until it was lunchtime. She logged off and turned to the others.

"So, what is a chutney then?" she asked. "Did anyone find out?"

"It's a preserve, just like jam or marmalade, but it can also contain vegetables, spices, vinegar, all sorts really, in addition to the fruit. Or berry," said Justin.

"What are you talking about?" asked Ford. Where did he come from? Jolene hadn't seen him since she'd been in his office this morning. Linda hadn't been around either and she assumed they had been training.

"The difference between jam, marmalade and chutney," Jolene told him.

"I know the difference. You can't chutney a door open. You can't marmalade your cock up a tight hole!"

"Ford! That's disgusting!"

Tanya looked at him like she wanted to throw up. Justin

and Chip both looked a little taken aback too. Jolene was about to walk away. She didn't need to hear this from anyone, let alone her new team leader. The same fuckwit who had given her a late form.

"All right, I'm sorry," said Ford, "I was just trying to have a laugh." He seemed sincere, but it was hard to tell with this guy. Anyway, it was lunchtime. Jolene wasn't really that hungry though. She'd just have something small. Maybe some toast and jam. She thought about what Ford said. Maybe just the toast.

#

Chip finished his cigarette and stood up. It was time to get back to work. It was a nice day, so he'd had lunch in the park and had taken a little walk too, but he'd misjudged the time and had to hurry back. Ford was standing at the official smoking area as Chip arrived, panting a bit from the brisk pace he'd set.

"Chip," called Ford, "you having a smoke?"

"I don't really have time. I start back in thirty seconds."

"Don't worry about it. I'll take care of it. Stay and have a quick one."

"Okay then."

"How's it going? I've hardly been out of that office today. Linda's really pushing me to get trained up."

"Well, you do need to know what to do."

"Mate, it's not that hard. I can just pick it up as I go along. I suppose today's a good day to do it though. I'm all rested up. Stayed in last night for the first time in a long time."

"How was that?"

"It was okay, mate, but I like to get out and meet the girls, you know? I had an epic wank last night, but it wasn't the same."

"I don't know what to say to that."

"You know what it's like. I mean, it was all right, I enjoyed it well enough. It was a bit difficult getting that second finger up my arse, though."

"Again, don't know what to say."

"Mate, don't be shy. There's nothing to be ashamed of. We all do it. A wise man once told me you're either a wanker or a liar."

"Who told you that?"

"My dad."

"For the third time, I have no response."

"Well, I'm not staying in two nights in a row. If you fancy a pint, let me know."

"Busy tonight. And actually, I should head back up now."

"All right. Well, give me a shout if you change your mind."

Chip headed inside and quickly went upstairs and logged back in to his computer. The first call hit as soon as he made himself available. It was a simple reboot issue that was easily dealt with. He saw Ford come back in as he was on wrap-up and tried to avoid eye contact. He desperately wished he could unhear what Ford had told him. Chip was no stranger to Pamela Hand and her five sisters; as a teenager, he'd helped put Mr. Kleenex's kids through college, but that wasn't information he cared to share with anyone else. He was slightly curious about the finger and arse situation, however. Not that he would try that. That was disgusting. No, he'd never do something like that. Almost certainly never.

Another call, another reboot. Shit. He really hoped that was coincidence and not some issue that was developing. If there was a problem that affected a lot of people, he'd be slaughtered for the rest of the shift. On the plus side, if that were the case, the day would pass quickly and then he'd be done and get home. He had another gaming session lined up tonight. This was his chance to get back into the guild's good graces. A top performance might give him some credit to get one of those strikes retracted. Fingers crossed.

The next few calls were about various issues and thankfully there were no more reboots. It looked like he was in the clear. The call count had died down after lunch too, as people got back from their break to share the load a bit. Linda came back from her lunch and took Ford into the office again. Chip looked at the call board. Just two in the queue. He looked at Justin, who nodded.

"Are you two going for a smoke?" asked Tanya.

"Er, yeah," said Chip. "Just a quick one."

"Mind if I come with?"

"Sure."

The three of them sneaked out and headed down to the fire escape area. It was empty and they each lit up a cigarette.

"How's Ford?" Justin asked Chip.

"What? What do you mean?"

"I saw you smoking with him at lunchtime. Are you two mates now or what?"

"No, no. He was talking shit as usual. He mentioned going out for a pint tonight, though."

"Are you going?"

"No, I have another game tonight and I'm not missing it this time. He was just talking about getting out on the pull."

"That's all he ever talks about."

"Maybe you should go with him, Justin," said Tanya.

"No fucking way. Maybe you should."

"Maybe I should. I'm single at the moment," she said. "I split up with my boyfriend last month."

"I didn't even know you had a boyfriend. You never talk about your private life," said Chip.

"Well, this is work. I've never really seen it as a social club. This isn't my life. I get paid so I do the job properly and to the best of my ability and I want to do well and move up and get paid more, but once I walk through the door, that's it."

"Maybe I should be more like that," said Justin. "When I go home, I put on the TV and think about how much I hate my job."

"That and Jolene," said Chip.

"What? No, I er..."

"Come on, Justin," said Tanya. "We all know you like her. There's no need to be coy about it."

"I like her, sure, but that's all. She's okay."

"You're not fooling me. It's all right, I get it. She's a nice girl, plus she's gorgeous. I definitely would."

"You definitely would what?" asked Chip.

"You know what I mean. I *would*."

"But she's a girl."

"I know. A hot one."

"So, you're..."

"Bisexual? Yeah, but I hate that word. It implies that we're just greedy and want the best of both worlds, or can't make our minds up. But it's not like that, it's more about an attraction and a connection with another person regardless of gender."

"Well, I connect with Justin, but I wouldn't."

"You wouldn't?" asked Justin.

"Would you?"

"Well, probably not. You're a bit short."

"That's your reason?"

"I was just trying to let you down gently."

"I'm not let down. I wouldn't want you to."

"Well, that's good, because I wouldn't."

"Guys," said Tanya. "Don't worry about it. You're friends. Plus Justin's in love with Jolene."

"I'm not in love with her."

"Okay then. Whatever you say. You finished smoking? Let's head back up."

The rest of the afternoon was steady and there were no obvious patterns to the calls, thankfully. Chip never felt overwhelmed, but there were no more chances for a sneaky smoke break and he was on his own during his official break. It was a pretty boring afternoon, all in all.

He noticed Jolene leaving early again, quarter past five. What was she up to? No matter, it was almost time for them all to go anyway. He took one more call, then sat on 'Not Ready' for the last two minutes of the shift. Justin took off his headset and moved over to Jolene's desk. He pressed a few buttons on her computer then moved back to his own desk. Chip caught his attention, but he just shrugged.

"What?" he asked.

"Nothing," replied Chip.

"You sure you're not heading out for a pint with Ford?"

"I'm sure."

"You want to have one with me?"

"I can't. Can't miss the game again."

And he was determined not to. He had plenty of time to get home and have dinner before the game started. He absolutely wasn't going to get distracted on a leather fetish website tonight. And there was no way he was going to crack one off while sticking a finger up his arse. No way. Absolutely not.

Chapter 8

Ford was practically shitting himself. He'd been called into Phil's office as soon as he arrived. This wasn't a good sign considering he'd only been team leader for three days. Not even a full team leader, he was still in training! He had no idea what he'd done. Apart from the odd sneaky drink, he'd been on his best behaviour. He hadn't even gone out last night after all. In fact, he hadn't been out the last two nights and had only had a couple of cans of lager at home, followed by two of the best nights' sleep he'd had in months. Now, he was feeling so nervous he considered a quick dash down to the fire escape to see if there was any gin left. Vik had probably finished it. Bastard.

"Jim? Are you coming?"

"Yes, Phil. I'll be right there."

Ford walked slowly into the big office. The blinds were closed despite it being another nice day and the only lighting came from a lamp on the desk. Phil was already sitting down and nodded for Ford to do the same. He slid a piece of paper across the desk.

"Take a look at that," he said.

Ford's eyes turned down to the page as a feeling of dread washed over him. He saw four names written on it. He let his eyes focus on them slowly. None of them was his. What was this?

"What is this?"

"This," said Phil, "is the list of sign-ups for the inter-call centre football match on Saturday." Ford let out a deep breath. Thank fuck for that. There was nothing to worry about after all. In fact, there was an opportunity here. Victory from the jaws of defeat.

"Only four? We can't put a team together from that."

"I know, Jim. What are we going to do? The game is only two days away. This has been on the noticeboard for two weeks. I was hoping more people would sign up closer to the day, but no one has and I'm getting desperate now. Those pillocks in broadband have won the last two games and I'll never hear the end of it from that Brian over there if we lose three in a row."

"We've always been able to put a full team together before. What's the difference this time?"

"It's always been on a weekday before, so we just let the players out an hour or two early."

"So, they got out early. What if you were to offer an incentive this time too?"

"What sort of incentive?"

"Time in lieu."

"You mean pay them to play?"

"Not exactly. Just a few extra hours holiday later on."

"Well, it's not exactly standard procedure, but it could work. Yes, that will get them interested. This is why you got promoted, Jim. It's that thinking outside the box that I was looking for in a team leader."

"Unfortunately, I can't play myself. Bad knee."

"That's a shame, Jim. It really is."

"Yeah, I wasn't half bad in my day. Had trials with County as a kid. I couldn't play for those bastards though. I'm Forest through and through!"

"I'm County."

"Oh."

"Never mind. It's just a bit of friendly rivalry, right?"

No. He hated those cunts. "Yes. Anyway Phil, who's the manager?"

"Well, I usually coach the team myself."

"Okay. I was just thinking that I might like a go at it. I have a few tactical ideas in mind."

"Well, I suppose I could hand over the reigns. Tell you what Jim, if you happen to get enough players signed up to make a team, then you can manage it. How does that sound?"

"Sounds good to me, Phil. Sounds good to me."

Vik hadn't arrived yet, but Ford wrote his name down anyway. He'd be playing whether he liked it or not. That was five. He needed at least fourteen including subs, so nine more then. A couple of boys in the Torvill and Dean team owed him favours for supplying alcohol and marijuana during working hours, so he'd start with them.

#

"Tech support. Jolene speaking. How can I help?"

"Hello, young lady. How are you today?"

"I'm fine, thanks."

"Well, I'm glad to hear that. Where are you?"

"Nottingham."

"Oh. Well, I'm in London. Well, not really London, although some people will say anything south of Watford is London, so I suppose I could say London, but it's more like Kent, really."

"What can I help you with today?" Get on with it!

"Well, I just got a new smartphone for my birthday from my daughter. It was my sixty-sixth birthday. I can't believe it. It feels like yesterday I was celebrating my eighteenth. You should have seen the cake, dear. It was beautiful, done up in a royal bunting. Oh, and it tasted wonderful."

"So you got a smartphone for your birthday."

"Oh, yes. I'm afraid I've been a little silly, really. I can't find the instructions. I may have thrown them out with the box, I'm not really sure. But I definitely put the box in the recycling bin, like I always do with card and paper products. When I realised that I might have left the instructions in the box, I went down to check, but of course it had been emptied. The recycling is collected every second Wednesday, you see. Except when there are five Wednesdays in a month, then they skip a week."

"So you've lost the instructions?"

"Well, I wouldn't say I've lost them necessarily. I may have. It's very possible that I set them down somewhere and haven't

73

realised it. So I don't want to say lost just in case they turn up somewhere. I'd feel very silly then if I said I'd lost them and they turned up a few days later!"

"I can help you. What do you need?"

"Well, I'm trying to send an email on my phone. Now, I've been sending emails for years on my computer, so I know how to do it. Don't think I'm an old biddy who doesn't know how to send an email. I use the hot mail. Do you know about the hot mail?"

"Yes."

"Well, I use it on my computer. But now I'm trying to send an email on my phone, and you know I can't find the instructions, so I'm not sure what to do next."

"What exactly is the problem?"

"Well, I can make an 'a' but I don't know how to get that little circle around it. You know that little circle around the 'a' you use when you send an email?"

Jolene knew.

"Hello? Hello? Are you there, young lady? You're awfully quiet."

"I'm here, madam. You don't need to put a circle around the 'a'. They've done it for you. Isn't technology wonderful? Look at your phone, beside the 1?"

"Oh. Oh, yes! There it is! How wonderful!"

"Madam, I can send you a printout of the instructions if you give me your address and the model of the phone you're using."

"You can do that? What service! I haven't had service like this for years, young lady. Not since the little bakery on the corner closed down. Oh, how I miss it. They did a Berner Haselnusslebkuchen that was to die for. It would have brought tears to your eyes."

"So, if I can just get your details, madam."

Jolene took the woman's details and printed out a copy of the instructions for her phone. She didn't normally do things like this but she was in a good mood today. More importantly, it would take her off the phones for a few minutes. She walked over to the printer and waited. Forty pages. Yes! She noticed Ford running around the call floor with a sheet of paper. He'd been at this all morning, she didn't know what he was doing but she'd never seen him so busy. He caught her looking, nodded and sauntered over to her.

"Photocopying?"

"Printing."

"Reproducing, eh?"

Twenty-seven pages. Shit. She looked away from Ford and waited patiently for the printout. The printer hummed and ever so slowly spat out a page. Hum. One more. Why was it so slow? Hum. Fucking hell. It was going to jam, she could feel it. That was why it was so slow. It was knackered. Hadn't been replaced in years. The company was trying to go paperless. Hum. One more. She felt Ford's breath in the air. Hum. Was that a splutter? Shit. Don't break. Don't break. Don't break. Hum. She glanced from the side of her eyes to where Ford stood. He was gone! Off waving that paper in someone else's face. Still eighteen pages left. Nice!

#

That was four more signed up with no effort required whatsoever. He managed to get two of them just by asking and only had to offer time in lieu to the other two. Phil had better be impressed with that. Now for his own team. Justin had mentioned football the other night in the pub, so he was sure that he could get him involved. Chip he wasn't so sure about. Only one way to find out. He started to make his way across the call floor, but ran into Paisley Des on the way.

"Des! How's it going, mate? Haven't seen you for ages."

"Been mostly doing late shifts, pal."

"Did you know there was a call centre footy match on Saturday? Are you playing, mate?"

"No, pal, I'm retired."

"Retired? Since when? I thought you loved the game."

"I did, pal, but as I got older, the football was really starting to get in the way of the drinking, so I had to let it go."

"Fair enough, but won't you play one last game for us? We

need you. I'm still a few players short of a team."

"Nay, pal, sorry, but I'll be there to cheer you on, like."

"All right mate. At least bring a few cans, will you?"

"I will, aye, likes."

Chip was on a call when Ford got to his team section, but Justin was leaning back on his chair and swinging while looking at the ceiling. That was better actually. Divide and conquer.

"Justin," he said, "are you on a call?"

Justin shot back into a sitting position and turned to Ford with a guilty look on his face. "I'm just on wrap-up now," he said.

"Hit 'Personal Time' and we'll head down for a smoke."

"Okay."

They went outside and Ford lit his own cigarette then offered one to Justin, which he accepted. Then he lit it for him using his Zippo lighter with the burlesque dancer on the side. Yes, that was the way. Now Justin owed him. If he used tactics like this during the game on Saturday, there was no way they could lose. "How's it going today?" he asked.

"It's okay. Not too busy, not too quiet."

"Good, good. Here, do you remember the other night we were talking about Chip's sister?"

"I remember you were talking about Chip's sister."

"Would you bang her?"

"If she wasn't Chip's sister, you mean?" said Justin.

"Never mind about whether she's Chip's sister. Would you?"

"Well, she's a good-looking girl."

"So that's a yes, then?"

"Well, she is Chip's sister."

"Like that would matter if you got a chance! Racked?" asked Ford as he held his two cupped hands in front of his chest.

Justin nodded.

"He better keep her away from me!" laughed Ford. He flicked his cigarette into the bushes then started towards the door. He turned back to Justin. "Oh, by the way mate, I've signed you up for the call centre football game on Saturday. It's us against those broadband bastards from across the way."

"But I..."
"You'll get some time in lieu."
"... would love to play."
Vik had started his shift by the time Ford got back upstairs. He walked over to the section occupied by his old team. There were three guys left in the Robin Hood team now that Ford had gone. Patrick was at least fifty so he wouldn't play and Paul was gay. Not that there was anything wrong with that, but there wasn't much point asking him to play football.
"Vik, you're playing football on Saturday."
"Am I?"
"Yeah, it's the inter-call centre game."
"Oh right, great. I was wondering when that was. I've played the last two games and I wanted to sign up again. When did they put the sheet up?"
"Two weeks ago."
"Really? I never noticed it."
"When was the last time you looked at the noticeboard?"
"We have a noticeboard?"
"I'd love to play too," said Paul.
"Really?" asked Ford.
"Yeah. Why didn't you ask me?"
"Well, I, er, I was going to, but I thought you were on a call."
"Put my name down, Ford."
That was eleven signed up, enough for a full team. He would definitely need substitutes though. He had conservatively estimated three subs to be enough, but on reflection, there was no chance of some of these boys lasting ninety minutes. Some of them would be lucky to last ninety seconds, the shape of them. Back to Chip, then.
"Chip, hit your 'Personal Time' button."
"Can't. I've already taken too much today. Been on the toilet all morning. The guts are hanging out of me."
"All right, well, I'll just tell you quickly then. You're playing football on Saturday."
"I don't play football."

"Well, you're playing on Saturday. It's against those broadband bastards."

"I've got something else on."

"It's only a couple of hours. Plus, you'll get half a day in lieu if you play."

"Really?"

"Really. You in?"

"Yeah, I'm in."

Nice. This was going well. At this rate he'd have so many players he was going to have a proper selection headache. Nice problem to have, though. All the best managers would tell you that.

#

It had taken a couple of hours, but Tanya had calmed down a little. She had been fucking livid when she overheard Ford telling Chip he'd get time in lieu for playing football. What a disgrace this was. All the guys off playing football and getting time off while the girls got nothing. It was this fucking boys' club mentality that led to Ford getting her job in the first place. Well, she'd had enough of it. She intended to do something about it.

She waited until her lunch break, then calmly logged out and walked to Phil's office. She knocked the door and walked in. Jesus, it was dark in here. What was he doing sitting in the dark?

"Yes, Tanya, can I help you?" asked Phil.

"Well, Phil, I hope you can." She took a seat despite not having been asked to. "It's come to my attention that there's an inter-call centre football match on Saturday."

"Yes, we have one every year. It's against Brian and his broadband boys. Will you be coming to provide some moral support?"

"I want to play."

"What? But you can't play."

"Why not?"

"It's a men-only game."

"I thought so. Does that seem fair to you?"

"Well, it's football. That's how it generally works."

"Okay, if I can't play, maybe I can be a cheerleader?"

"We'd love you to support us, yes."

"Will I get time in lieu?"

"What? For supporting the team? No, don't be ridiculous."

"Well, the guys are getting time in lieu for playing."

Phil stammered here. He was clearly looking for an excuse and embarrassed to have been found out.

"Don't worry, Phil," said Tanya, "if we can't get paid to support the team, maybe the girls can represent the call centre in another way."

"Do you have something in mind?"

"I hear there's a basket weaving contest next weekend at the Church Hall. Maybe us girlies should enter that on behalf of the centre."

"Do any of you actually weave baskets?"

"Well, we're as much basket weavers as most of these lads are footballers. Plus we're girls, so things like basket weaving and flower arranging come naturally."

"Are you taking the mick?"

"Of course I am, you sexist pig. I'm telling you now Phil, if those boys get paid to play football on Saturday, I'm taking Monday off. The whole day. On full pay."

"But..."

"You don't even need to do anything. I'll sort it all out myself. In fact, I'll just go and see Donna from HR now. I have some time, it's my lunch break."

"Er, no. It's okay. Let's leave Donna out of this. Take Monday. Call it a rest day and I won't process you as absent for that day."

"That's very kind of you, Phil. Thanks very much."

"Listen Tanya, I'm only going to say this once. You might think you've got one up on me, but I have my eye on you now. I never thought that you of all people would do something like this, but here we are. Take Monday off and enjoy it, but if this gets out to the other girls, there'll be hell to pay. Do we understand each other?"

"Sure, Phil. Got it."

Sweet. An extra day off. She'd been thinking of checking out that new Mexican place on Broad Street. She might go there for lunch. And if she were to have a sneaky Monday afternoon margarita while everyone else was at work, what would be the harm?

#

"Tech support. How can I help?"

"Will you have sex with me?"

"What!?"

Click. The line went dead and Justin made himself available again straight away. It never did any harm to build up a bit of credit and get the average down, so that when his call handling time was reviewed, it didn't look like he was spending exactly eighty-nine seconds wrapping up every single call. He'd be at the back of the queue now too and it was relatively quiet today, so it should be a few minutes until he had another call to take.

He turned around to Chip. The poor guy wasn't feeling well. He'd been up and down to the toilet the whole day. He finished a call, then ran off to the toilet again.

"Are you all right?" Justin asked him when he got back.

"Not really," replied Chip. "My fucking arse is just flinging out... well, you don't need to know that much actually."

"You could go home, Chip," said Linda, "take the rest of the day as sick leave."

"No, I'll be okay, thanks Linda."

"Seriously, Chip? You look terrible. No offence. Why don't you just go home and lie down. Take tomorrow off too."

"No chance. I would never waste a sick day when I'm actually sick. If I take the day off work, it's either because a new game has just been released or I'm sitting in the sun somewhere."

"I'll pretend I didn't hear that," said Linda.

"Well, you're leaving anyway."

"So, those times before when you've called in sick?"

"Not sick."

"Not?"

"No."

"Okay, well. It's just as well I'm leaving. I shouldn't really know that. I thought you were one of the most diligent workers in this place. I've seen you work with the cold, sore throats, the flu."

"I've always worked through the sickness. It's the only way to do it. First of all, if you're sick and sitting at home feeling miserable, you might as well come to work and get paid. Second, when you then do actually call in sick, people will think you're really suffering and never question it."

"What about the rest of you? Do you do this too?"

Jolene turned back to her computer. Tanya suddenly took a call. Justin shook his head. "You sure you're okay though?" he said to Chip. "You really don't look too well."

"No, I'm not great to be honest. And it's not just my arse. I'm feeling a bit down I have to say."

"Why?"

"I missed my game again last night."

"Really?"

"Yeah. I er, got a bit side-tracked and lost track of the time. Fuck sake, I can't believe it. I didn't miss a game for months and now I've missed two in a week. I don't know what's wrong with me. Life is fucking shit."

"You don't mean that."

"I do. It's fucking shit. I work here, I go home alone, and now I don't even have a gaming group. Fucking miserable."

"I know life can be shit sometimes," said Justin. "but it's generally not that bad. There are moments of happiness all the time."

"Yeah, you're right. Sorry. I know. It's not all bad, I'm just a bit low today."

"It'll be fine. I mean, how can a world with tigers and dolphins in it be that bad?" He really believed this, but had said it just loud enough so Jolene would overhear. He sneaked a glance at her. She was smiling. It worked!

"I'll be good," said Chip.

Justin took a couple more calls before Ford arrived and sat down. He looked quite tired from running around all day.

"Eighteen sign-ups!" he proclaimed.

"Then you'll not need me," said Chip.

"I need you. I need options. This many players means different tactics will come into play. You'll be there. Remember our arrangement?"

"Yeah, of course. I'll be there. Hopefully I'll be feeling better."

Ford turned to Linda. "I'm free at last, Linda. Did you want to do some more training or...?"

"Nah, we can leave it for today. It's already after three and we've done a lot these last few days. Just take it easy for the rest of the afternoon."

"All right. Might just pop out for a smoke then. Anyone else fancy one?"

Justin, Chip and Tanya all swung their heads towards him quickly.

"No," said Linda. "None of these guys are going with you. It's raining. Wouldn't want them to get sick and have to take time off work."

He left and reappeared twenty minutes later reeking of cigarette smoke and a hint of booze. Justin wondered if he smelt that bad after smoking. He certainly hoped not.

"Anyone got any plans for the weekend?" asked Ford. God damn it. Just when it looked like there would be a chance to relax, Ford was going to start talking. No one really replied, there were just a few mumbles thrown in Ford's direction. This was a mistake, and left him with an open platform.

"Well, just stick with me and I'll show you how things are done," he said. "I live the rock n' roll lifestyle. Girls, booze, partying. Every weekend and often during the week, I'm living it up. Justin and Chip have had a glimpse into things already, right lads?"

"I suppose so," offered Chip.

"Well, there'll be a lot more fun this weekend. You should have been out last Saturday. I got into the VIP section of Pryzm. There were a few Forest players and that guy off the local news. The place was crawling with fanny. Oops, sorry girls. I meant to say that there were quite a lot of ladies on the premises. I picked up this one bird, bit older, mid-thirties I would say. Gagging for it."

"Ford," said Jolene. "we don't need to hear this."

"I'm just sharing a bit about my life. Getting to know each other better. We're going to be working together now, so we should know each other."

She shook her head. Tanya logged out and stood up.

"Where are you going?" asked Ford.

"My break."

"Now? It's nearly four o'clock."

"Late break today."

"I'll come with you," said Linda. "I haven't had a break yet today."

Linda left with Tanya. They both looked relieved that they were getting away. The others had no such luck. They were a captive audience to Ford and he was looking to take advantage.

"Well, anyway, I took this bird back to my place. And after I'd taken her every which way and she was lying there whimpering with satisfaction and exhaustion, I reached around behind her and slipped a finger up her arse."

"Fuck sake, man," shouted Chip. "What is it about you and sticking fingers up arses?"

"You think that's bad? That was just the start. So, I slipped my finger up her dirtbox, then I brought it out, held it up to her face and gave her the Dirty Sanchez."

Justin and Chip's faces glazed over in horror. The room was deathly silent for what seemed like several minutes.

"What's a Dirty Sanchez?" asked Jolene. "Like, those Welsh fuckwits?"

"No, *the* Dirty Sanchez is something else. Why don't you look it up, Jolene?"

"Are you fucking about with me? Just tell me."

"No," said Ford, "you'll have to look it up."

"Just tell me!"

"No."

"Fuck sake." She turned to Justin and Chip. "Is one of you two going to tell me?"

"HowcanIhelp?" said Justin into his microphone.

"Er," said Chip, "I'd rather not. I think it's better if you read about it rather than hear it."

Jolene tutted and turned to her computer. Several minutes later she screamed. "Oh my God! You filthy bastard! You actually did that. That's fucking sick."

"She's lucky that's all she got. I was going to give her a full fucking goatee."

"Would that be a Dirty George Michael?" asked Chip.

"Shut up!" shouted Jolene. "All of you. You're all dirty bastards."

"But I didn't say anything," protested Justin.

"You were thinking it though. Oh God, I need a shower. Shit, there's a whole list of these things on here. A donkey punch? Fucking hell, what sort of psychos do these things? The Bismark? A jam donut? Jesus Christ."

"What's a jam donut?" asked Justin.

"Why don't you google it?" snapped Jolene.

"Oh, holy shit," said Justin after he'd looked it up. "I can't believe anyone would do that. That's bullshit, somebody has just made that up."

"What's a jam donut?" asked Ford.

"Oh, so you've never done that, then?" asked Chip.

"Well, I might have. I might know it by another name."

"Well," ventured Chip, red-faced, "it's when a man comes in someone's face then punches them in the nose, so the spunk mixes with their blood."

Ford turned pale. "Fucking hell. Nope. Never done that. There's a line that should never be crossed and that's the line."

"I don't know what disturbs me more," said Justin, "the jam donut itself, or the fact that there's enough people out there doing it that it has a name. How do people get into this shit? At what point in your life do you sink that low? These fetishes and shit, pretending you're a baby during sex and stuff, how do you find out that you're into that? What makes you try it in the first place? Hot candle wax? Fucked if that stuff is getting within two feet of me. It might be amazing, but fucked if I'm ever finding out."

"Try anything twice, Justin," said Ford. "Apart from the jam donut. No one should try that ever."

Thankfully, a call came in and took Justin away from this conversation. Although an easily-resolved issue with mp3 playback, he stretched it out until Linda came back from her break. He hoped that with her there, Ford would be more restrained. He was. He was talking about football and the tactics he might employ on Saturday. No one really seemed to be listening, but Ford was talking anyway.

Jolene had been quiet for a while and Justin hoped she wasn't still annoyed or disgusted. She was either on a call and listening to someone on the other end or she was just sitting there quietly. He'd try to talk to her.

"Jolene? You speak French, right?"

"Yeah."

A little cold, but could be worse. "Well, I was just thinking about the three musketeers. They're French."

"Yes..."

"And what weapons do they have?"

"What? Well, swords, right?"

"Exactly! Why are they called musketeers then, if they don't have muskets? Unless it means something different in French."

"It doesn't. It's the same. That's a good point. Surely they were around before muskets were invented?"

"So you're saying the gun is named after the musketeers?"

"It would seem that way, but that doesn't make sense. They carry swords. Why name them after a gun? Or the gun after them? That's crazy, Justin."

"Isn't it? I've often thought that."

"Often?"

"Yeah, all the time. Keeps me awake at night."

"Haha. We'll need to look into this deeper."

"Yeah. Jolene, sorry about before."

"That's all right. It was Ford, not you."

"Yeah, but still."

"It's okay."

"So, you want me to log you out again today?"
"Sure. That would be great. Thanks, Justin."

Chapter 9

The last Friday of the month was always the best. Not just because it was pay day, but it was also a marker of having survived another month. Chip had survived thirty-nine months and counting. He hadn't always thought of it this way; in fact he'd been happy to get the job at first. He had applied to over a hundred jobs, got rejected outright by five, had interviews with three and was completely ignored by all the rest. This was the only actual job offer he got and he was glad to be earning money after years as a student living off loans and his parents' goodwill. Not that the money here was anything to jump up and down about; it was barely over minimum wage. It paid the bills though and if he had a good month on the poker, he had more than enough to get by on.

He was feeling much better today. That sharp pain that ran through his stomach and arse yesterday had gone, thank fuck. He'd been a little worried about that, he hadn't felt that type of pain before and wondered if it was perhaps self-inflicted. Anyway, it was gone again as soon as it had arrived, so all good. In fact, now that he felt better, he was thinking that maybe he should have called in sick. Ah well, there was only today to go then the weekend could get started.

Jolene was checking her Facebook when Chip looked over. Fucking social media. "What are your friends having for breakfast?" he asked.

"What?" she replied.

"Facebook. People posting pictures of their food. We've talked about this before."

"No food pics today. Inspirational quotes, though. Want to

hear?”

“Yeah.”

“'We're all stars covered in skin. The light we're looking for is within'.”

“You just made that up.”

“No, it's for real. Here's another one. Ooh, this one has a Minion. 'When my arms can't reach those I care about, I hug them with my thoughts'.”

Chip couldn't take this and almost fell off his chair laughing. “No fucking way.”

“Yeah, it's right here. My friend Nancy shared it.”

“You might want to rethink who your friends are.”

“She's lovely. A bit special, but lovely.”

“Is she hugging you with her thoughts?”

“Right now? Yeah, I think so. It's a little creepy, actually.”

Click. Shit. Time to get this day started then.

“Tech support. Chip speaking. How can I help?”

“Is that technical support?”

“Er, yes.” What the fuck did he just say? “How can I help you today?”

“Are you really technical support? I mean, I've been trying for half an hour to get through to you, but I couldn't. In the end, I had to go through directory inquiries.”

“Well, we just opened a few minutes ago, so you won't have been able to get through. There should have been a message saying that.”

“There was no message.”

“What number were you calling?”

“0800 2200.”

“Where did you get that number?”

“I got it from your company's website.”

“Which section of the website?”

“The 'Contact Us' part. I'm looking at it right now. There it is, right beside your opening hours.”

“Those are the opening hours. Eight in the morning until ten at night.”

“Well, that's a coincidence! Your opening hours are the

same as your phone number!”

“Er, sure. Massive coincidence. Never noticed that before. So, what were you calling about?”

“You know, I can't actually remember. It's taken so long to get through, I've forgotten why I called in the first place. How silly of me.”

“Well, you can give us a call back when you remember.”

“This is terrible. How can I not remember? Anyway, yes, I'll call back when it pops into my head again.”

“You have our number, right?”

“Oh yes, 0800 2200.”

“0800 2200. Good luck with that. Bye now.”

Chip hung up and let his timer tick down. He got distracted from doing nothing by the muffled sound of an angry voice from the cubicle next to his. He looked over to Tanya, who had pulled her headset to the side to avoid taking the full brunt of this man's rage. The words were unclear, but he was kicking off about something. Tanya let him go on for a minute before putting her headset back on properly.

“Thank you for sharing that, sir. Goodbye.”

“What was all that about?” asked Chip.

“Nothing really. His mobile broke again and he wanted to get his frustration off his chest. It was nothing, he was just ventilating,” said Tanya.

“What?”

“He was ranting. You know, ventilating.”

“He was letting cooling air into a hot area?”

“What are you talking about?”

“Ventilating.”

“That's what I said, Chip.”

“Was he venting or ventilating?”

“Are you trying to be smart? I don't know what you're talking about. Get back to work.”

The rest of the morning passed quickly and it was coming up on lunchtime when Linda brought a pile of payslips from the office and set them down on her desk. Chip pushed his chair over to the stack then started flicking through the payslips to find his own. He liked to get in first and take his out of the pile, so no one would see his real name. Linda generally indulged him in this. She knew his name, of course, but had never revealed it. He stopped halfway down the pile.

"Doctor Leslie Jones? Doctor? She's a doctor?"

"Yes," replied Linda, "we have three doctors here."

"Three? Doctors? Working in a call centre?"

"Mmm, they can't get other jobs. I mean, they're not real doctors, medical doctors, but they have PhDs. I think Leslie's is in Himalayan bee-spotting or something obscure like that, but still."

"Is that spotting bees in the Himalayas or the spotting of Himalayan bees?" asked Justin.

"That's a good point," replied Chip. "You know, I've always wondered a similar thing about the Manic Street Preachers. Are they street preachers who are manic, or are they preachers from Manic Street?"

"They're from Cardiff, aren't they? Do you think there's a street in Cardiff called Manic Street? Seriously?"

"I don't know. It's Wales, isn't it? Who knows what they have there."

"Fair point."

Linda rolled her eyes but said nothing. Ford suddenly appeared from somewhere and noticed the payslips on the desk. "Yes! Pay day! Here we go!" he said. "There's going to be some partying tonight. I should celebrate this promotion. I'll be living it up like a champion! Anyone want to come out and help me celebrate?"

Tanya ignored him completely; she was either taking a call or pretending to. Linda and Jolene said they were both busy with prior arrangements. That left Chip and Justin. Thankfully, they too had other plans for this evening.

"Can't, mate," said Chip. "Got plans."

"Me too," said Justin.

"What sort of plans? If you're just going for a pint together, you can come with me instead."

"No, it's something else," said Chip.

"What?" asked Ford.

"Does it matter?"

"If you can't help me celebrate becoming team leader, of your team I might add, then yes, it does matter."

"We've got a gaming night set up with a couple of other friends. It's been planned all week, so we can't cancel it."

"If it's not a sex gaming night, then you can fucking well cancel it."

"It's not, and we can't."

"What is it, computer games? Cards? What? Maybe I'll join you."

"It's D&D," said Justin.

"What the fuck is D and D? Drinking and dicking?"

"Dungeons and dragons."

"Dungeons and dragons? What the fuck? Like sex dungeons? Whips and leather and shit?"

"No."

"Do you really not know?" asked Chip. "You've never heard of D&D?"

"Never."

"Well, it's a role-playing game where you play a character in a fantasy world and use various skills, talents and magic and stuff to defeat evil creatures such as dragons and orcs. The player decides exactly what to do and the gamesmaster, that's the guy who tells the story, will roll dice with a varying number of sides to determine the outcome of your decisions."

Ford was silent for a moment. "I don't know what you just said there. But that's okay. You lads play your D and D and I'll play mine. Drinking and dicking!"

He turned away from them and picked up his payslip from the desk. "What the fuck?" he said after opening it. "Linda, have you seen this?"

"How could I have seen it? You've just opened it."

"Well, it's not right. This is my old salary. This doesn't reflect the fact that I'm the team leader now."

"You're not technically the team leader yet."

"I've been taking escalated calls like a team leader! I understand that the whole month can't be paid at the new rate, but

I've been a team leader for a week. That week should at least be paid at the higher rate."

"There's nothing I can do about it, Jim."

"I'm not having this. It's fucking outrageous. I'm going to take this up with Donna from HR."

He stormed out of the room. Ten seconds later, he was back. He snatched his payslip up off the desk and stormed out again.

Chip hadn't realised it, but he'd been sitting on 'Not Ready' and now it was lunchtime. He and Tanya had the same break schedule today, so they both went for a smoke as soon as they logged off.

"So, I tried a chutney," said Chip.

"Oh. What kind?" asked Tanya.

"Mango."

"What did you think of it?"

"Mind blown. It was the best thing ever. I don't think I can go back to simple jams or marmalades after that. The blend of the fruit, the spices, vinegar and onions. It was amazing."

"Told you."

"You were right."

"Got any plans for lunch?" she asked.

"No, but we just got paid, so I'll probably go and eat out somewhere."

"Me too. I was thinking about the Indian on the corner. They have lots of different chutneys. And a lunch buffet, so you can sample them all."

"Sounds good."

"All right. Let's go."

#

The call floor was strangely quiet. Ford had disappeared in a fury a little while ago and hadn't come back. Chip and Tanya had gone on their lunch break and Linda had gone into the office. It was just Justin and Jolene left. There were no calls in the queue and he was sitting waiting for Jolene to finish with the caller she was talking to so they could have a chat.

"So," he started after Jolene had finished her call. "How are you? We haven't really talked much recently."

"Yeah, I know. There's always been something else going on. Like that fuckwit Ford!"

"Do you know him? I said to Chip that I've always seen him around and known who he was, but I never spoke to him before. Never wanted to, to be honest."

"I know him a little bit. He used to go out with a friend of mine. Years ago, like, maybe five years ago. He was different then. Not so... full-on."

"What happened?"

"I don't know. I didn't really know him that well back then either. She dumped him and then I didn't see him again for years until I started working here and there he was, screaming at the end of the call floor."

"Did he remember you?"

"No, he didn't, or at least he pretended not to, but we didn't really know each other anyway. He spoke to me on my first day here and we've exchanged a few words here and there, but this is the most I've seen of him in years."

"We'll be seeing a lot more of him. Anyway, what else is happening with you?"

"Oh, nothing special. Just the usual, working and watching TV and stuff."

"Me too, that seems to be all I do. Work, watch TV and have a pint at the weekend."

"What are you watching now?"

"Lost. For the fourth time."

"Oh, I love that show."

"Me too. It's the best ever. I never get tired of it. It still really pisses me off when people say they didn't like the ending. Most of them don't even get it. They're just like well, they were dead all along."

"I know! Idiots. It clearly states that they weren't dead all along and that it all happened for real!"

"Right? And then there's those people who didn't like that

they didn't explain the island. Like any explanation they could give wouldn't be shit. Oh, it's Atlantis. It's a crashed alien spaceship or whatever. No way, it's better not to know. Anyway, it was about the characters, not the island."

"Exactly. I loved it. I've only seen it once though. Four times? Isn't that a bit much?"

"Maybe, but it's not like I have a lot else going on in my life."

"Yeah, I hear you. Sometimes watching TV is just so you don't have to think about how bored you really are."

"It's funny," said Justin, "you know, we should be happy. We have everything; education, health, money and we're still not happy. People in other countries would bite your hand off to have a quarter of what we have and we don't appreciate it. We're bored. We're a generation of spoilt bastards is what we are."

"I agree," said Jolene, "but it's hard to be happy working in a call centre."

"Yeah, it is. But I don't just mean working, we're unhappy with our lives, we feel like the world owes us something."

"We were told that it did. Our parents, the government. Get an education. So we do and the only jobs we can get are in here. You heard Linda say that there are three people with doctorates here and they can't get other jobs."

"True. They did say get an education. A degree equals happiness and a job for life, but it's bullshit. My brother has been on benefits since he graduated more than a year ago."

"Really? What's his degree in?"

"Media."

"That explains it then," laughed Jolene.

"Yeah, but the thing is, he's happy. He plays golf all day then sits around at night with his mates watching movies and smoking dope. He's free."

"Is that what you want to be free to do?"

"Well, no, not really. Not the golf, anyway."

Click. God damn it. Why could callers just not call the call centre? Couldn't they fix their own problems? Didn't they have anything better to do? At least it was an easy call to resolve, the idiot simply needed to know where his mobile's volume control was located, but by the time he finished and turned to Jolene to resume their conversation, she had taken a call. Just as she was finishing, Justin took another. And it went like this, with them just missing each other until the others came back and the moment was gone.

Of course, they didn't have lunch at the same time either, so Justin just sat in the break room with a cheese sandwich and flicked through the same few websites on his phone until it was time to go back.

The afternoon was slow but steady, much as it had been all week, except for Monday. And with it being Friday, Justin was feeling the fatigue of a week's work. He auto-piloted his way through most calls while watching the clock slowly drift towards finishing time. His half-awareness was shattered by a familiar angry voice.

"I want to make a complaint," said Mr. Fucking Abbott. At half past four on a Friday afternoon. What a cunt.

"What's the problem, Mr. Abbott?"

"How do you know who this is? I didn't tell you my name."

"It's Justin, Mr. Abbott. We spoke earlier this week. And last week. And twice the week before that."

"Very well then. Anyway, my phone was down for forty-seven minutes earlier today and I was unable to use it. This is unacceptable and I demand compensation."

"Was it the signal or the phone itself? If it was the signal, then it was the network, not us. You'll need to take it up with them. I'm sure you've been told this before."

"I already called them and they said it was a technical problem that led to my phone not working, so you should be responsible for compensation."

"There's nothing I can do."

"Are you sure? You should be able to send me a voucher against my next purchase or something."

"Let me look into that for you. How much is your monthly bill?"

"Thirty-nine of the Queen's pounds, and ninety-nine of her

pennies."

"Okay, well, if you were down for forty-seven minutes and you pay, let's call it forty quid a month, that works out at four pence. I'll get a voucher for four pence printed up straight away and sent out to you."

"I don't often sully my tongue with profanity, Justin, please don't make me do so now."

"What do you mean?"

"I mean I'm about to become very angry unless I am given adequate compensation for my troubles, not a paltry and frankly derisory four pence. You are clearly unable or unwilling to help me, so I want to speak to your manager."

"Absolutely. Hold the line."

He didn't even bother asking Linda and went straight to Ford. He was honest with him this time about who the caller was and why he called. Ford's eyes tightened and his jaw clenched, but he took the call. If he'd managed to get his pay sorted out earlier, then he was getting paid to take these calls. If not, well, fuck him.

Justin transferred the call, pressed 'Not Ready' and sat back. Just like the last time he passed a call from Abbott to Ford, it was fun to watch. Ford visibly grew more and more frustrated and struggled to get a word in until finally he'd had enough.

"Listen, Mr. Abbott. Whoever gave you that voucher previously shouldn't have done so. It was against our policy. You shouldn't have got it and you will never get any form of compensation from us again. Good day."

#

Well, that was lucky, thought Linda. She managed to avoid that escalated call without actually having to avoid it. Justin went straight to Ford, bypassing her altogether. That was definitely the beginning of the end, being overlooked in favour of Ford. Ah well, it was her choice to leave so she had to live with it. One more week to get that record broken. That last call probably wouldn't count as she didn't have to dodge it directly. She'd need to discuss it with the other team leaders, but she wasn't expecting the vote to go her way. Her leaving would be looked at either as betrayal or with jealousy, so they certainly weren't going to do her any favours. That meant she still needed three more to draw level and four to win. With only a week left, it wasn't going to be easy. She hoped it would be a really nasty week next week.

Then there was this shoe situation. They arrived this morning, amazingly fast delivery, but of course they were the wrong size. Too small. They always were when she ordered online, despite ordering a size bigger than she actually wore. Now she had a huge dilemma. Send them back and hope they could be changed in time? She doubted this. Even though they had arrived quickly, by the time she sent them back and the shop sent a new pair, they probably wouldn't arrive in time for her starting her new job. Did she just wear them anyway? They were so awesome and would make such a great impression that having sore feet would be worth it. The only other option was to check out the local shops, see what they had. This was a bit of a lottery and she didn't like taking risks like that. It would be a good excuse to go shopping though. Maybe she could find a nice top too? She could go tomorrow. It would mean missing the football match though. She didn't mind that so much, but the pub afterwards would probably be fun. It usually was. She could just turn up at the pub anyway. Even if she did go, her heart might not really be in it. Could she give her full support to the call centre team when she was leaving? No, she'd hit the shops, maybe find a nice pair of earrings as well, then go home and chill out with a bottle of wine.

She sat back in her chair and listened to the sound of the call floor. Lots of voices were talking at the same time so she couldn't make out any of them individually. There was the sound of people walking and the floor squeaking a little by the door. A faint hum from the tube lighting. A buzz. It was full of life and activity, for all its other faults. There was an energy to this place that she was going to miss. One more week. My goodness. One week then it would all be over.

Chapter 10

That microwave burger was absolutely disgusting and would have been inedible if it hadn't been smothered with ketchup. But Chip didn't have time for anything else, he was already in a hurry. He took a shower and considered having a swift wank, but he didn't have time for that either. He walked over to the bed and pulled on the first clothes that he found. Thank fuck that this D&D group didn't insist on costumes like his previous group had. They had been very strict about the actual role playing element of the game, meaning everyone had to stay in character the whole time. Justin's group did this a bit too, but there was more of a piss-taking element to it rather than anything formal. Even Elliott was quite flexible about breaking character. It was a bit of a shame though, that shadow mage suit had cost a hundred and twenty quid and now it was just gathering dust.

Time to go. He did a quick sweep of the flat to make sure the lights were off and to grab the booze from the kitchen. He started walking to Tony's place. It was already five to seven and it was a fifteen minute walk. That was good, he wanted to be a little late. Tony was Justin's friend from his school days and although he and Chip were technically friends now too, sometimes the conversation dried up when it was just the two of them. It was better to let Justin get there first so there would be no awkwardness.

Justin wasn't there when Chip arrived. He usually waited outside if he got there first. Chip decided to wait a little to see if he turned up. He smoked a cigarette, but there was still no sign of Justin. He considered smoking another, but then it started to rain.

Fuck it, it's a quarter past seven, I'll just go up anyway, thought Chip.

He knocked the door and Tony opened. "Chip, come on in. Justin's not here yet, but Elliott is. He's just getting set up," he said.

Chip looked over to Elliott, who nodded in his direction. His lank, greasy hair fell into his eyes and he swept it up and tucked it behind his ear. He was a nice enough guy, thought Chip, but he could do with washing his hair a bit more often. And that Undertaker t-shirt was at least two sizes too small, not a great look.

There was another knock at the door a couple of minutes later. Justin opened it without waiting for Tony and walked in. A streak of black flashed past Chip and jumped straight at Justin.

"Tony," he said, "can you do something about this dog?"

"This dog, Justin?"

"Can you do something about Sergeant Shinynose?"

"He likes you, that's all. He just wants to be pals, don't you Sarge?"

"Tony, you know how I feel about him."

"Okay, okay. I'll take him into the bedroom."

Justin was shaking a little, even though Sergeant Shinynose was possibly the least intimidating shih tzu Chip had ever seen.

"He'll be fine in there," said Tony after a few minutes.

"Are you sure?" asked Justin warily.

"Yeah, I put on a DVD. How I Met Your Mother. It's his favourite show, we'll not hear a peep out of him all night."

"Are we ordering pizza or what?" asked Elliott.

"Pizza? No one mentioned pizza. I've just eaten a shitty micro burger. I'm feeling a bit queasy to be honest. I didn't know there would be pizza," said Chip.

"You don't have to have any if you've already eaten," said Elliott.

"No, I want some. I can eat again. What are we getting? I can have anything except for pineapple. Does anyone take pineapple?"

"I do sometimes," said Tony, "but I'm not married to it, I can take whatever."

"One ham and mushroom and one pepperoni? How does

that sound?"

"Perfect, Elliott. Call it in will you?"

"But I'm setting up here."

"Okay then," said Tony, "I'll do it."

Elliott continued to set up while Tony called in the pizza order. He seemed to be taking his time.

"What's taking so long?" asked Chip.

"I've got some complicated story threads planned, so I just need to make sure I'm on top of everything. I'll be a little bit longer."

The pizzas arrived after twenty minutes. Sweet. The boys gathered round the table and got stuck in to the pizza and beer.

"So, how's work?" asked Elliott.

"Shit," said Justin.

"Shit," said Tony.

"Shit," said Chip.

"Well, you two I understand, working in a call centre, but Tony, why is your job shit? You just piss about in that shop all day reading the paper and eating pickled onion crisps."

"Yeah, it's not so much that side of things, it's the fucking customers that do my head in. Always wanting something. So demanding."

"I was in there the other day," said Justin, "and you were just taking the piss out of them. I thought you enjoyed that."

"That's just to keep me sane. But if they're nice to me, I'll be nice to them. It's just that so many people look down on shop workers."

"And call centre workers."

"Yeah, and call centre workers. They think just because it's our job to serve them that we should bend over backwards to suit their every whim. And they think we have these jobs because we're stupid or not capable of getting anything better. I don't think they realise how betrayed we've been by our consecutive, self-serving capitalist governments that make it impossible for any real upward movement among the working and lower middle classes. Both sides are as bad as each other, claiming to be left or right but they're the same party really. I'm a big believer in democracy, but it doesn't seem to be working as intended. It was supposed to replace the monarchy and do away with ruling classes. Our politicians are supposed to be elected representatives of the people, but in actual fact they think they're our rulers. They think they know better than us. The only real difference between them and the monarchy is that one ruler is born into the power and the other is elected by an apathetic and cowed public."

"And that's why we can't get good jobs?" asked Chip.

"Exactly. We're being held down by the man."

"It's not because we're lazy bastards that take what we can get and can't be arsed looking for something else?"

"Well, speak for yourself. I applied for dozens of jobs before I got this one."

"Me too, actually," admitted Chip.

"It's Justin that's the lazy one," said Tony. "He loves to moan about his job but I don't think he's bothered looking for another one."

"There's nothing out there," said Justin.

"How do you know if you haven't looked?"

"I just know. Anyway, how's your job Elliott?"

"It's great. I love it."

"You just sit in a security hut all day reading comics."

"That's why I love it. But that's not all I do. I have to walk round and check things."

"Yeah, for like five minutes every hour."

"Yeah. You're right, the rest of the time I do just read comics or work on my fantasy series."

"How long have you been writing that for?"

"Years. It's going to be a twelve volume epic."

"How many books have you actually written?"

"Well, I'm not writing in chronological order, so it's hard to say. Just now, I'm having a few problems with the magic system. It draws its power from the earth, but I'm not quite sure how to explain that."

"Don't then. Just say it's magic and leave it at that," said Chip.

"I can't! These things need an explanation. Just saying it's magic would be as bad as those fuckers who wrote Lost never explaining what the island actually was."

"I don't want to get into this again with you, Elliott," said Justin.

"Things don't always need explained," said Chip. "Would you say that Star Wars was improved by the explanation of the Force coming from midichlorians?"

"That's different."

"How?"

"It just is. I don't have time to get into this with you right now as I'm setting up, but I've made my feelings perfectly clear all over the internet. You can read my blog."

"Can't you just sum it up in a nutshell?"

"In a nacho?"

"What?"

"What?"

"Never mind."

"Well, in a nutshell, the entire Star Wars saga can be looked upon as a myth, a story being told at a later date, hence the 'A long time ago' bit. This explains plot inconsistencies and the newer technology in the prequels, because even though the story takes place earlier, the narrator tells it at a later time, in a similar fashion as the movie release dates. It's also possible that he's an unreliable narrator. By that token, we can say that the storyteller has only heard of midichlorians as one of a number of theoretical explanations for how the Force works. If you are familiar with the original drafts by George Lucas, the entire Star Wars saga was written in the Journal of the Whills, so if you take this as truth, then we can see the prequels as a second-hand account of what happened at that time, but relayed verbally at a later date to the keeper or keepers of said Journal. Some people even think that there are two different storytellers, one for the original films and another for the prequels, again explaining inconsistencies between the two."

"That's a nutshell? Fucking hell, what's the full explanation like?"

"As I said, I refer you to my blog. However, I will say that if you view the prequels this way, they become much better films. Except Attack of the Clones. That's a fucking abomination no matter what way you look at it."

"What about Batman v Superman? Have you seen that yet?"

"Yet? It's been out for weeks. I saw it on release day, as I do with every genre film."

"What did you think?"

"Dreadful. It was a Batman film in name only, because that character was certainly not the Batman. I don't know who it was masquerading as the Batman, pretending to be him. The real Batman simply does not kill, but this, this... cos-player gleefully slaughtered at least fifteen people. He's also the world's greatest detective, not the idiot we see in this film, stumbling from plot point to plot point, manipulated by a pantomime villain complete with the requisite vocal tick. An utterly empty experience and a betrayal of the true fans."

"You say that now," said Tony, "but come Blu-ray release day, you'll be standing in a queue outside Tesco with saliva dripping down your chin waiting for midnight so you can buy the collectors' edition."

"Well, that's the collectors' edition. It has twelve minutes of extra footage. It could be a whole different film. Plus I'll be listening to the commentary to see how the director explains some of the frankly absurd choices he made. On top of all that, I've heard that there's a hidden Easter Egg that may go some distance to explaining how DC's on-screen multiverse ties together."

"Where did you hear that?"

"I don't know. The grapevine."

"The grapevine? Nerd rumour websites, you mean?"

"Well, yes, but they can be very accurate."

"Don't you have to get that game set up?" interrupted Justin. "Time's ticking on."

"Yes, I just need ten more minutes."

Twenty-five minutes later, Elliott was finally ready to get started.

"Before we continue, make sure your character sheets are

up-to-date. If you remember, we finished the game rather abruptly last time and didn't get a chance to do it."

"We finished abruptly because the sun was coming up and kids were on their way to school," said Chip.

"Well, yes."

"Can't have that happen again. Me and Justin have been forced into playing football tomorrow, so we need to get some sleep."

"We better hurry up then."

Chip opened another can of beer while Elliott started describing the scene, complete with a long recap of the last session's events. It was well after ten by the time they were ready to actually start.

"So, you wake up in the tavern after a good rest. Any new skills can now be added to your character sheet. The owner and his son are serving the tables when you go downstairs. They're overworked as they're still short of wenches due to the necromancer kidnapping them and using their life energy to resurrect the dead."

"Why is it always a necromancer?" asked Chip.

"What?"

"I've been playing with you guys for over a year now, and this is the fourth time we've been up against a necromancer."

"Is it?" asked Elliott, looking horrified. "I need to check my notes, but that does seem a bit excessive. Anyway, no more out-of-character talk, let's get after this evil bastard."

"Yoho," said Justin.

"Yoho," said Tony.

"Yoho!" said Chip in his best dwarvish, or Scottish, accent.

It took a little while and a couple more beers to slaughter their way through the hordes of goblins guarding the bottom of the tower. Individually, they were weak and easily dispatched, but if the little shits flanked you, it could be a tricky battle. They had been outnumbered six to one and only Tony's inspired play had saved them in the end. Now the tower gates wouldn't open.

Chip's dwarf warrior had tried to bash them down, but brute force wasn't the answer here. Justin's elven archer was of no help whatsoever in this situation and was meditating in front of the gates while Justin mixed vodka and coke in the kitchen. It was up to Tony's wizard now. He'd been doing most of the heavy lifting up to now anyway, it had to be said.

"Yoho," said Tony. "I'm going to use my rain spell in a localised area over the lock."

"Why?" asked Elliott.

"To create a rust effect that weakens the lock, which can then be destroyed by Chip, sorry, I mean by Torvid Ironhelm."

"Okay," replied Elliott, "maybe we should have a little break. Stretch our legs, go to the toilet or what not."

"I could do with a smoke," said Chip.

"You weren't expecting this, were you?" asked Tony.

"What?" said Elliott.

"You don't know what to do. That's why you want a break, you need to look up the rules."

"No, I know all the rules."

"What do we do now then?"

"Er..."

"Aha, you don't know!"

"Fucking bastard. Okay, I don't, I need to check the rule book."

The break lasted over half an hour, as Elliott become more and more exasperated at being unable to find an answer to Tony's once again unorthodox play style. Chip and Justin had lost count of just how many times they's gone out for a smoke. And indeed how many drinks they'd had. There had been a lot of beer and now they were on the vodka. It was already one o'clock, but the football didn't start until three tomorrow, so there was still time to play and to sleep. They were coming back upstairs from another smoke when Elliott told them he had figured it out and it was time to continue. A couple of dice rolls later and the gates were open.

Inside the tower it was surprisingly empty. They looked around and found some stairs leading up. As they ventured upstairs, the opposition got stronger and stronger. It started with a few random goblins on the lower floors, but by the time they reached the third level from the top, they were locked in heavy warfare with a pair of rock trolls. Justin's elf, Tómas Detankinjin, had fallen, but was happily restored by a resurrection stone they found a couple of months ago in another necromancer's tower.

Suddenly, there was a fumbling of keys at the door of the flat, which then opened to introduce a figure shaded in the haze of alcohol and darkness.

"Mark," said Tony, "you're home. What time is it?"

"It's two o'clock."

"Two? Already?"

"Yes. I thought you might be finished by now."

"Not yet, we still have a necromancer to slay."

"Okay well, I'm tired and a little drunk, so I'm just going to go to bed."

"Sergeant Shinynose is in the bedroom."

"Okay, he can sleep on the bed tonight. Good night. Don't be too late. See you in a bit. Night boys."

"Good night."

Chip was so drunk by the time they reached the top floor that he could barely focus. All he knew was that he was being swarmed by skeletons risen from their eternal slumber by the last necromancer in the known world. After clearing a wave of walking dead, they confronted the necromancer himself, who tried to explain his actions as benevolent and how he was misunderstood and had had a tough childhood. Torvid, Tómas and Harsted of the Golden Pond looked at each other, said 'yoho' and attacked the evil bastard without a second thought.

Now the necromancer was raising the dead like it was going out of fashion and was flinging rotten corpses at the heroes with abandon. Torvid was swinging his axe wildly and hacking them down like weeds, but they just kept coming. Harsted had erected a light shield to protect himself from the onslaught, but it was weakening with every shot. Then Tómas stepped into the light, his slender elvish frame illuminated by the last of the sun's rays through a small rectangular window. He notched an arrow to his bow and fired.

"Yes!" screamed Justin. "Crit!" He'd made a perfect dice roll, scoring a critical hit on the necromancer himself and putting a swift end to his reign of terror. The skeletons and zombies collapsed to the ground now that they had no netherworldly power to animate their soulless cadavers. They had done it. They had defeated the necromancer and freed the realm, and the tavern wenches, from his icy grip. Chip took a long swig of whatever was in his glass to celebrate.

"Well done," said Elliott. "You've defeated the necromancer. Now what do you want to do?"

"Let's free the tavern wenches," said Justin.

"Okay, you open the dungeon door. Inside the cell are six buxom tavern wenches."

"What are they doing?"

"What? They're waiting to be rescued."

"Oh. They're not... making the most of their time together, so to speak? I mean, they had no idea if they were going to live or die. It would only be natural if they turned to each other in their hour of desperation."

"It would be. Shit, sorry, I didn't write that into the script. I should have thought of that. I mean, I do think of that sort of thing. All the time. I don't know why it escaped me this time. I could rewrite it now."

"Don't worry about it. You did say there were six, right?"

"Yeah, two for each of the heroes."

"So, you were thinking of us, after all."

"Well, yes. Anyway, there's also a huge pile of treasure behind the wenches. You can see a resurrection stone and what seems at first glance to be a Staff of Wailing Agony. Do you want to search the treasure to see what else is there?"

"The treasure can wait, let's get these wenches back to town and see how grateful they are."

"We should start to go through the experience and loot," said Elliott, "so we can start straight in next time."

Chip didn't want to sort out experience and loot. It was late and he'd had a lot to drink. This armchair was the most comfortable place in the world right now and he just wanted to get some sleep and dream of buxom tavern wenches.

Chapter 11

Chip wouldn't wake up, no matter how hard Justin pushed him. It was like he'd become a part of that armchair and wouldn't be separated from it under any circumstances. At least he was snoring a little, so Justin didn't have to worry about him too much. It had been a rough night in the end and the last thing he remembered was falling asleep on the sofa. Chip was already sleeping at that point and Tony had gone to bed too. He had no idea what happened to Elliott, but he wasn't there when Justin woke up. He shoved Chip again but there was no reaction other than a snort, so he decided to leave him while he tried to shower this hangover off.

The bedroom door was closed and he didn't know if Tony was up yet. He didn't want to disturb him anyway, so he just went into the bathroom and took the first available towel. It didn't smell great and was probably due to be rotated out, but it would do. Unfortunately, the shower didn't help that much. Justin's head was still pounding and stray thoughts of paranoia were beginning to tickle his brain. What had he said last night? Had he spilled his guts? Talked about Jolene? God damn it.

Chip was still snoring when he came out of the shower, but he had at least moved, so Justin hoped he was starting to wake up. Where was Sergeant Shinynose? Surely he couldn't still be in the bedroom? Were there any fucking headache pills around this place? He'd scoured the bathroom cabinets and discovered a bit more about Tony's private life than he was comfortable with, but couldn't find any. He checked the kitchen and found some at the back of a drawer. Thank fuck.

He went back over to Chip and gave him another push.

This time he woke up with a start and looked a little baffled. Then he immediately put his head back down on the chair.

"Oh fuck. It feels like you just hit me between the eyes with a sledgehammer. Why would you do that? We're friends."

"What are you talking about?"

"Jesus, my head. What time is it?"

"It's ten past twelve."

"In the afternoon!?"

"Yes in the afternoon. When else would it be? We didn't sleep until like five, so it's not too bad."

"Oh, my fucking head. I don't remember much after we killed that necromancer. We did kill him, right? My memory's a bit fuzzy."

"I think so."

"I need some food. The greasier the better. We still have time before that fucking football game. Fry-up?"

"Yeah, good idea."

Justin found a note on the living room table. He picked it up. "Mark is walking the dog and it seems like Tony has been called into work. Poor bastard. It says to just close the door when we leave, it locks itself."

"Let's go then."

"I just need to pop home and get my football gear first."

"You have football gear?"

"Yeah, haven't used it for a while, but yeah."

"I don't. I had to borrow a pair of rugby boots from my brother-in-law, but they're the same thing, right?"

"I don't know. I assume so."

"Anyway, I'll meet you at the Roll in say, half an hour?"

"Yeah, that should be enough."

Justin smoked a cigarette on his way home, which probably wasn't a great idea considering he threw up as soon as he got through the door. He just about made it to the bathroom in time. After spending several minutes with his head over the toilet bowl in case of a follow-up, he sighed and got up. He grabbed his football kit from the bedroom and packed it before heading out again.

Chip was already at the café when he got there, standing outside smoking. They went in, sat down and both ordered the Full Monty, the biggest all-day breakfast on the menu. Chip ordered both tea and coffee with his food. The waitress gave him a strange look, but took the order and walked away.

"Tea and coffee?" asked Justin.

"Yeah, coffee for the caffeine and tea for the flavour. You have to have a mug of tea with a fry-up, there's simply no other option."

"None."

"But I need a hit of coffee as well to get me going."

"Fair enough." Justin signalled the waitress over again and added a cup of coffee to his order too.

"I can't believe I passed out on that chair," said Chip. "I must just have been tired, I mean I know I had a fair bit to drink too, but I wouldn't say I was *drunk* drunk."

"You congratulated a potato for getting a part in Toy Story."

"Fuck off."

"Then you ran into the bedroom and got into the wardrobe and screamed 'where the fuck is Narnia?'!"

"Well, at least I wasn't going on about Jolene all night."

"What!? I wasn't, was I? Please tell me you're joking."

"I'm joking. You didn't actually mention her at all. At least, not that I can remember, but I did pass out on a chair. I don't know what you did after that."

"Me neither. Fuck."

"Don't worry about it. It was just Tony and Elliott."

"Yeah, I suppose so." Justin didn't feel so confident, but there wasn't much he could do. When breakfast arrived the boys tore into it like they hadn't seen food before. Justin almost felt like he hadn't. It helped a lot though. The greasy sausage and bacon mixed with runny egg yolk and tomato sauce from the beans, all covered in a thick layer of HP sauce was just the thing. Chip still looked a bit ropey, but hopefully some fresh air would do him good.

"What time is it now?" asked Chip when he finished eating.

"I know you won't have a mobile phone anywhere near you, but you should at least get a watch," said Justin.

"Yeah, maybe."

"It's coming up on two. We're supposed to be at the pitch at half past so Ford can pick the team. We should probably head there now."

"Don't say head. Mine is still splitting. Fuck sake."

As they made their way to the football pitch, they walked past Tony's Tesco. "Let's pop in for a minute," said Justin.

"Yeah, good idea, I need to pick up a few things."

Tony was once again at the back of the shop, this time he had his head stuck in the milk fridge.

"What are you doing?" asked Justin.

"I'm dying, that's what I'm doing."

"Why did you come to work?"

"They called me at nine and said they were desperate. Offered me time and a half. I was still drunk and thought I was feeling great."

"Oh, you should never make decisions when you're drunkover."

"I know. Ah well, just a few hours to go then I'll get home and get back to bed. Was a good night though. I had fun."

"Me too," said Justin. He looked around to Chip, but he wasn't there. "Have you seen Chip? He was here a second ago."

"He's over there."

"Oh, yeah. So, we have to go and play this fucking football game. I just wanted to see how you were."

"I'll be okay, thanks."

"Oh, and by the way, I didn't say anything last night, did I?"

"About Jolene, you mean?"

"What? What did I say?"

"Nothing. Not last night anyway. You fell asleep on the sofa just after Elliott left."

"Oh, yeah, of course, just after Elliott left."

"You don't remember Elliott leaving, do you?"

"No."

"Well, don't worry. You were fine. Now please let me get back to cooling my head down."

Justin left Tony and went to find Chip. He was standing outside smoking again and swigging gulps from a bottle of Lucozade.

"How can you smoke so much when you're hungover? I had one earlier and I threw up."

"I don't know, it tastes like shit, but I just can't stop. I'm always like this after drinking."

"Well, let's get moving."

They arrived at the football pitch in good time for the match. There were about ten guys already there, including Ford. Justin and Chip walked over to join them.

"All right, lads? Glad to see you could make it. We're still waiting for a few more, then I'll pick the team and go over the tactics," said Ford.

Chip lay on the grass and pulled a bag of frozen peas out from the carrier bag of stuff he'd bought at the shop. He put the peas on his head and closed his eyes. He was still lying there when the rest of the team arrived and Ford walked over to him.

"You're in some shape, mate."

"Fuck sake, I'm so hungover, I can't look left."

"Well, that bag of peas better do the job, we kick off in half an hour."

"I'll be okay by then."

"Good. You'll be playing at centre back, alongside Angry Gilmore."

"Centre back? Really? You know I'm not the tallest guy in the world, I'll not be able to get up for those defensive headers."

"I don't care, mate. Angry can clear the air and you clear the decks. I've seen how much you smoke when you're supposed to be working. There's no fucking way I'm having you try to run round the pitch with your lungs. You stay at centre back and butcher anyone who tries to come near you."

"But I could be the midfield enforcer. You know, the Makelele role."

"Just stay at the back and put the feet into anyone within

two yards of you." He then turned to Justin. "You're up front, mate."

"Really? Nice!"

"I'm sure your lungs aren't in great shape either, but you look like you've got a bit of pace, so try to get in behind their defence when the ball is played up. Don't worry about tracking back, I don't want you running too much either. Just hang on the shoulder of the last man and get past him when the ball comes your way. There's only one ref and no linesmen, so if you were to creep a little bit offside, I reckon you'll get away with it."

By the time Ford had walked around telling everyone their positions, there was just time for a quick warm-up before kick-off. Justin and Chip weren't the only ones suffering and it consisted of a few knees-ups and some of the most half-hearted star jumps ever seen on a football pitch.

Big boss Phil pulled up at the side of the pitch in his BMW and made his way awkwardly onto the field, trying to avoid getting mud on his Italian slip-ons. "Great," he said, "I made it in time. I just want to say good luck lads and let's get it into those broadband jerks! There's a pint in it for all of you if we win."

The game kicked off and Justin stuck to Ford's tactics and stood up front waiting for the ball to come to him. It never did. The guy that had started off marking him gave up on that after fifteen minutes and started to push further up the pitch. He had tried to start a bit of banter, calling Justin a 'phone fucker' but after failing to rile him up, had given up. Now he wasn't even bothering to mark him.

Justin looked up and noticed that Jolene had turned up and was watching the game from the sidelines. Shit. Now he was going to have to work harder. He might even need to drop into the midfield and try to win the ball for himself.

Just as he was contemplating this, the broadband team made a break and scored. The through ball had sailed right over Chip's head and one of their strikers latched onto it and buried it. God damn it. Still, one-nil down after twenty minutes wasn't great, but it wasn't insurmountable.

Three-nil down at half-time felt insurmountable. Justin

trudged off the pitch towards an angry-looking Ford, who was waving wildly at his team to get them off. "What the fuck is going on out there?" he screamed when the full team had assembled. "Did any of you listen to my tactics?"

"Yeah, we did, Ford and we're trying," said Vik.

Paisley Des, already looking a bit worse for wear, tapped Ford on the shoulder. "I've been watching the game and we're not a million miles away in spite of the scoreline. Get that Vik fella out on the wing so he can run past boys and for fuck sake, put someone in defence who can get up to head the ball."

Ford proceeded to make a few changes. Vik was moved out wide and Chip took his place in the centre of midfield, while Tommy Cornell, a guy that no one actually seemed to know, took the other centre back position.

"Right lads," he said after doing this, "get some of these half-time oranges into you. The vitamins will sort you right out."

"But you and Paisley are boozing away here on the bench. That's hardly fair. The other team is having a fucking half-time can and all," said Angry Gilmore.

"Calm down, Angry," said Ford, "there'll be plenty of time for a drink after the game. I know some of you boys could use a cure, but just hang in there."

Justin waved across at Jolene and she waved back. She was standing with the other spectators, who consisted of a few of the girls from the call centre, Phil, and a few feral kids from the nearby estate. He didn't have time to talk to her though, as the teams were due back on the pitch for the second half.

The changes seemed to improve the team and Justin found himself running more now. It was either the changes or the fact that the other team had a half-time beer. Regardless, he hadn't ran this much in years. At least since he started work at the call centre. He was only just realising how sedentary he'd become in the last three years. God damn it, now the sweat was lashing off his forehead. It got into his eyes and the alcohol that was dripping out of the pores stung like fuck.

All of a sudden, he found himself free on goal. Vik had slipped up the wing and crossed the ball to Justin, who was at least five yards offside. The broadband team were appealing to the referee, who apparently saw nothing. Justin had the ball at his feet and only the goalkeeper to beat. He pulled his foot back and let fly. The ball went to the left of the keeper. Goal! Fucking hell, he'd scored. He couldn't believe it. He turned to around to locate Jolene, but he couldn't see her. All he saw was an angry Ford shouting at him from the sidelines. He jogged over to him.

"What the fuck was that?" asked Ford.

"What are you talking about?"

"How the fuck did you miss that? You were clear through."

"Miss? But I buried it. Shit, I must be seeing double, I thought I tucked it in to the left of the keeper."

"You tucked it in to the left of the corner flag, mate."

"Sorry. I'll do better next time."

Justin went back onto the pitch and ran around like a headless chicken for about five minutes and didn't touch the ball once. When the referee blew the whistle, Ford signalled for him to come off. He walked over to the sideline. Not only was he being replaced, he had the indignity of making way for Big Bazza.

"You're subbing me? Come on."

"Listen mate, you managed nearly an hour and that's not bad, the state you're in, but let's be honest here, you weren't going to contribute any more to the game."

"I was just limbering up. I'm feeling great, just about to hit my stride."

"Are you having a laugh?"

"What? No, I'd just found my feet, I was ready to start banging them in."

"Come on, mate."

"What do you...?"

"Goal!!!!" Ford started jumping up and down and running along the touchline. He clenched his fists and threw them in the air. What was the big deal? That goal was little more than a consolation. They were still three-one down with half an hour to go. Fucking Big Bazza though. He'd been on the field for less than a minute, strolled up the pitch and casually nodded a corner past the keeper. The big guy could barely run the length of himself but he'd managed more in a minute than Justin had in an hour.

Justin pulled on a hoodie and sat on the sub bench. He lit up a cigarette and sat down to watch the rest of the match. Fucking hell, Big Bazza was at it again. That was two! Once again, he barely moved, just swung his foot at a cross from Vik and delivered a thumping volley into the corner of the goal. Unbelievable! Ford slid on his knees across the side of the field screaming like a mad man.

Then the referee was running across to the bench. Now what? He pulled out a yellow card and waved it at Justin.

"What are you doing?" he asked.

"You're booked, son. Put that cigarette out."

"You're booking me for smoking?"

"I'm booking you for smoking in an officially designated player zone."

"The bench? And it's not really even a bench, it's more like a log with a few jackets on it."

"It's the official dug-out area."

"You know I've been subbed, right? Booking me won't make any difference now."

"It will be in my official report and will carry over to the next match," said the referee before turning and blowing the whistle to restart the game.

Justin stubbed out his cigarette and looked up just in time to catch the equaliser. Big Bazza once again powered a shot past the goalkeeper. Three goals in three minutes from the big lad. Fucking unbelievable. Ford was going absolutely mental now.

"Fuck you, you broadband bastards, that big man there, that's my secret fucking weapon. You didn't see that coming, did you, you bastards!?"

Justin couldn't take any more of this, so he walked across to join the spectators. Phil wasn't quite in the same state as Ford, but was quivering with excitement. Justin went and stood beside Jolene. "Hi," he said.

"Hi, did you enjoy the game?"

"Not really. It did help with the hangover though, I have to say. I'm feeling much better now than I was before."

"Big night last night?"

"Just a few drinks with the boys."

"I see. Well, you can rest up a bit now."

"Yeah, but I should still be out there. The game's still not finished and I was playing all right."

"Erm, yeah."

"What?"

"Nothing." She burst out laughing.

"I was shit, wasn't I?"

"Absolutely terrible, haha."

"Fucking hell. I blame the drink. On that note, are you coming to the pub after?"

"No, sorry, I can't, I have something on tonight."

"What, like a date?"

"No, just a family thing, but I have to go."

Justin was pulled out of the conversation by Phil cheering. No fucking way. They'd scored again. It was four-three now. Vik was wheeling away with one arm in the air. At least it was him who'd scored and not Big Bazza. Bazza was actually doubled over now, holding his chest and coughing up a hefty chunk of his lungs. He looked like he was dying, but he'd banged in a three-minute hat-trick so his job was done anyway.

With five minutes to go, Tommy Cornell got up and got his head to a free kick to make it five. Justin couldn't believe it. What a comeback. Ford would be talking about this one for a while. Justin didn't feel like a part of the team. In fact, he'd just held them back. They were on fire as soon as he left the pitch. He said goodbye to Jolene and walked back around to the bench and waited for the match to finish.

There was an almighty roar of triumph when the referee blew the whistle. The broadband team were sitting on the pitch as if they'd just lost the Champions League final. There were even a few tears from what Justin could see. Ford eyes were bulging out of his head as he cheered. He looked terrifying. Chip came and sat beside him on the bench. He looked a lot chirpier than he had before the game.

"Well done," said Justin.

"Thanks. It was a good second half. I was much better as the water carrier."

"The what?"

"The water carrier."

"What are you talking about?"

"I'm not sure really, but that's what the commentators on telly say. Anyway, you were part of the team too."

"Yeah, but the team didn't start to play until I left the pitch. I was the weakest link."

"No, your job was to tire out their defence so Bazza could rip it apart when he came on. Good tactics if you ask me."

"You're full of shit, but thanks. And don't tell Ford you liked his tactics. Ready for the pub?"

"Can't fucking wait. I didn't think I'd be saying that a couple of hours ago, but that run out did the world of good."

Ford walked over to them. "We're off to the Lion. The first round's on Phil. You coming?" he asked.

"Yeah," said Justin.

"Good, some of the others are going for a bite to eat first, but I say fuck that. I'll grab a burger in the pub. Or a bag of nuts, whatever they have. A few are heading home to get washed, but I brought a can of deodorant, so I'm just going to have a Manc shower."

"Can I borrow it?" asked Chip.

"Sure. Here you go."

A quick spray of deodorant later and they started for the pub. One of the local kids who was watching the match earlier was kneeling down by a bike that had been chained up at the side of the pitch. He had a pair of bolt-cutters and was trying to cut through the chain.

"Is that your bike, mate?" asked Ford.

"No, not yet."

"What do you mean? You're not fucking stealing that bike."

"Are you going to stop me? Come on then!" The boy took up a fighting stance and started throwing weak-looking air punches in Ford's direction.

"Are you serious? I'm not going to fight you. Those

punches of yours wouldn't break the foam on top of a cappuccino. What do you think you'll do to me?"

The kid's eyes darted around, then he turned and ran off. When he was at a safe distance, he turned and started shouting obscenities at them. His mate joined him and they yelled something about how their brothers were going to come down and 'do some fucking wrecking'. Ford and a few of the other players laughed this off and continued on to the pub. Justin couldn't help but sneak an occasional glance over his shoulder on the way there though.

Chapter 12

It was a generic Italian chain restaurant but she'd been here before and at least the food was good, if unremarkable. She looked around but couldn't see Danny. Oh wait, there he was, at the table in the corner. He could've at least waved, instead of just nodding at her. Now he was looking her up and down as she walked over. A little grin on his face. Cheeky. She'd liked that about him last week when she'd met him when she was out with some friends, but now she wasn't so sure. He had been so confident that it was hard to resist when he asked her to dinner. Now he just looked arrogant. Still pretty hot though. Good hair, cheeky smile, a little stubble.

He stood up and pulled her chair out and let her sit first. That was a surprise! He then took his jacket off to reveal both arms with full tattoo sleeves. Ugh. It wasn't that she was against tattoos as such, but this guy could be no older than twenty-five and to have two full sleeves already seemed so forced. Like he'd got them done in a rush just to have them rather than put any thought into what he wanted and let them build organically over the years. Nice muscles though.

"All right, love," he said and winked as he sat down.

"Call me Jolene," she said.

"Sorry, lo... I mean Jolene. Don't take it the wrong way, I don't mean nothing by it. Not trying to sexist, like. Just trying to be nice. Hope you're not one of those bloody feminists. A bloke can say nothing these days." Why was he speaking with a Cockney accent? He told her last week that he was from Hucknall, just a few miles up the road. Did he talk like this then? She couldn't really remember, but didn't think so.

"How are you?" she asked.

"I'm great, yeah." His phone beeped. "Sorry, love, I just gots to answer to this, yeah?" He spent the next five minutes fucking about with his phone. Jolene was just about to get up and leave when the waiter came to the table.

"I'll have a bottle of Perroni," said Danny. "And a white wine for the lady? Or a Prosecco?" He looked at her. She shrugged. That would do.

"And to eat?" asked the waiter.

"We'll have an antipasti to start. For the main, I'll have the seafood ravioli. Jolene, what do you want? The carbonara, probably."

"That'll be fine."

The waiter repeated the order then left. Jolene watched him walk away then turned back to Danny just in time to notice his eyes darting away from her cleavage. She'd agonised over which top to put on and realised she'd probably made the wrong choice.

"How's work?" he asked. "You said you work in a call centre, yeah?"

"Yeah. It's not great, but you have to do something."

"I couldn't be doing with that. Answering phones all day. Would do my head in. Nah, I like to be out and about. Odd jobs and that. Bit of building and a bit of decking. Good money too. Can fucking charge whatever you like. People will pay it."

"Good for you."

"Yeah, me and Trev, that's my mate that I work with, we painted a fence today, charged three hundred bar for it. Nice one. Plus, it was for a forty-something divorcée. Trev's round there now giving her a right good seeing to. Would've been there n'all, tag team, but I had this date lined up. You're a lot fitter then her anyway."

"Lucky me."

The drinks and the starter arrived and they ate in silence. Danny fucked about a bit more on his phone, laughing out loud occasionally. When the appetiser was finished, he set down the phone and started talking again. "So, you want another drink?" he asked.

"Sure."

"Doesn't hurt to be a little tipsy, eh?"

"It wouldn't hurt at all."

"Where the fuck is that waiter?"

"It's busy. He'll be here soon."

"He fucking better be, the Mario-looking cunt. Ah, wait, yeah, there he is."

The waiter brought their mains and Danny ordered more drinks for them. Again, the eating was done mostly in silence. Jolene didn't mind. After they had finished, Danny ordered two tiramisus for dessert. "Fucking love a tiramisu," he told her breasts.

"Me too," replied Jolene.

After they finished dessert, Danny declined coffee for both of them. "So, you want to get out of here?" he asked.

Yes. "I, er, I actually have to go home now. I've got an early start in the morning."

"But it's only half past nine. What do you need to go home now for?"

"It's a family thing, I can't get out of it."

"What time in the morning? I can wake you up early and drive you home."

Her eyes tightened. "No, thanks. I'll just go now. Thanks for dinner."

"What? I'm not buying your dinner if you're leaving now."

"But you asked me out."

"You think just 'cos you're a bird that the bloke should pay for dinner? Fucking ridiculous."

"No, I think whoever asked should pay. If I'd asked you out, I would pay, but you asked me."

"Thought I was getting a fucking ride out of it or I wouldn't have bothered. Blowie, at least."

"You are a fucking arsehole. Here!" She pulled two twenty-pound notes out of her purse and threw them at him. "Keep the change, fuckwit."

She stormed out of the restaurant and walked around the corner to calm down. She took a few deep breaths and wished she'd had more than two glasses of wine. Maybe Justin and the others were still at the pub? Probably, if Ford was with them. She took out her phone and started typing.

#

"Then Big Bazza came on, banged in three in three minutes and the comeback was on! I was holding him back until just the right moment. Those broadband bastards never saw it coming! They were so bad in the second half, they managed to snatch defeat from the jaws of victory! Of course, it was us that made them look bad."

This was the sixth time Justin had heard this story tonight. Every time someone new arrived into their company, Ford told it again. He wouldn't have minded so much but every time Bazza came on to the pitch to take the glory, Justin had to go off. Just as Ford was about to start telling Angry Gilmore's wife Jessie about Vik's majestic goal that put the team into the lead, his phone beeped. It was a text from Jolene! It said 'Finished early. U still at pub? Where?' Justin fumbled to reply. He wasn't that great at texting in the first place, plus he was on his sixth pint of the evening with only a packet of salt and vinegar crisps and some pork scratchings to line his stomach. After a few minutes, he managed to reply 'Yes. In the Lion. Come!'

He sent the message and turned back to the others. Ford had stopped talking now and Vik was up and miming the goal he scored. He almost knocked a table over and the couple that were sitting there made a few angry, but ultimately half-hearted, gestures in his direction. Ford and Vik then broke out into Nottingham Forest football chants until the bouncer came over and told them to be quiet, that this was a colourless pub.

A few minutes later, Jolene walked in. Justin had been watching the door for her. Jesus! She looked amazing. Even hotter than usual, if that were possible. She was wearing a skirt to just above her knees and boots to just below them plus a top with a generous neckline. Justin would have to try really hard not to stare. If that's what she wore to a family party, his mind boggled as to what she would wear on a date. He waved at her and motioned for

123

her to join him at the bar.

"Hi," he said after fighting his way through the crowds.

"Hi."

"So, you got out early then?"

"Yeah. I fancied a drink, so I thought I would join you."

"Good. Great. That's fantastic. I've had a few already." Justin really felt his head going a bit now and he thought he might be swaying.

"I can see that."

"What can I get you?"

"It's okay, I can get my own, thanks."

"Well, I'm just getting one for myself anyway. And for Chip, so I might as well get you one too."

"Okay then. I'll have a pint."

"A pint? Great!"

"You don't think it's unladylike?"

"Has someone told you that before?"

"Yeah, lots of people. They think women should drink bottled beer or white wine spritzers."

"Who gives a fuck about that? Drink what you want. A pint, then?"

"Yeah!"

Justin ordered the drinks and waited. A guy next to him was leering at Jolene. He tapped Justin on the shoulder. "Is that your bird?"

"You do know she can hear you, right?" replied Justin.

"So? You shagging her or what?"

"Er, no, she's just a friend."

"Yeah, thought so. There's no way you could pull a bird like that."

"What? What's it got to do with you?"

"You want to make it something to do with me, do you?"

"What?"

"Come on, then!"

Justin's head was swimming. Jolene stepped in between him and the guy at the bar. "You think that sort of behaviour is going to make me want to shag you?" she asked him.

"No. Look, I'm sorry, love. I didn't mean anything by it. I've had a few, that's all."

"All right, then."

Justin picked up two of the pints and Jolene grabbed the third and guided him back to the table.

#

Jolene manoeuvred Justin and the drinks through the crowd to the relative safety of the table. That guy looked like he was one Stella away from smashing his girl up and she was glad to be away from him. She sat Justin down beside Chip and, as there were no free seats, she sat on the arm of his chair. She said hello to the others, mostly the boys who played football today, plus a few other girls. It had been a while since she'd been out for drinks with her workmates but no one seemed surprised to see her. Ford was actually standing up and telling a barely believable shagging story to the group. She'd known that he had a flexible approach to telling the truth but now Jolene was beginning to suspect that Ford was one of the biggest shit-talkers ever to walk this earth. But, she had to admit, he was quite amusing. He was lying now with abandon, spurred on by a receptive audience and strong drink.

"So there I was, up to my knees in fanny batter when her husband walked through the door. Didn't even hear him come home we were going at it so hard. He was shocked to say the least. I just turned to him without breaking thrust at all and said 'you want to join us, big man?' Needless to say he didn't and I was running for the door a minute later, grabbing whatever clothes I could on the way out. Good times."

Most of the boys laughed at this. Most of the girls pretended not to.

"She wasn't the best-looking woman in the world, mind you," Ford continued, "but that's all right with me. In fact, it's better. Good-looking women think they're fantastic but the truth is that most of them are shit in bed. Don't think they need to make the effort 'cos they're fucking good-looking. Don't get me wrong, some of them are like dynamite, but a lot of them are like a sack of

125

potatoes in the sack. An ugly bird or a fat bird, they're the ones that'll fuck you so hard your head spins. Both your heads!"

Justin looked dubious. Chip looked interested.

"Well, that sounds about right," said Chip, "but I've got no real point of comparison. I've never shagged a good-looking woman."

There was a brief moment of stunned silence. Jolene had long suspected that men never told the truth about shagging when they were in the pub. This was uncharted territory.

"Well, I've had a lot," said Ford, "and there's been plenty of mingers in my past too but they're the best. Fuck you like a pig on a stick."

Jolene had no idea what this meant, but she just went along with it. Everyone in the group was listening intently to Ford, so she let him continue.

"I knew this girl at school. Big lass. They called her Jabba the Garage."

"Why?" asked Angry Gilmore.

"Because she was bigger than a hut. Anyway, she was my first. I was fourteen, and no one else would touch her with a bargepole, they wouldn't have ridden her into battle, but I was in there like a shot. I mean, the only time I'd seen an arse like that before, there was someone at the other end feeding buns into the trunk but I didn't care, she rode my fourteen-year old cock dry. There was only salt coming out in the end. It was fucking amazing. Shagged that for two years until I moved on."

"Is sex all you ever think about, Ford? You're so shallow," said Jolene.

"Shallow? Me? You don't know what you're talking about, no offence. I've got more layers than an onion. Go on, ask me anything. I'm interested in all sorts of things. Art, cuisine, travel, politics, you name it."

"Is it possible for ethical Capitalism to function alongside Socialist ideals in 21st century Britain? Is there even such a thing as ethical Capitalism?"

"Well, we could talk about that, but it's a bit boring for the pub. Look at Paisley Des there, he's half-asleep already. I was reading this thing yesterday about the world record ejaculation. That's a bit more fun to talk about."

It did sound a bit more fun, actually, if not a little disgusting.

"World record? By what? Volume or distance?" asked Justin.

"Distance."

"Who measured it? Is there a Guinness Book of Records representative going to a wanking competition?"

"Never mind that. What do you think the record is?"

"I wouldn't have a clue."

"Well, you must know how far you can squirt yourself, so you do have some sort of clue. Just give me a distance."

"I don't know, Ford. A metre?"

"Chip?"

"Two metres."

"Jolene?"

"Jesus. I can't believe I'm... I'll say a metre and a half."

"Four metres," said Vik, "but I could break that if I entered."

"Anyone else have a guess?" asked Ford. A few of the others had guesses ranging from a few centimetres to a few metres. "Six metres," he said.

"Six? That's like twenty feet? No fucking way can anyone shoot that far," said Paisley Des, now wide awake.

"You should give it a go, Des," said Ford.

"Where did you read this, Ford?" asked Jolene.

"Online."

"When you were supposed to be working?"

"It was quiet yesterday."

"Fuck sake," said Chip. "How do you even know you can do that? Do you just think one day you're going to see how far your spunk travels? How do you know you're good at it?"

"It's a bit like pole vaulting," said Justin.

"What?" asked Ford. "Fucking pole vaulting? What the fuck are you talking about?"

"Well, at school, I always wanted to try pole vaulting, but

we were never allowed. Health and safety. It's probably the same at every school in England. So, how do you know you're good at it?"

"You have a point," said Ford, "but you can't practice pole vaulting in your bedroom. This, you can."

"Can you improve the quality, I wonder?" said Chip. "You know, if your were to have a lot of dairy, for example. Would that make it thicker and easier to travel further?"

The conversation continued as the boys discussed the logistics of breaking this record. Jolene sat back on the arm of the chair and listened. It had been fun at first but now she was getting bored and desperately wanted to change the subject. The boys, however, were quite into it and starting to get a little rowdy. At that point, a bouncer walked over to the table. Thank fuck!

"Excuse me, folks, you're getting a little noisy. Can you keep it down please? There are other customers to consider."

"Fuck off," said Angry Gilmore.

"What did you just say?"

"Leave us alone. We're just having a laugh. Go and bother someone else."

"Listen, I'm the doorman here."

"You should've worked harder in school."

"What the fuck? Are you taking the piss?"

"Sorry, mate," said Ford. "He's had a few drinks. He doesn't mean to be rude. I know you're just doing your job. You're working hard, why don't you sit down for a minute and take the weight off your knuckles?"

"Right! That's it! Out, the lot of you."

Fucking hell, thought Jolene. She was going to have to do something about this. She hated taking advantage of being a woman but there were times when only tits were good enough to get the job done. She undid a button of her already-quite-daring top. "Excuse me," she said, smiling. "We promise we'll keep it down. Give us one more chance."

"One more chance," said the doorman, his eyes darting in several different directions at once. "If I have to come over here again, you're out."

"Thanks. We'll be good," said Jolene.

They broke off into a few smaller groups after this. Justin had given Jolene his seat while he went to the bar. She found herself discussing chutneys with Chip. He had discovered a whole new world and she was happy for him. She kept her eye on Justin as he got more drinks in but there wasn't any problem this time. That guy from before had either left or been chucked out. She didn't care which.

As the time drifted on, the group began to thin out. Soon, there were only a few of them left. Paisley Des had passed out and was snoring. Justin was talking to Ford about something and the two of them looked in her direction from time to time. She was listening to Chip wax lyrical about fruit preserves when Vik joined them.

"All right?" he asked.

"Yes, thanks. And you?"

"Good, yeah. Thinking about hitting a club."

"Great."

"What about you?"

"What about me?"

"Do you like clubbing?"

"No."

"Oh."

She got up and went to the bar. She bought drinks for herself, Chip and Justin. They had both bought her drinks earlier and she wanted to get her round back. Both of those guys were starting to look like they didn't need any more, especially Justin. He was swaying in the corner as Ford talked at him. She caught his eye as she approached and he smiled.

"Hey, Jolene," said Ford, "we were just talking about you."

"What? What were you talking about?"

"Nothing special. Just that you're a nice girl."

"Well, thanks. Justin, here's your drink. Maybe you want to make it your last one?"

"You didn't get me one?" asked Ford.

"No."

Jolene went to rescue Chip from Vik. Whatever Justin and Ford were talking about, she didn't want to know. After a while, those two came and sat with the others and they all discussed work for a while. Out of the blue, Vik announced he was going clubbing and asked if anyone wanted to come with him. No one did. He looked a little relieved and Jolene suspected he was in fact going home.

"Just the Brian Clough team left," said Ford.

"And Paisley Des," said Justin.

"Yeah, well, he's out of it. Maybe we should get some scissors and give him a haircut."

"No, Ford," said Jolene.

"Okay, okay. I was just messing. His hair's that short, he probably wouldn't notice anyway. Plus, it would grow back."

"You know," said Jolene. "I've often wondered how hair grows."

"What do you mean?" said Chip. "It grows out of your head. And other places."

"Yeah, but I mean, how? Where does it come from? And more importantly, where does it go?"

"What?" asked Justin.

"Where does it go when it's cut? Or when it falls out? My hair falls out all the time, so where does it go? There are billions of people in the world whose hair is falling out every day, so why is the world not full of hair?"

Ford started laughing like crazy. "Where does hair go? Jolene, what are you talking about?"

"I'm serious. Where does it go? Does it disintegrate? What?"

"Why is the world not full of hair?" asked Justin, catching up on the conversation.

"That's what I said."

"Yeah, I know, Jolene, but you're right, why isn't it?"

"I have no idea."

Ford jumped up off his seat and shouted around the bar. "Does anyone know why the world isn't full of hair?" Everyone ignored him, if they even heard him over their own conversations. Everyone except the bouncer.

"Right people, I've already told you once to keep it down.

Now, it's time to go."

"What? Why?" asked Ford.

"Because you've had too much to drink."

"Well, you've had too much to eat, you fat bastard."

The bouncer looked furious, but took a deep breath and managed to control his temper. "Last warning. If you're not out of here in two minutes, I will literally throw you out."

Jolene still had half a pint left, but set it on the table while the men gulped down whatever remained in their glasses. Ford then lifted her glass.

"You going to finish this?" he asked.

"No, you can have it."

Ford necked the beer swiftly and headed for the door.

"What about Des?" asked Jolene.

"He'll be all right. He's made his way home in worse shapes than this."

Hitting the cold air didn't seem to agree with Justin and he almost fell over. Chip caught him and held him up.

"Don't worry," said Chip, "I'll get him home."

"Are you sure?" asked Jolene. "You're a bit unsteady there yourself."

"Yeah, we'll be fine. It was a good night. Thanks. See you on Monday."

"Good night, then. Be careful on your way home."

"Night night Jolene," said Justin.

"Night Justin," she said.

Chip pulled him away and put his arm around his shoulders as he guided him down the road. They were both swaying a bit but they looked all right. Justin turned and started to make his way back but Chip grabbed him again and they were off.

"Just you and me left, then?" said Ford. Shit, she'd forgotten about him.

"Yeah."

"It's not even midnight yet. Fuck me, I never leave before midnight. But then again, I don't usually get kicked out either. You want to go to another bar?"

"No, I'm good."

"What about a club? Or we can go back to my place. I have plenty of drink at home. We can have a nightcap."

"No thanks, Ford. I'm good. See you on Monday."

She turned and walked away without looking back. She'd had a good night but now she just wanted to go home and get some sleep. Taxi!

Chapter 13

Justin's eyelids felt like they were stuck together and would require a tremendous effort to open. His mouth tasted like a wet dog that had smoked a hundred cigarettes and he gagged and dry retched. Someone was banging a drum inside his head. His eyelids had started to force their way open and the glare of a thousand suns burned his retinas. He snapped his eyes shut again and rolled over. Too fucking early.

The next time he woke up, an undefined amount of time later, his head was still pounding but he was at least able to prise his eyes open. The worst of the brightness had gone and now his vision was slightly hazy. His stomach reached up and punched the back of his throat and he jumped out of bed and made for the bathroom. The contents of his stomach, which was mostly liquid, emptied into the toilet and Justin sat back panting and wiped strings of saliva from his mouth. He waited for a few minutes, but no more was coming. That was the second time in two days he'd thrown up in this toilet. He hoped this wasn't becoming a regular thing. He stood up and popped a few pills and swallowed them down with tap water from his cupped hands.

He trudged back to bed and picked up his phone. It had just gone twelve. He didn't remember what time he got home but they had been kicked out of the pub around midnight, so it was possible he'd slept for almost twelve hours. His head felt like he'd slept for two. What the fuck had happened between leaving the pub and now? He had nothing. How did he get home? Did he say something to Jolene? To Ford? Shit, this wasn't good. Not good at all.

Maybe he could piece this back together if he just relaxed. A few deep breaths. He'd been talking to Jolene about, oh Jesus, ejaculation! No, wait, everyone talked about that. Then what? Hair, jam, smoked versus cured bacon, faster than light travel. Then there had been some football talk. They talked about work, giraffes and Eddie Vedder. That was it. Okay, now what had he said to Ford? Fuck. He had no fucking idea. He could have told him anything. Anything.

Fucking Chip. If he had a mobile Justin could text him and get some peace of mind. Why did he have to be so stubborn about fucking mobile phones!? He worked for a fucking tech support company for mobiles for fuck sake. He could call him, he did have a land line so he could get broadband, but they never did that. Answering phones all day had given them both a total hatred of telephonic communication. They usually just talked at work and made any arrangements they needed to there. No, he couldn't call Chip.

Ten minutes later, he called Chip in a total panic.

"Hello?"

"Chip. It's Justin."

"Yeah. How are you feeling?"

"Like shit. You?"

"Not great, but I'll survive."

"Listen, I, er, don't remember getting home."

"I brought you home. It took a while. We were both swaying all over the place and singing That's Amore, but we made it in the end."

"That's Amore?"

"Yeah, you know. When the world hits the sky like a big piece of pie."

"I know the song. I don't think I've ever sang it before though."

"Trust me, you have."

"I have? Shit. Are you sure those are the lyrics?"

"Yeah."

"Positive?"

"Well, not any more. Anyway, what's up?"

"Did I do anything last night?"

"Like what?"

"Anything stupid."

"No, you were fine."

"You sure? What happened with Jolene?"

"Well, after we left, you wanted to go back and rescue her from Ford and snog her or something but I held you back. And you don't have to worry, I saw her getting in a taxi. On her own."

"Thank God. Did I say anything to her?"

"I don't think so. You just had a laugh and got pissed and then we staggered home. You were talking to Ford for a while though. What was that about?"

"I haven't a fucking clue. Oh God. What the fuck have I said to that bastard?"

"Probably nothing. You worry too much. Listen, I'm going back to bed."

"Me too. I need to calm down. Thanks. See you tomorrow."

Justin turned around, pulled the duvet over his head and tried to ignore the thumping in his head and the tug of paranoia in his brain. He could have spilled his guts to Ford, told him anything. Told him everything. He couldn't remember a single word they'd shared and it seemed like he never would. Fuck. This was a nightmare. Breathe. There was absolutely nothing he could do about it now. It was perfectly reasonable to assume they had just talked about Forest or something, so why did Justin think the worst? All he could do was try to get through today and tomorrow at work he'd face up to whatever he'd said. If he could even go to work. The thought of seeing Ford and even Jolene tomorrow made him want to never set foot in that place again.

He jolted awake. It seems like he'd managed to get a little more sleep after all. He reached for his phone. No messages. He wasn't sure if that was good or bad. It was two o'clock now, so he should probably get up. His head wasn't pounding as much as before. He was due at his parents' house for dinner at five, so if he was to get any sofa time in before then, he had to get up.

Getting to the bathroom took longer this time, now that the need to vomit had passed. He felt nauseous as soon as he saw the toilet. He pulled off his t-shirt and boxers and clambered into the shower. The water felt great flowing over him, washing away the fear. He stood there for twenty minutes until his skin started to shrivel.

He had time for a couple of episodes of Lost before he left. It actually wasn't so bad to be hungover just then, as he'd reached the early season three slump and it was a bit of a slog to get through, so being a bit spaced out didn't really bother him.

It was a good half hour's walk to his parents' place and he hoped the fresh air would sort him out. As he walked, he had a pervasive feeling of dread that usually came the second day after a particularly heavy session. It was early this week, probably the result of basically drinking the entire weekend. It wasn't the hangover as such, that was still there but fading, but more a discomfort and uneasiness that felt like it was deep within his bones. Everything made him jumpy as the paranoia swept over him in wave after wave. Even people he knew for a fact had absolutely no knowledge of the weekend's events made him suspicious as they passed on the street. He kept his head low and pulled up his hoodie so no one would recognise him. He made it to his parents' house without anyone telling him off for his behaviour.

His mum answered the door seconds after he rang the bell, almost as if she was standing there waiting.

"Are you all right, son?" she asked.

"What? Yeah. Why do you ask?"

"No reason. It's just that you look a bit tired."

"I suppose I am."

"Burning the candle at both ends?"

"You could say that. I've been out the last couple of nights. Had a few drinks."

"Do you have to drink so much?"

"Who said I had so much?"

"It's written all over your face. You should take it easier, son. You don't need alcohol to have fun, you know."

"Fair enough, Mum. You don't need trainers to run a marathon either, but they help."

"There's no need to be like that. Why don't you head into

the living room? Nathan and your dad are both in there. Dinner won't be long."

Justin made his way into the living room where his father and brother were sitting on the sofa, laughing at something. His dad jumped up and ran over to him and shook his hand. He did this sometimes and other times, he just said hello or nodded. There was seemingly no rhyme nor reason to how he would react upon seeing his oldest son. Probably depended on how much he'd had to drink.

"Justin! What are you drinking, son?"

"Eh, I don't know. Maybe a Schloer or something?"

"Schloer? What are you talking about? I meant a drink drink. We don't have any Schloer anyway. Your gran isn't coming today."

"Oh? Is she all right?"

"She's better than all right. She's great. She's off on some bus tour to Skegness with her pals."

"I suppose I'll take a beer then."

"A beer? Right."

Justin sat down beside Nathan. "How's it going?" he asked.

"Yeah, good," said Nathan. "You?"

"Same old shit. Plus a hangover. I've had better days."

"Yeah, you look rough as fuck."

"Still? I'm feeling a bit better than before."

"Been on it?"

"All weekend. This beer will either sort me out or have me running for the toilet. Either way, I'll probably feel better, so it's okay."

His dad came back with a bottle of San Miguel. The three made small talk about the weather and football until Mum came through and said dinner was ready. They made their way into the dining room, where Justin took his usual seat next to the window.

On the table was a huge hunk of roast beef with all the trimmings. Roast potatoes, mashed potatoes, carrots, peas, Yorkshire puddings, gravy. It looked delicious but Justin felt his stomach hit the back of his throat when he smelt it. There were also two bottles of red wine on the table. No Schloer. Well, in for a penny. He stacked his plate so high that things were falling off the sides and the gravy was flowing down the mountain of mash and creating a pond at the edge of the plate.

"So," asked Mum after everyone had plated up, "how's work, Justin?"

"It's the same as it was when I was here two weeks ago, Mum. Shit."

"Why do you stay there? You've hated that job for years."

"Mum. You ask me this every time I come round here. There's nothing else out there.'""

"You don't look, Justin. A boy with your education can get a job doing anything you want."

"My degree is in IT. Everyone has a degree in IT these days."

"Or Media," said Nathan.

"Or Business Studies," said Dad.

"Or those too. But it's not easy, there's a lot of competition."

"Plus, there might be another reason why you stay there, right Justin?" said Dad.

"What do you mean?"

"Like maybe a girl you have your eye on?"

Justin felt his face going red and there was nothing he could do about it. There was no point denying it either, so he had to go on the defensive. "Has Nathan said something? Nathan, have you said something? You don't know what you're talking about."

"Calm down, son," said Dad, "just having a laugh with you. But seriously, it's about time you got yourself a girlfriend. It's been a couple of years since that last one. What was her name?"

"Sandy."

"Sandy, yeah that's it. She was a nice-looking girl, you should have held on to her."

"I caught her with her mouth wrapped..." he looked at Mum, who had the beginnings of a scowl on her face. "I mean, she cheated on me."

"I know, but still. Anyway, aren't you a bit lonely? You must be getting some good upper arm workouts."

"Sam!" shouted Mum. "That's enough of that talk at the

dinner table."

"Sorry, Karen," he said while rolling his eyes at the boys.

"These things will all fall into place at the right time. He just needs a better job so he can meet new people."

"Mum, would you stop going on about the job? You never say anything to Nathan about a job and he doesn't even have one. At least I'm earning." He shrugged an apology at Nathan for bringing him into this, but he didn't mind, really. It wasn't like this was the first time they'd ever had this conversation.

"Earning minimum wage! Anyway, Nathan is working on a project with his friends."

Yeah, thought Justin, working on how to build the perfect bong and seeing how many Nicolas Cage movies they could get through in one sitting.

"It's not minimum wage, Mum. Listen, that's enough about my work. Let's talk about something else."

Justin took a large swig of wine from his glass and got tucked back into his dinner so he couldn't be questioned any further. Dinner continued over a long description about how Dad was upgrading his caravan ahead of his and Mum's annual trip to the Lake District. Apparently there was some new type of fibreglass on the market that was revolutionising the privacy and comfort of the outdoors holidays industry.

When everyone had finished, Dad took the plates into the kitchen and started loading them into the dishwasher. Justin poured himself another large glass of wine. He was feeling a little tipsy again already and desperately in need of a smoke.

"You want to pop outside, Nathan?" he asked.

"Yeah."

"You boys and your smoking," said Mum. "Me and your father are going to watch Midsomer Murders. You can join us if you want."

"Thanks," said Nathan, "but we'll be fine outside."

As soon as they were outside, Justin lit up a cigarette and took a big drag. That was better. He offered one to Nathan, who took it but didn't light it. He started turning it between his fingers, pouring the tobacco into a rolling paper that had suddenly appeared in his other hand. He sprinkled some hash resin over the tobacco and rolled up the paper.

"This is a bit more like it," he said.

Nathan took a few puffs and passed the joint to Justin. He wasn't overly keen, seeing as how he'd been drinking for three days and had to face work tomorrow. The paranoia from earlier had gone but there was more in the post as soon as he took a puff of this spliff. He took it anyway.

"So what's this project that Mum thinks you're working on?" asked Justin.

"There is an actual project, you know."

"What?"

"We're working on a film. Just a little one, low budget, intimate. We've got a great script and a cracking lead actor. I have a good feeling about it."

"Seriously? I didn't know that. Since when have you been working on that?"

"For about a year, I suppose. Ever since I finished uni but it's only getting off the ground now."

"What are you doing?"

"I'm the cinematographer."

"I don't know what that is."

"Well, I basically set up the shots and the lighting and stuff like that."

"You can do that?"

"Yeah. That's what I studied. Plus, I've watched thousands of movies, so I have a good idea of what I want to do."

"Wow. I'm impressed, I have to say."

"Yeah, you know, you have to try to follow your dreams. When we were kids, well, not kids, teenagers, that's what you always told me. Do what you want to do, worry about everything else afterwards."

"I said that?"

"Yeah. You were going to travel or write a book or play in a band, or something. Something different. Now you work in a call centre."

"Yeah. Where did it all go wrong?"

"It didn't. You just got sidetracked. You're only twenty-four, you still have time, but Mum's right, you should get out of that place."

"I know I should. It's just..."

"That girl? Jillian, is it?"

"Jolene. It's not just her, it's money and not knowing what to actually do. But yeah, her too. Sometimes it feels like we're connecting and other times not at all. I just don't know what to do about her."

"Just ask her out. If she says yes, that's great. If she says no, move on. Simple."

"It's not that simple. We work together and we're friends and I don't want that to be a problem. I don't know, I'm just lonely. It's been a while. I haven't even seen a nipple in months, never mind anything else. Sometimes, I think it's better to be alone, at least that way, I don't get hurt, like with Sandy."

"Justin. You're my brother and I love you, but you can be a right boring bastard when you talk about this stuff. Either ask her out or don't. Quit the job or don't. It's up to you, but you should start following some of your dreams before it's too late."

"When did you get so smart? I'm the older brother, I should be the one giving out the advice."

"It's this new dope I've been smoking. It's turned me into a real philosopher."

Justin laughed and he felt the effects of the joint start to kick in. He thought about what Nathan had said about Jolene and work and following his dreams. Something would have to happen soon, he thought, before he ended up getting stuck doing the same thing for the rest of his life. His head started to drift slowly to the side. He felt it jerking inch by inch yet when he tried to pull it back to the middle, he found it hadn't actually moved at all.

"Boys! What's going on out here? I thought you were just popping out for a cigarette. That was half an hour ago." Half an hour? Shit, that passed quickly.

"We're just chilling out, Mum," said Nathan, "it's a nice night."

"It's bloody freezing. At least put your coats on if you're

going to stay out here getting high like two wasters."

Nathan went in to fetch coats for them and Mum went back to the TV. Justin's head was still spinning when Nathan got back. He took the coat and put it round his shoulders. He hadn't seen this coat in years, since he'd lived here. He was surprised his parents hadn't thrown it out when he moved out like they'd done with most of the rest of his stuff.

"Thanks," said Justin.

"No problem. Mum was right, it is a bit chilly."

"Why do you think chilli is called chilli when it's not chilly at all? Just the opposite in fact."

"That's a good question. Why indeed?"

The boys debated this for a while, along with what defined a curry, what was the difference between a chilli dish and a curry dish, was rice or naan the better accompaniment, and the necessity of poppadoms with an Indian. They lit up another joint and were just moving on to discussing chutneys when Dad came out.

"Are you two still out here? Your mum's been complaining that you're high as kites out here."

"We are a bit," agreed Nathan. "Maybe we should have been a bit more discreet in front of Mum."

"Don't worry about your mum. She's just being motherly. She loved a toke on the Devil's lettuce when we were your age."

"She did? I've never heard that before."

"Don't tell her I told you. Can I have a puff?"

"Sure. How was Midsomer Murders?"

"Oh, we didn't watch it. It was one with that new Barnaby and we don't like him. We only watch the ones with the old Barnaby. Watched a documentary instead. Attenborough."

Dad took a few drags and passed the joint to Justin, who also took a few draws before letting Nathan finish it. Justin's head was really spinning now, so he lay back on the grass and looked up at the stars. The air was cold, but the food in his belly and the wine in his blood warmed him. The stars seemed to be moving, dancing in the night sky. His father and brother lay down beside him and giggled about penguins. He was, at least in this moment, happy. He wished it would last for a very long time.

Chapter 14

What a fucking nightmare this was. Justin had arrived at work early to try to get a read on the situation and to show that he had nothing to fear. Now he was sitting alone in an empty call centre with only the hum of a vacuum cleaner to keep him company. At least the cleaners were there when he arrived otherwise he'd be standing outside in the rain chain smoking. It was a quarter to eight and for the first time in the three years he'd worked here, he was the first to arrive.

Linda was next and she looked genuinely shocked to see Justin sitting there. "What are you doing here?" she asked. "Did you get the time wrong?"

"No. I woke up early and just thought I might as well come in."

"Really? Why not just stay at home a bit longer?"

"Probably should have."

"Good weekend?"

"It had its ups and downs."

"Want to talk about it?"

"No, thanks."

"Coffee, then?"

"That would be great."

Linda left to make coffee and Chip arrived. He looked a little tired but not too worse for wear. Justin's stomach was in knots and he felt his leg shaking under the desk. He really wanted Ford to arrive so he could assess the situation, but he also wished he would never see that fucker again.

"How's it going?" asked Chip.

"So so. Still not sure what happened on Saturday night."

"Don't worry about it. You were fine. Really."

"I wish I could believe that. I mean, I believe you, I just don't trust myself."

"Nothing happened. You want a coffee?"

"Linda's making me one."

"Okay, I'll go and get her to make one for me too."

Chip left him alone again. His treacherous brain fired another shot of paranoia at him just as Ford walked through the door at one minute to eight. Justin looked straight into his eyes, which were barely open, making him look even more sinister. He wasn't getting any vibes from Ford at all. Shit. This wasn't good. Ford gave him a slight nod and a little smirk. Oh, fuck. He'd told the fucker everything.

Linda and Chip came back with coffee just as Jolene arrived. On time? What the fuck? Well, not quite on time, it was two minutes past, but still, this was the earliest she'd arrived in months. She looked amazing like always, and fresh, as if she hadn't had a drink at all on Saturday. She was wearing a pair of tight jeans with no knees and a t-shirt with a melting Rubik's Cube.

"Hi Jolene," he said.

"Hi."

"Nice t-shirt."

"Ha, yeah. I stole it from my sister."

"Looks great."

"Thanks."

"You have a sister?" asked Ford, with a wicked gleam in his eye.

"Two. And don't even go there."

Ford smirked and his eyes glazed over a little.

"So," said Linda, "it's my last week and Jim, sorry, Ford is going to be taking on a little bit more this week to get him used to doing the job once I'm gone. He's going to take the briefing today."

Ford handed briefing sheets to everyone. Was it Justin's imagination or did Ford hesitate when giving one to him? "There's not really a lot this week. If you look on the sheet, you'll see that there's a few new unsupported apps on the list. There's been a few reports of the new USB charger not working properly, so keep an eye on this. There isn't enough information yet to do a recall but management wants the situation monitored."

"How?" asked Chip.

"There's a file on the hard drive to add information to if you get a call like this. It's all there on the briefing sheet. The only other thing is the new policy towards our flagged nuisance callers. They are no longer to be given any vouchers under any circumstances. Some fucking idiot gave Abbott a voucher a couple of weeks ago and he hasn't stopped calling ever since trying to get another one. We're trying to cut down the amount of time lost to these repeat callers too, so try to wrap the calls up quickly. And if it's Miss Peal, you can just hang up on her straight away."

"But don't we have to treat all our callers with the same courtesy?" asked Justin.

"Yeah, but she's nuttier than a squirrel's vomit. I doubt she even knows who she's talking to. So, if she comes through with one of her crazy stories, just hang up and don't listen to her. It's wasting valuable call time with a legitimate caller."

What a fucking killjoy this Ford was!

"Also, Tanya's not going to be here today, so we're one down. Hopefully, you'll be able to deal with things without her."

"She's not here?" said Chip. "Why not? Did she call in sick?"

"No," said Ford. "I think she organised time off with Phil but he said she'll be back tomorrow. Any other questions? No? Well, let's get on the phones then."

Easy for him to say. That fucker didn't have to get on the phones. He looked at Justin again and held the gaze for a few seconds. What did he know?

Click. "How can I help?"

"Hi, what's your name?"

"It's Justin."

"Hi, Justin. My phone isn't charging, Justin."

"Can you take the battery out for ten seconds, please?"

"Already did that, Justin. Still not charging."

"Okay. Has it been working before?"

"Working fine, Justin. Got a new charger. It doesn't work."

Fucking hell. Already? The first call of the day and he was going to have extra work to do.

"Was it a new USB charger?"

"Yes, Justin."

Shit. He looked at the briefing sheet and found the file on the hard drive that Ford mentioned. "Okay. There might be a problem with these USB chargers. I'll need to get some details from you."

"Sure, Justin. My name is Hung Lee."

"Well, Hung. I'll just need some information so we can investigate the matter." He opened the file and starting taking Hung's details. This took fifteen minutes, so while it was extra work, at least it kept him from talking to anyone else.

As the day progressed, he felt Ford's eyes on him but every time he looked over Ford was looking in another direction.

"Tech support."

"Just to let you know, my brother Duncan has been kidnapped by Welsh insurgents. They have cut off all his limbs and he is now just a torso." Yes!

"Have they made any demands?"

"None just the now. They are, however, extracting his sperm and pumping it into women all over the country."

"Why would they do such a thing?" Justin had to be careful here. He wasn't sure if Ford was listening and he'd just told them not to talk to Miss Peal. Today of all days, he couldn't let Ford get anything more on him.

"It's the quality of the sperm. Duncan shares a genetic fingerprint with Genghis Khan, Blackbeard the dread pirate and Sammy Davis Junior. By my estimation, he'll soon be the father of over two hundred Welsh babies, many of whom are being forcibly removed from their mothers' wombs and being gestated in Rastamouse pencil cases and lunch boxes."

"That sounds serious. What's the endgame here?"

"Those sheep-shagging bastards are building an army in the Valleys. I'll be safe up here in Scotland for a few years but you English are in imminent trouble. Get that passed on as quick as possible. Thanks now."

He hung up and let the countdown tick. He had no intention of taking another call before those ninety seconds were up. Just then Ford came over to him and told him to go to 'Not Ready'.

"Can I borrow you for a sec, Justin? Come into the office." Well, this was it. Cards on the table time.

"What's this about?" asked Justin when they were in the office.

"Just a quick review. How would you rate your own performance, Justin?"

"I don't know. Good, I suppose."

"Out of ten?"

"What? Eight, maybe?"

Ford started laughing. "Eight? Come on, mate, be serious."

"Okay, nine then."

"Nine! Nine out of ten! More like a six on a good day. Listen mate, last week Linda trained me in call monitoring and I've been listening in to some calls."

"Some of mine?"

"Not just yours, but yes."

"What's the problem?"

"Well, there's not much wrong with your support. You could be a bit nicer but that's by the by. How long have you been working here now?"

"Just over three years."

"Yeah, it's been a while since you've done any training, right?"

"Yeah."

"I thought so. You do know that every time you take a call you're supposed to use the proper greeting?"

"No."

"Well, there's a prompt on the screen telling you exactly what you're supposed to say, so I don't know how you don't know. You're supposed to say 'tech support. Thank you for calling. You're speaking to Justin today. How can I help?' or 'how may I help?'"

"That's a bit long-winded."

"I agree, mate. And when I was an agent, I was just like

you. I just said 'tech support' or whatever. Sometimes I just said 'hello', so I know where you're coming from. But I'm team leader now."

"Not yet."

"Well, maybe technically not yet, but I will be next week. Now, I know that maybe it's a bit too soon for me to be throwing my authority around but I just want our team to be the best on the call floor. That's why I'm telling you this. I want to get off to a flying start and not have anyone in management able to question anything we do."

"Fair enough."

"So, what are you supposed to say at the start of every call?"

"The prompt."

"Yeah, say it for me."

"What?"

"Say the prompt."

"No."

"Come on. Just to practice."

"No."

"Come on Justin."

"Fuck off."

"Do it."

"No chance."

"I don't want to be a dick, but if you don't, I'm going to have to start monitoring all your calls to make sure you're saying it. If you don't, it's unfortunately a disciplinary matter."

"Ford..."

"Say it, Justin."

"Tech support. Thanks for...

"Thank you."

"Thank you for calling. This is Justin."

Ford tutted and shook his head.

"You're speaking to Justin. How can I help?"

"Today."

"Today."

"Now all at once. The whole thing straight through."

“I've already done it.”

“I want to hear the whole thing, Justin.”

“Tech support. Thank you for calling. You're speaking to Justin today. How can I help?”

“Not bad. Sounded a little forced though. One more time. Try to make it sound more natural.”

“Are you having a laugh?”

“Not at all. Like I said, I just want to make sure we're the number one team in the call centre. So, one more time then.”

“Tech support. Thank you for calling. You're speaking to Justin. How can I help today?”

“The 'today' was in the wrong place there, Justin. One more time.”

“For fuck sake.”

“You're just making it harder on yourself. Just say it one time properly and naturally and we're done here.”

“Tech support. Thank you for calling. You're speaking to Justin today. How can I help?”

“That was much better.”

“Is that all?”

“For now, yes.”

Justin stood up and left the office. He'd dodged a bullet there and no mistake. He'd been certain that Ford was going to call up some dark secret from Saturday night but there was nothing. Maybe they had just made small talk about football after all. Justin didn't care, he just wanted to put some distance between them. For the first time in three years, he was eager to get onto the phones and start taking calls.

#

Ford sat back in his chair and let out a huge sigh of relief. He knew he'd been talking to Justin in the pub on Saturday night, that much he could remember. He hadn't a fucking clue what they talked about though. He couldn't remember a single word of that conversation. He'd spent all day yesterday worrying about what he might have told that little bastard and what he could now possibly hold over him. He couldn't be worrying about these things, not now that he was team leader. Or he would be from next week at any rate. That was when the real responsibility began and he wanted a clean slate. New team, new direction.

But it seemed like Justin didn't have anything on him after all. He properly pissed him off there, making him say that greeting. That had been the plan, of course. Get him on his own, get him annoyed and see what came out. If there was something to be said, Justin would have said it, Ford was sure of that. The plan worked. It was a good one. He was full of good plans. That's why he was the team leader.

What was happening to him though? This was an entirely new concept to him. Guilt. Doubt. He'd never experienced these things before. Why were they getting in his way now? He never usually worried what he said when he was drunk, or even sober, for that matter. Why now? Was this the effect that responsibility had on people? He wasn't sure that he liked it. He wasn't sure that he disliked it either.

He went out for a smoke then joined the team on the call floor.

"Ford," said Linda when he sat down, "we've been wondering where you got your nickname from. Since it's my last week, I've been nominated to ask you. I need to know before I go."

"All right then, I'll tell you. Why not? I'm actually named after Harrison Ford," he said smugly. "When I started secondary school, all the kids thought I was like a cross between Han Solo and Indiana Jones, so they called me Ford and the name stuck."

This was a slight distortion of the facts. Ford was a huge fan of Star Wars and Indiana Jones growing up, that much was true. He had thought that Harrison Ford was the greatest man on the planet. Still did. On his first day at secondary school, he told all the other kids that people round his way called him Ford and they believed him and he kept the nickname to this day. Even as an eleven-year old, he sure as hell wasn't going to let the other kids pick his nickname for him. The nicknames kids came up with were awful and he didn't want to be stuck with something like Spike for the rest of his life just because his mum hadn't brushed his hair down one day.

"Harrison Ford? You?" said Jolene.

"Yes."

"Seriously?"

"Yes."

"Crystal Skull Harrison Ford, maybe. Or some of the other recent shit he's done. There's no way that name is based on Raiders, Blade Runner or Empire era Ford," said Chip.

"Well, Chip, as we're sharing nickname origin stories, where does yours come from?"

"What? Fuck sake, is that the time already? I was supposed to go on my lunch break five minutes ago."

Chip logged off and slipped out the door. Let him run, thought Ford, he hasn't heard the last of this.

#

He pulled the door open ever so slightly, just enough that he could see in without being seen himself. Good. Ford wasn't there. Hopefully he'd gone for his own lunch or was doing some training or something. Just as long as he wasn't there now. Chip had spent the whole of his lunch break wondering if he should just come clean about his nickname. He'd got sick of the lies and the avoidance over the years. It might be good to get the truth off his chest. Justin knew where the name came from already. And just because it didn't have as cool a background as Ford's didn't mean it was a bad name. It was better than his real name, that was for sure. Plus, he wasn't sure that Ford had been entirely truthful either.

Justin was the only one there when he went back in. "Where's everyone else?" Chip asked him.

"Lunch."

"All at the same time?"

"Yeah. I don't know who made the schedule today."

"So, I've been thinking of just telling them why I'm called Chip."

"Are you sure?"

"Yeah. It's been years since I've told anyone. You were the

last person I told.”

“I'm honoured.”

“You should be.”

“Anyway, I was just reading this thing. Some kid in Manchester is allergic to water.”

“He must fucking stink.”

“Well, he is from Manchester.”

“Yeah. So, how does he clean himself?” asked Chip.

“Well, that's what I was just wondering. It doesn't say here. I was thinking he maybe sticks tape all over himself then pulls the dirt off along with the tape.”

“What? Are you joking? He'd have to buy like twenty rolls of tape every day.”

“Well, how else would he do it?”

“I don't know. Sand, maybe?”

“Sand?”

“Yeah. Like rub sand all over his body. That would take the dirt away.”

“Maybe, but wouldn't it get into some uncomfortable places?”

“Price you pay.”

“Yeah, but, no, he uses tape. Sand would just make him even dirtier when you think about it.”

“It wouldn't. It has to be sand.”

“Tape.”

“Sand.”

“Here's Jolene coming back. Let's ask her.”

“Ask me what?” she said.

“If you were allergic to water, how would you get clean?”

She thought about this for a moment. “I suppose you'd stick tape on yourself then pull the dirt off.”

Justin looked at Chip and grinned.

“Fair enough. You win this one,” said Chip.

“Nice. Anyway, that's my lunch. See you later.”

Justin left for lunch, leaving Chip and Jolene alone. “What did you have for lunch?” he asked her.

“Salad. You?”

"Sandwich."

"What was that about with the water thing?"

"Oh, something Justin read online."

"I think I saw something about that actually. Some boy who's allergic to water?"

"Yeah, that was it."

"He's like a real-life mutant or something. His cells have evolved to his environment or something like that."

"You mean because he's from Manchester he's never seen water?"

"Haha, something like that! But seriously, he's evolved."

"I don't know. That theory of evolution? It's bullshit," said Chip.

"Er, I think you'll find there's scientific proof," said Jolene.

"There is no theory of evolution. Just a list of creatures that Chuck Norris has allowed to live."

"Oh God, what is it with you and Chuck Norris?"

"The man is a legend, a god amongst men. Do you know he doesn't sleep?"

"What?"

"Chuck Norris doesn't sleep. He waits."

"Your pop culture references are so dated, mate." Shit, Ford. He had this way of just appearing out of nowhere.

"What?"

"I don't think I've ever heard you talk about anything that became popular in the last decade. Chuck Norris? That guy must be a hundred years old. Did you know there used to be a street named after him somewhere in Texas, by the way?"

"No. What to you mean, used to?"

"Well, they had to change the name because nobody crosses Chuck Norris and lives."

"Nice. Anyway, I don't really like modern stuff. I'm a retro guy."

"Stuck in your teens, you mean. You don't even have a mobile phone. How do you ever get girls' phone numbers?"

"Er." This was a touchy subject for Chip. He never did actually get girls' phone numbers. "Well, it's been a while."

"Right. It's time to hear where that nickname comes from. You can't avoid it any longer. If you don't tell me now, I'm going to hound you day and night until you do."

"Day and night?"

"Day and night."

"Well, you know I like games, right?"

"Right."

"I like all types of games. Video games, role-playing games, pub games, whatever. I like to play a bit of poker too." Once every year or so, he would decide he didn't want to work for a living any more and fancied himself as a bit of a master poker player. That would be the life, sitting at home all day drinking coffee and wearing a robe while playing online poker, raking the cash in. This notion normally lasted a few days until he realised that just because he knew the basics and did all right in games with his drunken friends, he was no Phil Ivey. It usually cost him about a month's wages too, so not only did he have to go back to work, he'd end up doing lots of overtime as well. For years he'd alluded that his name came from his interest in poker. If people were prepared to think that the name Chip was somehow related to master poker skills, he wasn't going to point them in a different direction.

"So, it comes from poker chips, does it?" asked Ford.

"Yeah. No. Fuck sake. I can't lie any longer. I've been misleading people for years over the nickname. The guilt is getting too much to bear. I've been letting people think that for years. That it was poker chips, but it isn't. The truth is that I ordered a plate of chips for lunch on my first day at school and I've been called Chip ever since."

There was silence for a moment.

"Fair enough, mate. It's not the best origin story in the world but what are you going to do?"

This was odd. He expected much more shit from Ford. He'd got off lightly here and he knew it. At least for now. Ford was probably just a little sluggish in coming up with a witty response due to a weekend on the drink, but once he thought of something, Chip expected to get it from both barrels. He turned to Jolene, who just shrugged. She didn't care. He wondered what Tanya would think when she found out. It was a little strange that she wasn't here. She'd been part of the furniture for years, quietly getting on with her job in the corner. Her chair felt very empty without her in it. He hoped she would be back tomorrow.

Chapter 15

Tanya was glad to be back at work. Even though she was still angry with Phil, both for giving her job to Ford and for giving the boys time in lieu to play football, it was a relief to be back in the call centre. She thought yesterday would be great, living it up on a Monday, but she had actually spent the whole day feeling awful. She went into town to do some shopping but it had been practically deserted. The only people around were the unemployed and mothers with young children. She'd gone to that Mexican for lunch but her chimichangas tasted like they'd been seasoned with guilt. It was one thing to let the call wrap-up countdown run out or to take an extra smoke break now and then but she was finding it hard to live with the fact that she'd essentially blackmailed her boss into giving her time off. After she got home yesterday afternoon, she spent her time watching the clock waiting for bed time, so she could go to sleep then get back to work and put this whole episode behind her.

Ford beckoned her into his office when he arrived, which was after her, of course. He gave her a quick recap of yesterday's briefing and what she'd missed. Not much really, it was same old, same old. She could do this job in her sleep by this point. She could really do with a bit of a challenge. That's why it was so frustrating that this idiot got her job. She still found it difficult to make eye contact with him and being alone with him wasn't easy, so she was happy when he told her to get onto the phones.

There wasn't much of interest from the callers to hold her attention this morning. It was all pretty routine stuff. The usual broken screens, fading signals and battery problems. She was glad to slip off for a sneaky smoke with Chip and Justin when Linda took Ford back into the office to continue his training.

"So, you're back, then?" asked Chip when they got downstairs.

"Yeah. How was your weekend?"

"It was good," replied Chip. Justin nodded silently and looked at the ground.

"What did you do? Did you play football?"

"Yeah, we both did. Won five-three."

"Nice! Did you score?"

"No," snapped Justin. "But at least we won."

"We went to the pub after," said Chip. "You should have come, it was fun."

"Yeah, you know, maybe I should. I've never been on a work night out. Not even a Christmas party. Don't know why, really. I've just always tried to keep work and my personal life separate, but maybe I shouldn't have done that."

"Well, you'll go to Linda's leaving do, right?"

"Yeah. Yeah, I think I will, actually."

"What did you get up to with your long weekend?" asked Justin.

"Not much, to be honest. I went to my mum's on Saturday, watched some movies on Sunday and went into town yesterday. It was awful. There was no one around."

"What did you do, then?" asked Chip.

"I just wandered around for a bit, then went for Mexican, then home."

"That new Mexican on Broad Street?"

"Yeah."

"How was it?"

"Hmm. Okay, I suppose. Good salsa. I love salsa. It's my favourite type of salad."

"What do you mean, salad?" asked Justin. "It's not a salad, it's a sauce."

"I've always thought of it as a dip," said Chip.

"Really? I've always thought of it as a sauce," said Justin.

"It's a salad to me," said Tanya.

"A salad? How can it be a salad?" asked Chip.

"Well, it's tomatoes, onions and stuff and can be served as an accompaniment to a main dish. Therefore, a salad."

"No way. It's a dip. I can accept sauce but it never has been and never will be a salad."

"Well, when I eat salsa, it's a salad. It'll always be a salad to me."

"Dip."

"Actually," said Justin, "I believe the Spanish word salsa translates directly as sauce. Or a dance. But we'll go with sauce here."

"I don't care what the word means," said Tanya. "It's all about how you eat it and I eat it as a salad."

"I've never heard it referred to as a salad before," said Chip.

"First time for everything."

"We should probably be heading back in now," said Justin, "but this isn't over."

#

Linda was pleasantly surprised. Ford had been working hard the last couple of days and was picking up everything really quickly. It seemed like once he'd put his mind to the training, he was determined to give it his best shot. Just now, he was reading through a technical document ahead of sitting a test.

"How's it going there, Jim? Ford?"

"Good, yeah. I've just finished reading this."

"Ready for the test, then?"

"Yes. Bring it on."

She opened up the test on the computer and signed Ford in. She wasn't sure whether to leave him on his own or not. It was possible to cheat on the test but his recent behaviour made her want to give him the benefit of the doubt. Still, it was Ford. Even though he'd had a good couple of days, leopards didn't change their spots that quickly. She'd have to stay and watch over him. As he got stuck into the test, she sat back and relaxed. She thought about how great her new shoes were and how professional she was going to look on Monday. It was going to be fine, she told herself. They seemed to love her at the interview. She would fit in there for sure. There was nothing to worry about. Nothing at all.

Her eyes snapped open. She'd fallen asleep. Ford was still sitting at the desk working on his test. She really hoped he hadn't noticed her drifting off. What if she'd snored? Oh God.

"Finished," he said suddenly.

"Already?"

"Yeah. I think I nailed it."

"I hope so."

"Anything else?"

"No. That's it."

"That's everything?"

"Yes. Training's all done. I still have to mark that test of course but apart from that, it's done. You picked it up quickly."

"Well, I had a good teacher."

"Flatterer. But yeah, we still have a few more days allocated but there's no point stretching it out any longer. Get it done, that's what I say. That's how I rock."

"Don't you mean roll?"

"Whatever."

"So, you looking forward to the new job?"

"Yes. I mean, I'm a bit nervous, but it'll be good. I need a new challenge. I've been here for years. Good years for sure but it's time to move on. The money's a lot better too."

"Yeah. Well, I've just had a nice pay rise but I know what you mean. It's not for life or anything. I'll probably do a couple of years as team leader then look to move on myself. Should look good on the CV, though."

"Yeah, any management experience is good for the CV. Anyway, let's go through to the call floor. We've been away for a while. God knows how many smoke breaks that lot have been on."

"I'll just pop down for a quick smoke myself, then I'll come and join you."

Linda went through and sat down with the rest of the team. To her surprise, they were all there, although there was the faint smell of recent cigarette smoke in the air. She didn't really care, anyway. In fact, she usually let them take smoke breaks when it was quiet. Now that Ford was shadowing her though, she was worried about coming across as irresponsible or as a bad team leader. Why? She had three days to go, so what did it matter if Ford thought she'd been too easy on her team over the years? Why did she care now? And Ford? He was the most irresponsible of all. She still couldn't really believe that he was taking over from her instead of Tanya, who she'd been training and had lobbied Phil to give the job to.

"What are the plans for the weekend, Linda?" asked Chip.

"Oh, well, it's my leaving do on Saturday night, of course. I hope you'll all be there." They all nodded that they would be, even Tanya. "And on Friday, after I finish, my boyfriend is picking me up and taking me to Manchester. We're going to see Ed Sheeran."

"Ed Sheeran? I wouldn't go to an Ed Sheeran concert if it was in my back garden," said Chip.

"Well, he did come around this decade," said Ford. Where did he come from? Wasn't he smoking?

"He's great," said Linda. "I haven't seen him before, but I've heard his live shows are amazing."

"Does he sing completely different songs?" asked Chip.

"Well, just because floppy-haired indie pop didn't make it out of the '90s doesn't mean everyone else is rubbish, Chip." Ha. That shut him up. Justin and Jolene looked a little put out too. Oh, come on. Get with the programme, people. It's 2016. The future is here. Moving on. Looking forward. Growing up.

#

There was no need for that, thought Jolene. No need at all. They all used to love a bit of Britpop, even though they were kind of too young for it. Linda too. It had been introduced to the team by Bligger, a former teammate who was a bit older and who finally escaped the call centre a year ago for a job in a toothbrush factory. None of them had seen him since. But he'd loved '90s music. And drugs. He introduced the Stone Roses, Blur, Primal Scream, Oasis, Suede, and more to the team. That was back in the days when they were allowed to have music playing quietly in the background. Phil put paid to that when he got a complaint from a caller who claimed to have been called a motherfucker by one of the call agents. He'd actually just overheard the Wu Tang Clan, but that was the end of the music. What a shame.

But she didn't want to dwell on that. She was feeling good. She'd come to a decision. It was time for a total detox. After this weekend, of course. She couldn't go to Linda's leaving do and stay sober! But then that was it. No drinking. No shitty food. No more dates for a while either. It was just a string of arseholes, one after the other. There had to be some good guys out there somewhere, though. She knew there was. She'd met one. Spencer had been lovely. She still missed him sometimes. Still, that shit with his sister was way too creepy. He had to go. Who said she needed to be in a relationship anyway? Society. Facebook. There was nothing that got more likes on Facebook than changing your status to 'in a relationship'. That or having a baby and that certainly wasn't going to happen for a while! She should probably stay off social media for a while too. Clean break from everything.

She should knock reading this shit on the internet on the head too. This couldn't be for real. She turned to the others. "I'm just reading that there's a town in Belgium that has put lights on the ground at road crossings, so that people on their phones will know they're at a crossing and won't walk out."

"What!?" screamed Chip. "That's fucking ridiculous. These people shouldn't have this, let them get crushed under a bus. If they can't look out for their own safety because of these fucking devices, they don't deserve to live. This is evolution we're talking about. Survival of the fittest. Darwin."

"It's evolution, Chip?"

"Yeah."

"Thought you said there was no such thing. Chuck Norris or something."

"It was a joke, Jolene."

"Really?" she said sarcastically. Silly Chip. He was a good guy though. So was Justin.

"I'm very sorry to hear that, madam. However, we will need you to send your phone back to us so we can repair it."

"No fucking way! This is ridiculous. Your fucking phone is shit."

"Language, please, madam." Tanya hated it when callers swore at her. She didn't care about the language; she swore plenty herself, after all. It was the lack of respect that it implied, as if the callers felt they had the right to talk down to her. She was pretty sure most of them would never speak to her like this face-to-face, but somehow it was acceptable over the phone. It was the great problem of the digital age. Everyone with a wi-fi connection felt they could get outraged with impunity and spout their feelings over Twitter. This extended to phones too; as long as someone couldn't see you, they felt they could say whatever they wanted.

"Never mind about my language. I'm angry and you're not helping. My phone is broken, so you need to send your engineers round to my house to fix it."

"We don't do that, madam."

"Well, you'll do it this fucking time!"

"Please refrain from using foul and abusive language. That's twice I've had to point out your language. One more time and I'll have to terminate the call."

"You're not terminating with me. I want to speak to a supervisor. They'll get the engineers round."

"I don't think they will."

"I'm not talking to you anymore. I'm done with you. Get your manager."

"Okay. What's your name, madam?"

"It's Kelly, bitch!"

"Okay, Miss Bitch. Please hold."

"What did you call me!?"

"What? Nothing."

"You called me a bitch!"

"No, I didn't. You just said your name was Kelly Bitch."

"You're in so much fucking trouble. I'm getting you fired,

you whore."

"That's three times, Miss Bitch. I'm terminating the call."

Tanya hung up. No doubt that woman would call back and speak to some other poor bastard. She was even angrier now and obviously didn't see the irony in getting upset at being called a bitch by someone she'd just called a bitch. Ah well, Tanya was confident she could talk her way out of that one if need be. Hopefully the next callers would be nicer.

"So," said Justin during a quiet moment, "I've translated salsa and it's a sauce. It can also be a gravy, a dressing or a relish, but neither a dip nor a salad."

"Gravy? It's not a fucking gravy. It's a dip. I dip tortilla chips into it," said Chip.

"And I eat it as a side dish. It's a salad," said Tanya.

"You can't just make up your own definition of words, Tanya. That's like saying just because you eat a spag bol with chopsticks that it's a chow mein. No. Google Translate says it's a sauce, therefore it's a sauce."

"Google Translate is hardly the fucking Oracle of Delphi," said Chip.

Tanya laughed. This was amusing, but she wasn't budging. Salsa was a salad and that was it. They'd have to agree to disagree.

"Tech support. You're speaking to Tanya today. How can I help?"

"Hello, Tanya. I'm calling because my phone is broken." Great. Another broken phone.

"Okay sir, we're here to help. Could you explain how the phone got broken?"

"It was eaten, devoured in fact, by Winston, my pet bulldog."

"Okay, so, we normally need to take the phone back to repair it, sir. If Winston ate it, is there anything left of it to send back?"

"Nothing. We should probably take him to the vet, actually. He's swallowed the whole thing."

"That's probably a good idea, sir."

"Well, I still need a new phone."

"We can't replace or repair a phone without getting the old one back."

"I can't send it back. It's inside my bulldog."

"I'm afraid that the warranty doesn't cover inside of bulldogs, sir."

"Well, I used to own a sail boat and my wife always wears something purple. What do you say to that?"

"Uh..."

Click.

It wasn't for everyone, this type of job. You had to be patient and thick-skinned and put up with a lot, not to mention the low pay, but it wasn't that bad, really. Sometimes, it was genuinely surprising. She was starting to enjoy the banter too. She realised that she'd been taking the job too seriously before and that there was fun to be had here too. Her initial instinct upon hearing that Ford had got her job had been to quit immediately and storm out. She was glad she hadn't done that. She was still angry, of course, but maybe that job wasn't right for her after all. Having to deal with escalated calls from people like Kelly Bitch on a regular basis would get very tiring. There had to be something else for her though, being a regular call agent wasn't enough any more. Even though she felt guilty about taking yesterday off, it felt good to stand up to Phil over an injustice in the workplace. Maybe there was a way she could do more to help others deal with similar things. She'd think about that. Either way, it was nice to be back.

Chapter 16

The week had flown in. Chip couldn't believe it was Friday already. In one sense it was great because it was the end of another working week. On the other hand, life was flying by with nothing to show for it. Chip didn't hate the job in the same way that Justin did, he was fine with just getting on with things and taking his pay check. It was okay, but he was twenty-six now and had been doing this for years. He figured it was all right so long as he was still in his twenties but maybe someday he would somehow find a woman that would want to spend some time with him. They might even get married and start a family. He couldn't very well support them on a call centre salary, especially one that was subject to occasional poker-related fluctuations.

His lack of ambition worried him at times, and it truly terrified his parents. He wanted to do something with his life and accomplish something, but what? For now, things were okay. He had a job, his own flat, a few friends and a lot of gaming time. That was what he'd always wanted and it had been great but there was something in him now pushing for more. He'd been encouraged in the past to go for team leader positions when they became available. He'd always resisted. Was it due to lack of ambition, or did he just not want to commit to responsibility in a call centre? He really wasn't sure. He hated when thoughts like this crept into his head and tried to dismiss them.

Justin arrived just before eight o'clock. He sat down and logged into his computer before turning to Chip.

"I just got a text from Tony. He can't play D&D this week."

"What? I thought it was all organised. You said it was on.

On like Donkey Kong, you said."

"It was, but he's sick, so now it's off. Off like Gorbachev."

"Shit."

"Yeah. You want to go for a pint or something anyway?"

"I don't know. Tomorrow will be a big night. It's probably best to leave it actually. Maybe it's good that D&D's cancelled. I don't know if I could take another double whammy like last weekend."

"Good point. Me neither. Let's leave it then."

The morning rushed past in a steady stream of calls, with nothing specifically taxing to deal with. Chip was just about to go on 'Personal Time' and have a smoke break when another call came through.

"How do I take a bug out of my phone?"

"A bug, sir? What kind of bug?"

"A listening bug. They're in my phone lines."

"They?"

"Can't you hear it?"

"Hear what, sir?"

"The tapping. They're tapping my phone line."

"Who's tapping your phone line, sir?" asked Chip innocently, occasionally flicking his index finger against his microphone.

"The BFI! They're after me. They're everywhere. Any time I leave my house, I'm followed. They listen in to my phone calls. I've put tin foil all over my walls and ceiling but they still get through."

"The FBI? I don't think they have any jurisdiction here in England, sir."

"Oh. Don't let them fool you. They have ears everywhere. They don't like it when I talk about the government. The warmongers in the government. Oops, I've said too much."

Click. Fuck sake. It had been ages since Paranoid Paddy had called. Why did he have to hang up so quickly? That could have been fun. Anyway, it was time for that smoke. Justin and Tanya were both ready too, so they all headed out.

"So, you're definitely coming tomorrow night, then?" Chip

asked Tanya.

"Yeah, I'll be there. I'm looking forward to it, actually. My first work night out."

"Should be fun," said Justin. "There's going to be something this afternoon too. I saw Davey Jones taking a cake and party hats into the office earlier."

"Party hats?" said Tanya. "Like paper crowns? I hate those."

"What's your favourite type of hat?" asked Chip.

"I don't often wear hats," replied Tanya.

"No, but if you did, what would you wear?"

"Probably a trilby or something like that, I don't know. I wouldn't really be too fussy as long as it had a decent brim. I like a brim."

"*I* like a brim! I always say to Justin that I like a brim."

"He does," confirmed Justin.

She would look pretty hot in a trilby, Chip thought. He was slightly confused. He'd never looked at Tanya this way before. She'd always been the quiet, responsible one. She came in and did her job, then went home. She rarely participated in group discussions and never spoke about her private life. Now, she'd changed. She was taking smoke breaks with him and Justin and talking shit like she'd been doing it all her life. And ever since he found out she was bisexual, he found her ludicrously attractive.

#

"My neighbour breaks into my house every night. Well, not on Tuesdays, I think she has bingo on Tuesdays, but she comes into my house and steals my electricity every other night."

"How does she do that? Does she take it out in a bag?"

"A bag, or a hold-all of some sort. Maybe a rucksack. But that's not the point. The point is that she uses this electricity to power a stasis field in her basement that she thinks will allow her to discover the secrets of time travel."

"Time travel, eh? Maybe she's already discovered it and is secretly changing history."

"I'd no put it past her. She's an evil bitch. She always had her eye on my brother Duncan but he wasn't interested. As we speak, she may well be altering the fabric of the space-time continuum to make sure she gets her claws into him. It's a shame he doesn't have limbs anymore."

"If you could go back in time, when would you go to?" asked Justin.

"Obviously, I would go back to the 30th of May 1431."

"Why?"

"To save myself from being burned at the stake, of course."

"Oh, so you have the same genetic fingerprint as Joan of Arc as well?"

Ford's head popped up from behind the partition. "Is that Miss Peal you're talking to?" he asked.

"Er, no?"

"Wrap it up, Justin. Now."

Fucking killjoy. "I'll pass that on for you. Bye now."

He let the wrap-up countdown tick away. Fucking Ford was like Batman, seeming to appear and disappear at will and when you least expected or wanted him. That was the only way he was like Batman though. Batman was cool. Justin was glad it was almost lunch time, so he could get away from that lurking bastard listening to his every word.

He thought about going out for lunch but on his way past the break room, he noticed that Jolene was already in there and on her own. He quickly popped over to the vending machine instead. There wasn't much left. God damn it. Only a couple of packets of those mini biscuits and a shitload of Mars bars. He always wondered who actually ate Mars bars. It was weird, the whole company was named after this bar and yet he'd never seen anyone either eat or buy one. Most people went for a Snickers or a Galaxy. Or anything Cadbury. No one ever took a Mars, yet it was one of the most famous chocolate bars in the world. It was a bit like the confectionery equivalent of Coldplay, really. Lots of brand awareness, acceptable if there were no other options, but no one really liked it if they were honest about it, yet it somehow still generated boatloads of cash. He really needed to discuss this with

Chip. Later. He hurried back to the break room and went in. Good, Jolene was still alone.

"Mind if I join you?" he asked.

"Of course not," she said and smiled, "sit down."

"How's it going?"

"Much the same as always. Just getting on with things. Hoping something happens. I'm going to try a detox from next week, see how that goes."

"What do you want to happen?"

"I don't know, something. I just feel like every day is the same, you know?"

"I do know. I'm trying to shake things up too. Look, I have a Mars bar."

"A Mars bar! You know, I've never tried one. Isn't that weird?"

"No. No one has. There's loads of them in the machine. No one wants them."

"You bought one."

"It was the only thing left. So I'm doing something different by eating a Mars, but it's not even through choice. That's a bit sad."

"Then, tomorrow, you should choose to do something different."

"Like what?"

"I don't know. Maybe drink something new?"

"Like a cocktail instead of a beer?"

"Maybe you should. You might love it."

"I might. I will. A mojito. I don't even know what that is but I like the sound of it. What about you? If I do something different tomorrow, you should too."

"Okay. I'll think about it."

"Maybe that's what's missing in our lives. Doing different things. Different jobs, different places, different people."

"Doing different people?"

"Yeah. I mean, I didn't mean it like that. I meant meeting different people, talking about different things. We should all do that, try different things until we find something that fits. And when you do, then that's what you keep doing."

"We should. But it's easier said than done. This place doesn't fit you, but you're still here."

"I'm leaving."

"I know. When?"

"I'm not sure yet but I want to explore things and do different things. I want to travel and sing and dance in the sun and swim with dolphins."

"I want to do those things too."

"Well, you should. We should. We should do those things. And other things. Anything. Everything."

"Yeah. Got to get out of there first, though, eh?"

"Yeah. Yeah, we just have to get out of here."

#

"Okay," said Linda, "its time for my last word of the day. What have we got?"

"Analphabet and catharsis were the best I've had," said Justin.

"Bad day for me," said Jolene. "Only craven."

"It's a good word but it won't be good enough, I think. Chip?"

"Er, let's see. Bamboozled, bivouac, discombobulate and nefarious."

"Wow. Any one of those could win on a normal day and you have all of them? It's no wonder you're running away with the competition."

"He won't beat my word," said Tanya. "It's spitchcock. It's an eel that has been split before being cooked. I was talking to a fisherman who couldn't get a signal when he's at sea and he told me that."

"Well, that's the winner, then," said Linda. "I think we should finish the competition here. Maybe Ford will want to take it over but if he does, you should restart the scores. For me, the final scores are Chip with 156, Justin and Jolene both have 115, Alex and Nicola, both still not here, have 97 and 57 respectively and Tanya has 3. Chip has won comfortably, so he'll get a prize, but there's a bonus prize for today's best word too, so well done Tanya."

"What's the prize?" asked Chip.

"It's a twenty pound voucher you can use towards a new phone or accessories."

"But I don't have a phone."

"I don't know how you can live without one."

"Well, fucking phones. It's the end of days, people can't put the fucking things down..."

"Chip?"

"Yeah?"

"I'll stop you there. I've heard this before. Many times."

"Oh."

"Linda, he just wants to ventilate. Let him be," said Tanya.

So she did. She turned to her computer while Chip ranted about the evils of smartphones. He had a point, at least to some degree, but she couldn't imagine living without her phone now. How the hell did anyone manage to exist just a few years ago before they were invented? It was hard to believe that humanity as a species had managed to survive into the 21st century without handheld personal computers and constant access to social media.

Chip was still going on when Phil came out of his office carrying a cake and walked over to Linda's desk. He told the team to go on personal time when they finished the calls they were on. Linda suspected they were all already on personal time. He passed party hats to each of the team members. Tanya looked at hers with disgust but put it on anyway.

"So, as you all know, it's Linda's last day today. We're very sorry to be losing you, Linda. You've done a wonderful job for us over the years. I'd like to take this opportunity to wish you all the best both in your new job and life in general and I think I can speak for everyone when I say how much we're going to miss you. Three cheers. Hip hip. Horrah. Horrah. Horrah!"

Shit, was that a tear? Yes, in fact, she fully burst into tears and gave Phil a big hug.

"Speech!" said Ford.

"Okay, okay," said Linda, wiping her eyes. "It's been an

absolute pleasure to work with you all. Some of you for longer than others. You've been a wonderful team and are wonderful people. I'll miss you all but I know that Jim will have it easy because he's taking over the best team in the whole call centre. Thank you all."

"Guys, you have ten minutes extra break today, so have a bit of cake and say your goodbyes to Linda," said Phil. "The other teams will get five minutes at intervals Linda, so anyone who wants to can come for a piece of cake and to say goodbye."

"Thanks, Phil."

It was good cake. Chocolate with lemon icing. Linda ended up having five slices, which was way too much, but it was a special occasion, so whatever. Every time a new team came over to wish her all the best, she took another slice. She suspected that a lot of these well-wishers only came for the cake; some of them she'd never even spoken to, but she appreciated the gesture nonetheless. Davey Jones came over and gave her a hug, before taking her off to the side.

"I just want to offer my commiserations, Linda," he whispered, "thirty escalated calls avoided in a row. So close. It was a valiant effort but I'm still the champion. In fact, I doubt my thirty-one will ever be broken."

"You do know that Ford has taken over from me, don't you Davey? I give your record three months tops."

He looked a little worried about this prospect. He was going to have to up his game if he wanted to remain the biggest skiver in the call centre. The competition had gotten fierce.

After all the teams had eaten cake and said their goodbyes, it was almost four o'clock. She'd see most of these people again tomorrow anyway for her leaving do. But today was the official goodbye from the company, tomorrow night was when everyone would get wrecked and have fun. Most leaving dos were just an excuse for a party, so she was happy to get a sober send-off before the drunken one tomorrow.

Four o'clock arrived and it was her finishing time. She was leaving early today, as her boyfriend was picking her up and taking her to see the wonderful Ed Sheeran. His music was so touching and it was a great treat for finishing this job. She quickly told her team goodbye and said that she'd see them tomorrow, then she walked out the door and didn't look back.

#

Justin watched with envy as Linda left the call centre for the last time. It was strange to see her go. She was already a team leader when he started and was the only one he'd ever had. Now it was going to be Ford. He felt a little shiver move up and down his spine at the prospect. Even though nothing had been mentioned, Justin couldn't shake the feeling that he'd exposed his soul to Ford last weekend.

There wasn't long to go now to the end of the shift and the end of the week. It was a shame in a way that tonight's D&D game was cancelled but it would have ended up being a late one in spite of their best intentions. That, coupled with tomorrow's party, would have been too much and Justin couldn't take another weekend like last week. It would be another lonely night on the sofa in front of the TV. He should probably have a few drinks to get in some training for the heavy session tomorrow.

As five thirty arrived, Justin managed to time his last call perfectly so he could ride out the last minute on wrap-up without taking another. Jolene hadn't been so lucky though and was still on a call as Justin put his coat on. He waited a couple of minutes until she finished.

"So, I'll see you tomorrow night, then?" asked Justin.

"For sure. See you then," she smiled. Justin waved goodbye and left. He couldn't fucking wait until tomorrow night.

173

Chapter 17

Justin couldn't make up his mind whether to shave or not. He preferred to be clean shaven but facial hair was in at the moment, so it couldn't do any harm to keep his five-day fuzz. It's not like it mattered anyway. Who was going to notice? Tonight was going to be the same as any other; he would stand at the bar with Chip making comments about other people before getting drunk and moaning about being single.

A glance at the clock decided for him. It was already ten past six and he was supposed to meet the others in the pub at half past. He simply didn't have time to shave now. He pulled on his best jeans and the shirt he'd ironed earlier. It was still a bit wrinkly, but he'd just have to walk the creases out. He lifted his arm and sniffed underneath. Not bad. The shirt wasn't completely fresh but he'd only worn it a little bit before tonight, so it would be fine. He put on his shoes, left the flat, lit up a cigarette and walked to the pub.

Chip was already there when he arrived but his pint glass was still almost full, so it looked like he hadn't been there for too long. There was a pint already set up for Justin on the table. Good old Chip. But who was that fucking weirdo with the lumberjack shirt and a massive beard sitting at the table? Justin looked closer. Oh, it was Alex. Nice. Unexpected, but nice. He hadn't seen Alex for a couple of months since he'd gone off sick from work.

"Hey Chip, Alex." They both nodded and Alex bounced up off his chair and gave Justin a big hug. A hug?

"What was that for?"

"It's just good to see you, that's all. It's been a while. And it's just Lex now, by the way."

"Yeah, it has been a while. Good to see you too, but a handshake would have been enough."

"Don't be so uptight, Justin. Hugging is in now. Like beards and cold coffee. It's acceptable for male friends to give each other hugs."

"In public?"

"Anywhere. Any time."

"What's gotten into you?"

"What? Nothing. I've just re-evaluated some things recently. I had my priorities all wrong before. I was getting upset about work and life and letting things get to me but since I've been off work, I've been looking at things differently."

"Have you been on the happy pills?"

"Well, yes, but it's not just that. I've gotten into meditation and healthy living too. I was just telling Chip about the teachings of Guru Muhk when you arrived."

"He was," confirmed Chip, his face unreadable.

"So how does drinking factor into your new, healthy lifestyle?" asked Justin, nodding towards Alex's already two-thirds-consumed pint.

"Well, it's not ideal but it's all about balance. I had a bok choy and ginger smoothie before I came out and I've prepared a high-citric solution for when I get home tonight. That should balance my chi."

"Your what?"

"My chi."

"Is that anything like feng shui?"

"Nothing. But I've had my flat fully feng shui'd too, according to the teachings of Guru Muhk. You wouldn't believe what he has to say about the world. He's changed my life, Justin, and he could change yours too. I might not even be able to go back to work now."

"What? You're quitting?"

"I didn't say that. But I do have to consider my position in working for a corporation that values profit above all else. I have two weeks left on my sick line and I need to think about how my actions affect the fragile state of the harmony of the planet."

"You're waiting to see if the doctor will extend your sick line, aren't you?" asked Chip.

"Erm, maybe. If she doesn't though, I'll have some serious things to consider."

"Not least that Ford is your new team leader," said Justin.

"Yes, so I heard. How on Earth did that happen?"

"You can ask him yourself," said Chip. "Here he comes, right on cue."

"Did you invite him?" asked Justin.

"He invited himself. He called me earlier and demanded that I meet him for a pre-party drink. I couldn't say no, so I had to tell him I was coming here to meet you."

"He called you?"

"Yeah."

"On the phone?"

"Yeah."

"Your home phone?"

"Well, I don't have a mobile."

"I knew you two were becoming mates."

"We're not becoming mates. But he is my team leader, so I have to at least be civil to him."

Ford bounded up to the table. "All right, lads? How's it going?" He turned to Alex. "Who are you?"

"I'm Lex. I'm in your team at work but I've been off for a while."

"Oh yeah. I've seen you before, I just didn't recognise you with that fucking hipster beard."

"It's not a *hipster* beard. It's..."

"Never mind. It's nice to meet you."

"You too." Alex stood up and held his arms out to Ford.

"Sit back down there, kale breath. You'll get no hug from me. We've only just met. At least buy me dinner first. Justin, give me a hand carrying the drinks. What are you having?"

"Just a lager," said Chip.

"Cider," said Justin.

"Well, I'm drinking a lager that Chip bought for me but I

wouldn't mind switching to an ale. Maybe an Old Speckled Hen or a Magic Hat No. 9 if they have it," said Alex.

Ford nodded and went to the bar with Justin. "A cider and three Carlsbergs," shouted Ford at the barman.

"What about Alex's ale?" asked Justin.

"What about it, mate?"

They waited at the bar for the drinks to be poured. When the barman set them on the counter, Ford motioned to one of the pints. "Mate, look at that pint there. Could you put a whiskey in there?"

"Er, you want a whiskey in your beer?"

"Could you put one in?"

"Well, yes."

"That's because it's not full, mate. Look at it, it's an inch below the rim. How would you like going into Tesco and buying a loaf of bread with three slices missing? Fill it up there, would you?"

The barman's eyes tightened and one of them flickered as he took a few deep breaths before smiling at Ford. "Certainly, sir. I apologise. I'll sort it out straight away and I hope you'll enjoy your beverages and your time in our establishment. Will you be dining with us this evening, sir?"

"I think we should. It's going to be quite a session, so we should get our stomachs lined first."

"Certainly, sir. Here are some menus and I'll send someone to your table to take your order."

"Cheers, mate."

Justin lifted the cider and one of the lagers and went back to the table, closely followed by Ford.

"Ah," said Alex, "did they not have any ale, or...?"

"Don't know, mate. I asked the barman but he didn't have a fucking clue what he was doing. Anyway, let's get something to eat."

After they had studied the menu for a few minutes, a waitress approached the table. "What would you like, guys?" she asked.

"I'll have the steak," said Chip, "medium."

"Me too," said Justin.

"I'll take the steak as well, but medium rare," said Ford.

Alex was still looking at the menu and appeared undecided. "I was just wondering where the produce comes from. Is it locally sourced?" he asked.

The waitress was silent for about ten seconds. "I'll just go and ask the chef," she said.

She returned after a few minutes. "I'm afraid not. Some of it might be but it's just brought in from our supplier at the best possible price, so we can give our customers the best value for money."

"Oh, that's a shame but there's nothing to do about that. I don't eat much meat these days but that turkey melt sounds good. Do the turkeys come from an ethical farm that uses sustainable methods of agriculture?"

"I could go and ask the chef again but I think I'll just go ahead and say no on that one."

"No?"

"Just to be on the safe side."

"Well, I'll just have the radish salad then, and hope the vegetables aren't subjected to too much chemical treatment or genetic modification. Trying to find ethical food is a nightmare. It's a minefield out there."

The waitress looked as if she'd like Alex to be in a minefield as she smiled through gritted teeth and took their orders to the kitchen. Justin hoped the chef would only spit in Alex's food.

"It's going to be a good night tonight, lads!" said Ford. "There'll be plenty of booze and plenty of women! Anyone you've got your eye on? We know you have your eye on Jolene, Justin. We all do!"

"I don't know what you're talking about," said Justin.

"Fuck off, mate. I've seen the way you look at her and I don't blame you. I'd ride the life out of her. In fact, if you don't, I will. You need to get in there before I do, or someone else does."

"Ford, we're just friends."

"Fuck that. You want in there and I know you do. I tell you what, I'll be generous and give you first dibs on her."

"First dibs? What are you, ten?"

"Ten inches!"

"Ford..."

"Justin, go for it. Seriously. You'll probably crash and burn but better to try than regret never trying. Anyway, what about you two? One of you should make a move on Linda. It's her last night and all."

"She has a boyfriend," said Chip.

"So? It's her last night. She'll be drunk and emotional and you'll never see her again!"

"That would be unethical," said Alex.

"Fuck your ethics, hemp shoes. When it comes to shagging, there are no ethics. It's the law of the jungle. He who eats radish salad goes home alone."

"That's not fair."

"Prove me wrong then."

Alex was saved by his radish salad, which arrived well in advance of the steaks. Justin, Chip and Ford took the opportunity to pop out for a quick smoke. Their steaks were on the table when they got back. They ate quickly and squeezed in another pint before heading to the hotel function room that was booked for Linda's leaving do.

"Here we go!" said Ford. "By the way, Alex, it's your round. Don't be trying to get out of it by disappearing into the crowd. Not that I'm accusing you of anything, mind you. Just saying."

"It's Lex, actually."

Justin walked in. It was indeed Alex's round and he'd have to keep an eye on him. He'd been caught out in the past. Alex had a habit of needing some fresh air or a piss when it was time for his round. He wondered how Ford could have known this. Maybe Alex's reputation preceded him.

There was quite a crowd already, even though the party only officially started at eight o'clock and it was now ten past. Most people were standing with their teams, talking to the same people they talked to every day instead of taking the opportunity to meet others when the whole call centre had been invited. Justin looked around for Jolene but he couldn't see her, or any of the girls from the Brian Clough team, for that matter. He hoped they would arrive soon. He didn't want to have to make small talk with someone from one of the other teams, nor did he want to get involved with the heated discussion that was brewing between Chip, Alex and Ford about art house films versus mainstream cinema. He walked straight back out and lit a cigarette.

As he was smoking, Tanya arrived. She waved and walked over to him and lit up a cigarette too. She was looking pretty good, thought Justin. He'd never seen her with her hair loose before and he couldn't believe how long it was. She was wearing a trilby. Suited her.

"Hey, Justin, how's it going?"

"Good, thanks. You?"

"Yeah, good. Are you the first here?"

"No, Chip and Ford are inside. Alex too."

"Alex? How's he?"

"He's, er, well, you'll see."

"What do you mean by that?"

"You'll see."

"Cryptic. Okay then. Look, here comes Jolene."

Justin's eyes nearly popped out of their sockets as Jolene approached. She was wearing a dark blue dress that was longer on one side than the other, showing off one thigh. It was quite low cut, giving a hint of cleavage but not too much. She was wearing a pair of sexy strappy heels too, making her almost the same height as Justin.

"Justin. Justin!" said Tanya.

"Er, what?"

"Close your mouth."

"What? My mouth isn't open."

"You're drooling, Justin."

He lifted his hand to his mouth and wiped it. He wasn't really drooling at all but just wanted to be on the safe side. He put out his cigarette. "Hi, Jolene," he said when she reached them.

She smiled brightly. "Hi, Justin. Tanya."

"Should we go in?" asked Justin.

"Sure."

They walked back into the function room and saw Chip, Ford and Alex standing at the bar. They made their way over.

"I can't believe you haven't seen Tokyo Story or Bicycle Thieves," Alex was saying, "they are all-time classics."

"I've seen Toy Story and Prince of Thieves. They are classics. Well, Toy Story at least, Costner was a terrible Robin Hood, an embarrassment to Nottingham," said Ford.

"You can't compare art to simple entertainment. Chip just tried to say that Empire Strikes Back is the best film ever made. Please."

"What is the best film ever made, then?" asked Chip.

"Well, my personal favourite, and you've probably never seen it, is..."

"Hello?" interrupted Jolene. "We've been standing here for like, two minutes."

Ford, Alex and Chip turned around, apologised and greeted the girls. Alex hugged them both for a long time. Jolene pulled back after a few awkward moments, shrugged and shook her head.

"At least he didn't hug you with his thoughts," Chip muttered under his breath.

Maybe that's exactly what he was doing, thought Justin and picked up the pint from the bar that Alex had got in for him. Lager. The bastard. Justin had been on cider. He turned around and saw Linda approaching with another team member that he hadn't seen for a while.

"Nicola," said Linda, "I'd like to introduce you to Jim, or Ford, as he likes to be called. He's taking over from me as team leader. Ford, this is Nicola, she's in your team but she's been on holiday. She'll be back next week."

"The week after," said Nicola.

"Yeah, sorry, the week after. I'll let you two get acquainted. Alex, long time, how are you?"

"Getting better, thanks. Maybe I should be at home, but I couldn't let you leave without saying goodbye. And I just go by Lex now."

"I'm glad you came, thanks. Thanks all of you. The whole

team is here. It's great."

Jolene and Tanya had moved over to talk to Chip, leaving Justin on his own with his drink. He struggled to keep his eyes off Jolene, but those legs were so hard to resist. He didn't want to go ploughing in there and seem desperate, so he stood by the bar and sneaked not-so-subtle glances at her every few seconds. He was glad her back was turned.

He felt someone arrive beside him at the bar and reluctantly turned around to see who it was. Vik looked at Justin and mouthed 'holy fuck' while pointing at Jolene. Justin could only nod.

"Want a drink, mate?" asked Vik.

"I have a pint here, thanks anyway."

"Have a shot with me. It's a party."

"All right."

Vik bought them a shot of Sambuca each and asked the barmaid to light them.

"Doesn't that just burn off the alcohol?" asked Justin.

"Does it? Never heard that before," said Vik. "Fuck it. Cheers!"

They knocked back their shots and Justin felt obligated to buy Vik one back, so they ended up having two before Ford and Nicola made their way to the bar.

"Ford!" said Vik. "Shot?"

"Always. Justin, you in?"

"I've just had two," said Justin, "I'm good."

"Wuss."

They slammed their shots and Ford bought another two, then they left, leaving Justin at the bar with Nicola.

"I see you've met our new team leader, then?" asked Justin.

"I've met him before. He doesn't seem to remember that though. We've worked in the same place for years though, just not on the same team. Of course I'd met him before."

"I hadn't. Not until a couple of weeks ago."

"How is he getting on?"

"Fff. I just can't believe he got the job."

"Me neither. I thought it was Tanya's. We all did. How's she taking it?"

"Remarkably well. She's out tonight. First time ever."

"Maybe she's drowning her sorrows."

"Maybe. Anyway, I thought you were in Spain?"

"Got back yesterday but I still have another week off."

"Nice."

Justin stole another glance at Jolene, just as she was turning around. Shit. He quickly turned his gaze to the floor and hoped she hadn't caught him. She was walking towards him now. He felt like his face was on fire. He looked towards the door. Was it too late to bolt outside for a smoke?

"Justin," she said.

"Hi."

"Hi. Do you want to get a drink?"

"Absolutely."

"Okay, can we go to the other bar? I kind of want to get away from Alex. He's dissing my taste in music. This is the same guy whose favourite band used to be Maroon 5."

"Sure. Nicola, do you mind if we go to the other bar?"

"No. Go," she smiled. "I'll smack a bit of sense into Alex."

Justin and Jolene made their way across the room to the bar on the other side.

"It's got to be a mojito, right?" said Jolene.

"It's got to be!" Justin ordered two mojitos. He took a big gulp from his when it arrived. "Oh, it's mint. Not bad. Not bad at all. I could get used to this."

"Don't get used to it. Try something else next. That's what we said yesterday, right? That we should try different things in life?"

"We did. Okay, what's next, then?"

"Let's get a cocktail menu. We can order different drinks and share, so we get to taste more."

They looked through the menu and selected the drinks that sounded the best. The Bloody Aztec and the Bushwhacker were great. The Flaming Volcano was just average and the Mickey Slim positively awful. Justin started to feel his head spinning. He thought he saw Ford standing at the end of the bar with his fist in the air in a shagging gesture. Shit, it *was* Ford at the end of the bar.

Now he was putting the finger of one hand through a circle formed from his other hand and winking at Justin. He tried to move out of Ford's line of sight but that didn't work. Ford just moved around and was now thrusting his pelvis back and forward.

"Is that Ford?" asked Jolene. Shit, she'd seen him too. This could be embarrassing. "What's he doing? Is he shagging the air?"

"Just ignore him."

"Yeeeeooooooh!!!!" screamed Ford.

"Or not."

"What the fuck? Is he implying that because we're having a drink together that we're shagging?"

"Who knows what he's implying," said Justin, his face now so red he actually felt a bit ill. "Just because two people have a drink together, it doesn't mean anything. We're friends. He's just being an idiot."

"Yeah, he's an idiot." Jolene leaned towards Justin and kissed him. "He doesn't know anything."

They kissed again. Justin was so shocked he barely registered what was happening. Jolene suddenly pulled back.

"I'm sorry. I shouldn't have done that. We shouldn't do this," she said.

"Why not?"

"Because we work together."

"So, we'll work together, it's okay."

"Hmm."

This time Justin leaned in to initiate the kiss. And this time Jolene didn't pull back.

Chapter 18

They were all looking now. Tanya noticed first and had nudged Chip, who had nudged Linda. Now everyone was staring across the room to other bar where Justin and Jolene were kissing. They broke the kiss then talked briefly before kissing again. Chip had a big grin on his face. He could see Ford dancing close to them at the bar, his hands waving in the air as he moved behind Jolene and sent a hip thrust in her direction. He really was a fucking prick. Luckily Jolene was too absorbed to notice.

Alex looked as if he was confused, although it was hard to tell behind that huge beard. "Are those two together now? When did that happen?"

"They're not together. This is the first time it's happened," said Chip.

"The first time for real, at least. It's happened in Justin's dreams many times," said Nicola.

"I think all the guys have been dreaming about her," said Linda.

"Some of the girls, too," said Tanya. "Probably."

"Not me," said Alex. "I mean, she's a beautiful girl for sure, but her looks are a bit too... mainstream... for my liking. I prefer someone with a bit more character in their face."

"You mean someone who's ugly enough to let you near them!" said Nicola.

"What about you, Chip? Have you ever fantasised about Jolene?" asked Tanya.

"Erm, no? No, I mean she's pretty and all but I always knew that Justin liked her, so I never thought about her in that way."

"Bullshit," coughed Tanya, then laughed.

"What?" he laughed.

"Okay, Chip, whatever you say," said Linda.

"Well, let's hope that this doesn't end in tears," said Nicola.

"Why would you say that?" asked Chip.

"You know, Justin has fancied Jolene for years and I'm happy for him but we've just said that she's a good-looking and popular girl. She could get any guy she wants."

"What if she wants Justin?"

"She hasn't wanted him before, so I wonder what's changed, that's all. I'm just worried about him, Chip. So should you be, he's your best mate."

"He'll be okay."

"I hope so. I don't want to say she's out of his league but, well, I suppose I just said it."

"That doesn't matter," said Alex. "We shouldn't be so superficial when dealing with relationships. Two people can connect on a deeper level than looks, you know."

"Yeah, you're right," said Nicola.

"I am. I mean, you're way better looking than your husband, Nicola but that works well, doesn't it?"

"Way better looking, Alex? Flatterer. But yeah, it works, so don't think you're flattering your way into my pants."

"What? Can't a man just pay a woman a compliment without any ulterior motives?"

"I don't know. Can they?"

"Yes."

"All right then, flatterer. Can you buy a woman a drink without any ulterior motives?"

"Okay. Let's go. Linda, you come too. I'll buy you a leaving drink."

"What about me?" asked Tanya.

"Someone should stay with Chip. I've already bought him a drink, I'm not buying him another one."

He hadn't bought Chip a drink at all, he'd just been getting his round back. Typical Alex. Even when he was being generous, he was still a stingy fucker. Chip didn't mind though, he was quite happy to be alone with Tanya.

"So, are you enjoying the party?" he asked Tanya after the others had gone to the bar.

"Yeah, it's all right. I mean, it feels like it hasn't really got going yet, but it's okay."

"It's got going for some people but, yeah, I see what you mean. I think we need some music."

"You can't really dance to your type of music though, Chip."

"I know, but I don't mind. I can dance to anything, really. Once I have a few drinks, that is."

"I'll hold you to that."

"No problem. You know, I don't even know what type of music you like. You never really talk about yourself at work."

"No, I'm trying to get better at that though. I mean, I know I've been sort of quiet but I've always just wanted to get on with the job. I suppose I've taken it a bit too seriously, really. It is just a call centre, after all."

"Yeah, but it's good to take things seriously sometimes. I know me and Justin joke around at work but I do take other things seriously."

"It's fun though, I guess. I mean, as long as you get the job done, there's nothing wrong with having a little fun too, right? I'm trying to see that but it's hard sometimes. I just want to do my best at things."

"You do. You should have got the team leader job. I don't know what the hell happened there."

"Well, it happened, so. Anyway, enough about work. Tell me what you're serious about then."

"Hmm, I'm serious about food."

"You should be. It's a serious matter. How serious? Like for work or? Would you like to work with food?"

"I don't know, really, that's the problem. The call centre is fine for now but I don't know what I want to do long term. I suppose working there just puts things off. I don't want to still be there in five years but I don't know where I do want to be. Sorry, too serious?”

“No, it's fine. I know what you mean. I thought it would be a good starter job, work my way up a bit, get some experience, then move on. Working my way up isn't quite going to plan though.”

“It'll work out.”

“Yeah, I hope so. Anyway, what else are you serious about?”

“I love gaming. Any type of gaming, really. Playstation, computer games, online, offline, D&D, anything. I'm a bit of a nerd, I suppose.”

“A bit? You don't say.”

“Everyone is a bit of a nerd now, though.”

“Yeah, I suppose. I'm a bit of a TV nerd. I watch a lot of shows.”

“Most people watch a lot of shows these days. Netflix and chill, you know?”

“Erm, yeah. I don't think that means what you think it does.”

“What?”

“Netflix and chill.”

“Well, you sit and watch Netflix and chill out.”

“Yeah, it's not that.”

“What else could it be?”

“Do you really not know?”

“What is there to know?”

“It's kind of slang for hooking up.”

“What?”

“It's a euphemism for people getting together and, well, getting together.”

“Really? Shagging, you mean?”

“Yes.”

“Do they watch Netflix while they're shagging?”

“No, Chip.”

“I had no idea.”

“I gathered that.”

“You learn something every day. What's your favourite

show, anyway?"

"It's probably the Sopranos. Boring choice, I know, but it's just so good. It was the show that got me into shows and it's still the best. I also love Breaking Bad, Mad Men, Battlestar Galactica, the Wire, all the classics. Twin Peaks. Game of Thrones is on its way to being an all-timer. I really hope they don't fuck up the ending."

A loud noise interrupted as microphone feedback echoed through the room causing everyone to hold their ears. Phil was on the stage and started tapping the top of the mic.

"Hello? Testing, testing, one, two," he boomed. "Sorry, can someone turn this down a bit?"

After a few minutes, someone gave him the thumbs up and he picked up the mic again. "Good evening everyone. First of all, I'd like to thank you all for coming. It's wonderful to see everyone together in the same place. It doesn't happen often enough outside of work, unfortunately. I hope everyone is having fun. There will be music soon, but before that, I'd like to talk about the reason we're all here tonight. Linda, would you mind coming up here please?"

There was a large cheer from the room as Linda made her way to the stage. Ford and Vik were chanting her name as she climbed the steps and Chip was tempted to join in.

"Linda, Linda, Linda," said Phil. "I never thought the day would come when we had to say goodbye to you. You've given us some great years and we're going to miss you. You've worked with most of the call agents over the years, and I think we can see their appreciation in the wonderful turn-out tonight. Three cheers for Linda, everyone. Hip hip."

"Hurrah! Hurrah! Hurrah!"

Linda looked a little overwhelmed as she took the mic. "Thank you so much, everyone. You have no idea how hard it is to leave this place. I never thought it would be like this or I would never have quit!" A little rumble of laughter came from the crowd. "Anyway, it's been wonderful working with you all and I'm going to miss you, but everything moves on. Thank you all and keep in touch."

There was a disturbance in the crowd. Ford's head began to rise above the others as if he was on a lift. Chip realised that it was Vik, whose shoulders Ford was sitting on, that was lifting him above the crowd.

"Linda!" Ford yelled. "Linda! You'll be hard to replace. Only one man is capable of..."

He started swaying a bit and the people standing around him moved back. Chip could see that Vik's legs were buckling as he struggled to hold Ford up. Ford's arms were all over the place now and he looked a little panicked. Boom! He hit the floor in a nasty looking spill, but bounced straight back up. Vik was still on the floor though.

"I'm all right. No worries. Get up, Vik. All good here. Sorry, Phil, Linda."

Phil took the microphone back from Linda. "Just as long as there's no one hurt. Jim Jefferson, ladies and gentlemen. Linda's replacement as team leader. He's not like this at work, folks. Haha. Anyway, its time for some music but before we start, I want to split everyone up. Everyone is standing in their teams, which is nice and I'm glad to see that team spirit. But, I want everyone to mingle a bit and get to know someone from another team. So, all the guys take a step forward."

There was a general reluctant rumble that went around the room, but after a few minutes, the guys did indeed step forward. Chip found himself next to Vik, who was rubbing his arm but didn't look too hurt.

"All the gentlemen start walking clockwise, please," said Phil. "No, the other clockwise, Mr. Bingham, that's right. Okay, keep going. And stop. Now, take a step back and join the ladies. Hopefully, you'll be standing beside someone you don't really know. There might even be a new romance or two tonight! Okay, and hit the music!"

Paisley Des, the DJ for the night, started up some house music shit and the half the people left the dance floor immediately. Seemed like Des had misjudged the audience. Chip walked off the dance floor and found himself with Vik and two girls from the Torvill and Dean team. They were both quite hot, although one of them had a strange tic in one eye. He nodded hello and began to introduce himself before Vik started talking over him. He knew how this was going to go and decided to bow out in case he was considered guilty by association. He looked around and saw Tanya just a few metres away, looking bored as she listened to Angry Gilmore kick off about something.

"Hey," he interrupted.

"Hey, Chip," said Tanya.

"Buddy," said Gilmore, "have you seen Jessie? This fucking splitting people up thing is bullshit. I just want to get fucked with my wife. Maybe get drunk as well, eh? Ha."

"I think she's over there," said Chip and pointed randomly across the room.

"Cheers, buddy," said Gilmore and he left.

"Fancy meeting you here," said Chip.

"I know! Thanks for the rescue. I don't even know who that guy is."

"No problem. That's Angry Gilmore."

"Oh, so *that's* Angry Gilmore. I've heard about him but never met him. Said his name was Tom. I should have realised. It's not an ironic name, then?"

"No."

"Have you seen Alex, by the way?" asked Tanya.

"What? No. I, er, are you looking for Alex?"

"No. I mean, have you seen the state of him? Look."

She pointed at the dance floor where Alex was jumping up and down roughly in time with the pounding music. His arms were like jelly as he shimmied back and forward across the floor. He looked like he was in a trance.

"Glad someone's enjoying the music," laughed Tanya.

"Yeah. He's supposed to be depressed, you know?"

"It affects different people in different ways, I suppose."

Chip saw Phil at the DJ booth talking to Paisley Des and within a few seconds, the music stopped. Alex seemed not to notice at first and continued dancing for a little while, before looking around and shuffling off to the bar while looking at his feet. Then the music started up again. It was a lot quieter this time around. And calmer. Fucking One Direction.

"Don't suppose you want to dance to this, Chip?" asked Tanya.

"I do not. What a lot of shit. It's always like this when I go to parties. They never play any good music. Fucking story of my life."

"Well, a lot of people seem to like it. The dance floor is filling up already."

"Yeah. People have no taste."

"It's easy to dance to."

"I suppose so."

"You said you liked to dance."

"If I'm drunk, I do. We'll see later."

"God, look at Phil. He's cruising all the girls on the dance floor. He must be fifty years old. How creepy. How embarrassing."

"He doesn't see it that way. I think he sees himself as a bit of a Clooney, a bit of a silver fox."

"A silver fox? He's more like that creepy uncle at a wedding who you won't let your kids within ten feet of when the Birdie Song comes on. I can't watch."

"Bar?" asked Chip.

"Bar."

"You never did tell me what kind of music you like, by the way."

"I like boy bands."

#

Justin was fucking furious with Phil. What did he think he was doing splitting people up like that? And for all his talk about starting new romances, he actually seemed determined to stop them happening. Justin looked around again but he still couldn't find Jolene anywhere. He'd already been around the room twice and felt he was starting to look a bit desperate, so he went to the bar instead.

He ordered a beer to take the edge off all the shots and cocktails. While he waited for it to arrive, Ford and Vik appeared beside him.

"Nice work. Where is Her Royal Hotness anyway?" asked Ford.

"She's er, at the toilet."

"You've lost her, haven't you?"

"No, we just got separated during the dancing. I'll catch up with her in a bit. Needed a drink anyway."

"I just have to say well done. Didn't think you had it in you. Suppose I owe this fucker Vik a tenner now."

"What?"

"Doesn't matter. Have fun tonight. Vik, pay for Justin's drink there, he deserves it. I'm off into the fray again."

Vik winked at Justin and set a pint down in front of him, then started talking about who he was going to pull tonight. Justin leaned on the bar and nominally listened to Vik, but his eyes kept darting around the room, looking for Jolene. The euphoria of the kiss was wearing off and the doubt was starting to creep in. Where had she gone? To the other bar maybe? No, it didn't take twenty minutes to get served at the bar. Not for Jolene anyway. Maybe it would take Justin twenty minutes as the barmen continually ignored him while serving the hot girls instead, but Jolene would be the first in line at any bar. Maybe she'd just bumped into a friend and got talking. She'd be back soon.

"I shagged her in a phone box," said Vik, snapping Justin out of his thoughts. He quite enjoyed Vik's lies, even though he didn't have the same charisma as Ford to pull them off, but this was stretching credulity to breaking point. There hadn't been any phone boxes in Nottingham for years.

"Really?" said Justin with barely feigned interest. He couldn't take any more of this. He ordered a shot of tequila, necked it and walked away from the bar. He hadn't necessarily intended to go looking for Jolene but that's what he found himself doing. Ah, there she was in the corner, talking to some girl from the DH Lawrence team. He thought about going over to them but he didn't want to look any more desperate than he was sure he already did. He headed back to the bar and rejoined Vik, who was now regaling Chip and Tanya with the tale of the time he joined the Mile High

Club.

"Where's Jolene?" asked Tanya immediately.

"She's talking to a friend. She'll be along in a bit."

"Sweet."

Chip shook Justin's hand. "Drink?" he asked.

"I don't know. I've had quite a bit already."

"Take one. It's on me. Pint?"

"No, I just had one. I'll take a tequila, I think."

Ford made his way to the bar, sweat lashing off him. "Fucking hell. That dance floor is packed. Great turnout tonight. Pretty much everyone is here."

"Yeah," said Justin, "even Alex and Nicola made it."

"I was hoping Donna from HR would be here but there's no sign of her. Shame. I was hoping to get to know her a bit better."

"There are plenty of other girls here," said Justin. "If you're as good as you say you are, you should have no problem."

"Yeah, mate, but I'm a team leader now, so the call agents should be off limits. I'm looking for someone a bit higher up the ladder, you know what I mean?"

"Whatever, Ford."

"Where's your girl, mate? I saw you half an hour ago and you were on your own and you're still on your own. What's going on?"

"Nothing. I'm just having a drink."

"Yeah, but where's Jolene?"

"She's mingling. She's with Linda now, look."

Justin pointed to where Linda and Jolene were standing and talking, along with Alex and Nicola. Linda spotted him and waved. She turned to the others, then they all made their way across the room.

"Hey, everyone," said Linda. "Great party!"

Justin moved away from Ford and towards Jolene. "Hi," he said.

"Hi," she replied and smiled.

"How are you?"

"I'm not feeling the best, to be honest. I feel a bit sick. I've been a bit silly."

"Silly? How?"

"We shouldn't have..." she gulped then took a few deep breaths.

"Are you okay, Jolene?"

"Yeah, sorry, but we shouldn't have mixed all those cocktails. My head is swimming. I went outside for a bit to get some fresh air but it didn't really help that much."

"Everyone gather round," shouted Linda. "We need a picture of the whole team together for the last time."

Justin took Jolene's arm and she was indeed swaying a bit but he held her protectively round the waist as the group posed for a picture. Ford stood on the other side of Jolene and Alex beside him as the other girls and Chip stood in front of them. Vik took Linda's phone and moved a few paces away.

"Say cheese," said Vik and took a picture. Tanya then gave him her phone, then Alex did the same. It took quite a while for everyone to pose again as they continued to swap phones until everyone had a picture.

"I'll have to get a copy from someone," said Chip. "I don't have a phone."

"I don't know how you live without one," said Nicola.

"Don't get me started."

Justin took Jolene's hand and started back towards the bar, but she pulled back.

"Sorry, Justin. There's no way I can have another drink. In fact, I think I need to throw up. Sorry, sorry, sorry."

"Don't be sorry. Go. It's fine."

Jolene half-ran, half-stumbled towards the bathroom. Justin watched her go, then sighed deeply and turned to the bar. Ford was buying shots for everyone. Justin thought about sitting this round out but had a glass shoved into his hand anyway. Ford made a toast to Linda and everyone knocked their drinks back. Nicola bought a round and made a toast to world peace, then everyone knocked their drink back again. Chip stepped up to the bar and ordered a round.

Justin had lost track of time and the amount of shots he'd had. He couldn't remember if he'd bought a round or not. He probably should buy one, just to be sure. He didn't want to be accused of being a round-dodger. He signalled the barman.

"Bar's shut, mate."

"What? When did that happen?"

"About ten minutes ago. You got another ten minutes to drink up and then you're getting kicked out."

Justin turned and walked away from the bar. Paisley Des was playing slow songs now and there were several couples snogging on the dance floor. For the third time tonight, Justin circled the room looking for Jolene and didn't find her. The music stopped and the hotel staff started moving people outside. Justin was swept along with the crowd and soon found himself out in the rain.

People made their way into their teams again as they left and started saying their goodbyes. Justin found Chip and Tanya and stood beside them while looking at the door as more people filed out. He couldn't quite find the power of speech, so he just stood there. Ford walked past with his arm round a girl Justin recognised but couldn't name. He just winked and walked on. A police siren cut through the mumble of voices. Most people took this as a sign to leave, including Chip and Tanya, who waved goodbye to Justin.

One of the police officers jumped out of the car and ran over to the hotel, where Vik was taking a piss against a wall. A heated argument took place, with Vik waving his hands in the officer's face. Justin couldn't make out the words but before long Vik was being led towards the car with his hands behind his back.

"Justin!" he said on the way past, "I can't fucking believe it, my cock's got me in trouble again."

Justin shook his head. He looked around again. He had no idea where Jolene had gone and most of the others had drifted off too. The rain was pouring down now. Vik was going home in a police car. Justin was going home alone. There would be no singing That's Amore on the way home tonight.

Chapter 19

Yesterday had been an absolute write-off. Justin woke up at one in the afternoon, threw up and went back to bed. He got up again at four, ate a microwave pizza, watched some football, then went back to bed again and watched more Lost until he fell asleep. Even now, at seven o'clock on Monday morning, he was still feeling the effects of Saturday night. The physical pain was starting to subside but the worst was yet to come. The fear and paranoia were in the post and the postman always came early on a Monday.

He looked in the mirror as he brushed his teeth. His beard was now a week old and starting to look patchy. He knew he should shave it but he couldn't be arsed. His eyes were bloodshot and had bags under them in spite of the twenty or whatever hours' sleep he'd had. If there was ever a day to call in sick, this would be it. He couldn't though, everyone would know he wasn't really sick and besides, he had to see Jolene.

They had texted briefly yesterday afternoon during Justin's short period of being awake. It had just been to check that the other had got home safely. There was no mention of anything else, although Justin had spent several hours trying to decipher the hidden meaning behind the words 'Got home ok. Feel rough. Hope ur good' and 'Yeh cu tomoro'. He had nothing, even the fucking Rosetta Stone couldn't have helped.

He finished brushing his teeth and went through to the living room and lit up a cigarette. He always enjoyed the first one after brushing, it tasted a little minty. He could actually see the appeal of menthol cigarettes, at least the odd one here or there. Morning television was terrible as always and Justin wondered why he even bothered paying his TV licence. He watched a lot of television but never what was actually on television, preferring DVDs, Netflix and occasionally, torrents.

He stared at the screen blankly for a while, trying to avoid thinking about the horrendous day ahead. Everyone was going to be staring at him; he and Jolene hadn't exactly been discreet the other night. On one hand he felt proud that he was the one who snogged Jolene and thought well, bring it on then. But on the other hand, half the call centre had seen him standing alone soaked and pathetic outside the hotel at the end of the night. Shit, this was going to be a nightmare. Deep breaths. Better to face it now than put it off.

He pulled on a hoodie and left his flat, keeping his head down and covered the whole way to work. He had that same feeling he always got; that everyone somehow knew what he'd done at the weekend and was laughing behind his back.

There were only a few people in the call centre when he arrived, thank fuck. It was the only good thing about this run of early shifts; that he was able to get in and sit down in the corner and hide, ignoring the other workers when they arrived later in waves. He made his way over to his team section where Chip and Tanya were already sitting, drinking coffee and having a chat. There was a steaming cup of black coffee on Justin's desk.

"I made you a coffee," said Chip. "Thought you might need it this morning."

"Thanks."

"How's things?"

"I don't know. I feel like shit, obviously, but other than that, I don't really know. I don't know what to think."

"Don't worry, Justin. Things will work out the way they're supposed to," said Tanya.

"Thanks, Tanya. We'll see."

"You'll be fine," said Chip. "By the way, we have our breaks at the same time today."

"That's something."

A couple of people from the other team on early shift walked through the door, laughing. Laughing at Justin. He could feel their eyes on him as they walked the length of the call floor, staring and judgemental. Time itself had slowed to a crawl, with every movement taking an eternity. He could see the whites of their eyes as they eased past him in slow motion, drops of saliva spilling slowly out of their mouths as they laughed. The worst voice in the world snapped him out of his trance.

"Morning, all," said Ford as he approached his desk. He was trying to look spritely and full of energy but Justin could see that all-too-familiar hint of darkness behind his eyes. He was either suffering the full hell of a second-day hangover or had tried a cure yesterday and another hangover was just about to hit. Justin nodded at Ford then turned slightly away from him.

"Morning," said Chip and Tanya simultaneously.

"Ready to get this week off to a great start?" asked Ford. He rubbed his hands together as he said this. Definitely faking it. No one replied. Ford left to get some coffee and when he came back, he started to give out briefing sheets.

"So, Linda's gone and I'm full team leader from now on. You all know this, so there's no need to go over protocol again and I've been around for the last couple of weeks, so you should all be used to me by now. I'll get straight to the briefing."

Just then Jolene walked in. It was only two minutes past eight. She kept her head down as she walked to her desk. She was wearing baggy jeans and a jumper today, almost like she wanted to hide herself and look insignificant. Her eyes flicked up to Justin's and she give him the smallest of smiles before looking away again.

"Good morning, Jolene," said Ford. "I was just about to start the briefing. There's a sheet on your desk."

"No, there's not," she said.

"Oh. It must have gone missing. I hate it when things go missing, don't you? Here's another one. Anyway, there's a couple of things of note this week. First, there's another few apps that aren't supported by our hardware. They don't work together. They're incompatible. We don't like incompatible things, do we Justin?"

"What?"

"Never mind. The next thing is that you may have heard

rumours about a merger with another big technology company. They've been floating around for a couple of weeks and some callers may have asked about it. Up to now, the policy has always been to deny any knowledge, but if anyone asks now, you can be honest and tell them there's no deal. The two companies weren't able to seal the deal."

Ignore the twat, thought Justin.

"The final thing for today is a bit of good news for you guys. Jeff Moreau handed in his notice on Friday, so there'll be another team leader position coming up already. He's going to try being a stand-up comedian or some shit, I don't know. Anyway, that could be something for you to think about, Tanya. I don't know if you've considered it before but I think you'd be good at it."

"Thank you so much," she said.

"And any of you others too, of course. You should all apply. No harm in trying. Speaking from experience though, Justin, management is looking for people who take affirmative action. People who seize the initiative and don't let opportunities go to waste."

"Whatever. Is there anything else?" asked Justin.

"No, that's all. Time to get on the phones, team. Let's make it a good day today."

Justin looked over at Jolene before turning to his computer but she didn't look in his direction. He made himself available and started taking calls. There was nothing overly difficult to deal with, which was good because he still felt terrible. Between calls he turned to look at Jolene but she was always intently looking at her screen. Ford came and went intermittently, and looked better every time he came back. Finally, it was break time and he and Chip both logged off and went downstairs.

Justin couldn't get the cigarette lit quick enough and those first few drags were amazing.

"I take it Jolene never reappeared on Saturday night, then?" asked Chip.

"No. I texted her yesterday and she got home okay but I haven't spoken to her today. She was quite drunk though. She went to the toilet and I didn't see her again. I think she pulled the Irish

Goodbye."

"Yeah, that's what I thought. Sorry, man."

"Hopefully things will be okay when she's feeling better. Anyway, you and Tanya seemed pretty friendly the other night. What's going on there?"

"Nothing. Well, we're becoming friends a bit, I suppose. Strange, considering we've worked together for ages and not really spoken much before."

"It was her that never spoke before. She just sat there like a jobsworth."

"Yeah, she's talking a lot now, though. I don't know what changed, but I like it. She's nice."

"You fancy her?"

"Maybe, actually."

"Go for it."

"Maybe I should."

"She'll probably get the team leader job this time, so you should go for it before she changes teams. Unless you're applying for it yourself?"

"I doubt it. I mean, I guess it would be okay to move up but I don't want to get in Tanya's way. Don't suppose you're going to apply?"

"Please. The only thing worse than working in a call centre is being a team leader in a call centre."

"For you. Not for everyone."

"Well, I'm not applying. Ready to go back in?"

"Yeah."

They put out their cigarettes and went back upstairs. Justin tried to get Jolene's attention as he sat down but she was still focussed on her screen and didn't acknowledge anything around her. This wasn't good. Justin liked talking to Jolene even more than he liked looking at her. He was sure this wasn't normal. He could probably get beaten up in the pub for even thinking such a thing. It was killing him not to be able to talk to her. After a couple of minutes, she logged off for her break.

"Jolene?" said Justin. She turned and looked at him briefly before looking at the floor.

"Yes?"

"So..."

"So."

"How are you?"

"Okay. You?"

"Okay. Feel a bit rough."

"Me too. Going to get some coffee."

"Okay."

"Okay. See you later."

"See you."

Justin sighed and logged back in. He started taking more calls. When Jolene came back, she sat down and turned to her screen once again.

It was coming up on lunch time when Ford walked over to Justin and told him to log off and come into the office. He finished the call he was on, then did so. The smell of alcohol coming from Ford in that small room hit him like a wave.

"What's this about, Ford?" he asked.

"I'm going to have to give you an official warning, mate."

"What? What for?"

"For not meeting the required standards."

"What the fuck are you talking about, not meeting the required standards?"

"I'm afraid your performance on Saturday night wasn't good enough. You pulled Jolene, but didn't take her home and finish the job. That's a warning in my book."

"Fuck off, Ford."

"Mate, it just wasn't acceptable. You've let down men all across Nottingham who can't get anywhere near Jolene and you manage to get in there but you don't bang her. It's just not on. I'm going to speak to Phil about getting you transferred to another team. I can't have a bottler representing Brian Clough."

"You can't be serious."

"Well, no," laughed Ford, "not about the transfer. Or the warning actually. But mate, what the fuck? I pulled some bird from the DH Lawrence team. Riding all night."

"I thought you said call agents were off limits?"

"We're not talking about me, we're talking about you. You should have taken Jolene home and shagged the life out of her. Bent her over and done her from behind while slapping that tasty arse, then got your cock between those glorious tits and shot all over them. You should have left her looking like a painter's radio."

"I'm leaving now."

"Go, then. But you'll not live this one down quickly, mate."

Chip had brought lunch with him today but Justin felt like being alone, so didn't join him in the lunch room. Instead, he wandered around town for his entire forty-five minute lunch break, chain smoking and thinking about what a mess his life was. How had it swung so quickly? Just two days ago he was kissing the girl he'd fancied for years and thought life couldn't get any better. He was already distraught that things hadn't progressed any further that night without that fucking Ford rubbing it in. And Jolene wasn't talking to him. Did she regret what happened? And everyone was still fucking staring at him! God damn it.

He stormed back into the call centre and pulled on his headset without talking to anyone.

"Tech support."

"Hi there. My name is Alison. I have a bit of a problem."

"Don't we all?"

"Excuse me?"

"How can I help?"

"Well, I can't put my phone down for more than a few minutes at a time. I always pick it up even if I don't need it for anything. I'm checking Instagram and Twitter constantly, even if I just checked them a few minutes before. It happens all the time. When I'm in a restaurant with my boyfriend, my phone is always beside my plate. So is his, actually, so he doesn't mind. I look at it when I'm walking down the street and even when I'm crossing the road. I even find myself cheating at pub quizzes, and I never cheated at anything before I had a smartphone."

"What does this have to do with us?"

"It's your company's phone. I was wondering if there's any way to restrict access?"

"Yes, as it happens. You can start by taking the battery out of the phone."

"Okay, I've done that. Should I wait for like ten seconds or so before putting it back in?"

"No. You should throw it away."

"Excuse me?"

"Throw the battery away and the phone won't work anymore, so you won't be able to check your social media feeds."

"Well, that's not really helpful, to be fair."

"And to be fair, this is tech support, not an addiction control helpline. Bye now."

Leave me alone, thought Justin. Why can't you just leave me alone? I don't want to speak to you idiots today. Just fuck off, all of you. Click.

"Yes?"

"Hello. Is that tech support?"

"Yes."

"Oh, okay. I thought I had the wrong number."

"You didn't."

"Maybe you can help me. My phone won't switch on."

"Tried taking out the battery?"

"Why would I try that?"

"Why wouldn't you?"

"What?"

"Try it. Leave it ten seconds, then put it back. Call back if that doesn't work."

Fuck off. Click.

"Tech support."

"I'm having a problem with my phone."

"What's the problem?"

"The speaker isn't working properly."

"Can you hear me?"

"Yes, I can hear you."

"It's working just fine."

Fuck off. Click.

"I'd like to make a complaint."

"Go."

"Go?"

"Yes. Go ahead with your complaint."

"What? Are you taking this seriously?"

"I need to hear the complaint first before I decide whether it should be taken seriously."

"All complaints should be taken seriously."

"Not all complaints. Some people just love to moan."

"Are you suggesting that I'm a moaner?"

"Not at all. I don't know you, so I couldn't possibly suggest that."

"I don't particularly like your tone. Do you want to hear my complaint or not?"

"Go ahead."

"I'm complaining about the battery life of my phone. It won't hold a charge for more than a few hours at a time. I'm a businessman and I need my phone available at all times. This isn't good enough."

"You're right, it's not. I'll send you a new battery. Can I have your details?"

"I'm afraid that's not enough. I want compensation for my trouble."

"Oh, fuck off."

"I beg your pardon?"

"Erm, I've a cough," Justin said and faked a few splutters. "I can't do that but I'll send you two new batteries in case you need a spare and will let management know you've registered a most vociferous complaint."

"Vociferous?"

"Extremely vociferous."

"Well, that will have to do."

Justin took the caller's details. That was another one down. Next. Click.

"Just to let you know, all the grapefruits delivered to Tesco supermarkets around London in the last week have been injected with a type of transmorphic potion. This potion alters the DNA code in the human body, turning people into beings of pure energy."

"What's the point of that?"

"I'm not privy to that information just the now but my brother Duncan has infiltrated the headquarters of a dangerous terror cell and is gathering data as we speak."

"Isn't he just a torso?"

"A very resourceful one, let me tell you."

"I want to ask you a question, Miss Peal."

"What?"

"How do you function in normal society?"

"I don't know what you're talking about."

"Well, you're easily the most insane person I've ever spoken to and I've spoken to quite a few. I'm just wondering how you go about your daily life. What happens when you need a pint of milk? Do you tell the shopkeeper all your crazy theories or do you just keep yourself to yourself? I don't understand how you can exist in our world. Why do you even call here? Do you even know who you're calling? This is tech support for..."

Click.

"Miss Peal?"

Justin made himself available once again and rattled through call after call. This was the hardest he'd worked in three years. He wrapped up each call swiftly and went available again straight away. This was all right, actually. While he was talking to these twats, he didn't need to think too much. Before he knew it, it was break time again. He and Chip went for a smoke as usual.

"What's wrong with you today, man?" asked Chip. "You're paradoxically being a diligent worker and being really obnoxious to the callers. I've heard you talking to them. It's funny as fuck but you need to be careful. Is it Jolene?"

"No. Yes, well, it's everything, really. I just need to get out of this fucking place."

"Why don't you take another depression break when Alex gets back from his?"

Justin had taken a two-month-long depression break the year before. It wasn't hard to convince the doctor he was depressed. He worked nine hour shifts talking to crazy people under tube lighting. He was a textbook case. After spending two months sitting in his underwear in his grubby flat playing video games and surrounded by pizza boxes, he actually started feeling depressed so went back to work.

"I don't think that will help. I'm not depressed, I'm unhappy. I want to be with Jolene. Or someone. Or be somewhere. India or Indonesia or Bolivia or somewhere. I just need a change. Besides, it's your turn for the depression break."

Chip had also taken a two-month-long depression break the previous year. He had likewise spent his time in his underwear playing video games in his flat. He considered it the best time of his life, but after two months he started to feel guilty about being paid for doing nothing so went back to work.

"I'm saving it for something special. I don't know what that is yet but I want to be ready. I don't mind going out of turn, anyway."

"Thanks, Chip. I appreciate it but I want to see what's going on with Jolene first."

"Fair enough."

They went back inside and Justin logged back in and started taking calls again. There was only an hour and a half left of the day and it flew past in a flurry of pointless calls. At five thirty, Justin logged off, waved a brief goodbye to the others, who were all still taking calls, and left. He went straight home, put a ready meal in the microwave, took off his clothes and sat in his underwear watching brainless television so he didn't have to think about his life.

Chapter 20

For the second day in a row, Chip was the first to arrive and the call centre was empty. He suspected it was going to be this way from now on. Previously, Linda was always there no matter how early he arrived. The others had varying degrees of punctuality. Even Tanya usually cut it very close to starting time, which had always surprised him a little. Jolene, of course, was never on time. He turned on his computer then walked to the break room to make coffee. He just made one for himself today; he didn't want the others to get into the habit of arriving after him expecting there to be a cup of coffee waiting for them. He made an exception for Justin yesterday, as he felt he needed it. Maybe he could make an exception again today. For Tanya this time. Tea. She didn't drink coffee.

Justin had arrived and was taking off his jacket when Chip went back through to the call floor.

"Oh, is that for me?" he asked.

"No, not today."

"Oh."

"What? I'm not going to make you coffee every day."

"Fair enough. Who is it for?"

"It's tea for Tanya."

"Fucking hell, that's milky."

"Yeah, it's like half and half. She likes it that way."

"It is even really tea? In fact, you could call it a mea."

"Yeah, or a tilk."

"Is it even warm? It'll be freezing by the time she gets here."

"Here she comes now. You feeling better today, by the way?"

"Yeah, I'm feeling fine."

"You look a lot better."

"Thanks. I'm going to go and make some coffee since you didn't make me any."

Justin waved to Tanya on his way past. She looked at the cup of tea on her desk, then at Chip.

"Did you make this for me?"

"Yeah. Milky, one sugar, right?"

"Right. Very observant. Thanks, Chip."

Ford was the next to arrive. He looked bright and was wearing what looked to be a new suit. This one matched and actually fit him. He greeted everyone and asked them to get ready to get on the phones at eight o'clock sharp.

They did and just as the first call came in, Jolene arrived. It was only one minute past eight; this must have been some sort of record. She was also looking fresh, like she'd had a good night's sleep and was full of energy. There must have been something in the water that morning. Everyone seemed like they were in good form. Chip had a feeling it was going to be a pretty good day.

#

Tanya hadn't slept much last night. She'd spend most of the night tossing and turning in bed, wondering whether to apply for the team leader position. She was very excited yesterday when Ford mentioned that Jeff Moreau was leaving, making another supervisor role available so soon after the last one. There had been no vacancies for the previous two years and now there were two in a month. Her first thought had naturally been to resubmit her application, with maybe a couple of tweaks, and this time get the job that should have been hers already.

The problem was, of course, that she didn't get the job that should have been hers already. She'd had a couple of weeks to get used to that but it still stung. The fact that it was Ford who got the job stung even more. He was clearly only interested in a higher salary and getting off the phones, he had no interest in the responsibility that the role entailed. Somehow he managed to convince Phil and the rest of the management team that he was the one for the position. He was a top-quality shit-talker who told people what they wanted to hear and they fell for it. Therein lay the problem. What if another shit-talker came along and talked the job out from under her a second time? She would definitely have to quit then. Storming out would be required. She was just starting to have a little fun at work for the first time, so she didn't want to leave now. But if Ford could be a team leader, there was nothing to stop Phil giving the job to someone like Paisley Des or even that fucking Vik. Imagine.

If she was going to go for the position again, she'd need something to set her apart from the competition. There was no point giving the same interview as before. If she said the same things again, she would lose the job, like before. What should she do differently?

She thought about this while taking calls. Her heart wasn't really into talking to the callers at the moment and she provided the bare minimum of help. She felt bad about not giving the quality of customer service that she usually did but by lunch time, she had a plan.

She logged off and walked over to the Lord Byron team section, where Jeff Moreau was sitting with his feet on the desk chatting with one of his agents. She waited for him to finish and acknowledge her. They had never spoken before but it was time for that to change. Depending on what Jeff had to say, it could turn out to be a pretty good day.

#

Ford was feeling a bit stressed. Yesterday wasn't the best first day as solo team leader. He'd been ridiculously hungover and while the sneaky drinks he'd gone for had helped a bit, it wasn't until the end of the day that he felt normal again. He resolved to try harder today. He didn't have a drink at all last night and he was wearing that new suit he intended to wear yesterday.

He looked at his team. Tanya had just got back from lunch and was logging in, Chip and Justin were both on calls and Jolene was spinning on her chair. She didn't talk to him between calls, none of the fuckers did. He needed to change that, inject a bit of team spirit into things and make his own mark on the team. Linda had played that stupid word of the day game, which gave them all a little fun while on the calls, but he didn't want to do that. He could think up something better than that. He was Ford.

Jolene was still spinning around and Ford was hoping to catch a glimpse of her tits jiggling as she did so, but her bra was too fucking supportive. What a shame. She was so fucking fit. Jolene. Jolene. He started singing that song in his head. That was it!

"Team meeting, guys. If you're on a call, finish it up. If not, go on 'Not Ready' and wait." He waited until everyone was ready. "So, things seem a bit dull today and I've been trying to think of a way to make the calls more interesting for you guys. There will be a new competition to replace word of the day. The aim is to try to get song titles into your conversations. We'll check at the end of the day and the best one will get a point. The most points at the end of the month or quarter or whatever will win a prize."

"It's gonna be me," said Chip.

"Well, everyone has a chance," said Ford. "We're starting the scoring from scratch."

"So, what's the prize?" asked Tanya.

"I don't know yet, but I'll think of something. Something better than vouchers."

"So, the winner takes it all, then?" asked Justin.

"Yeah, yeah. There's no second prize."

"This could be tricky," said Jolene. "I might burst out laughing while on a call. I'll have to try to keep a poker face."

"Yeah, you don't want to sound like a desperado," said Justin.

"No, try to make it sound natural," said Ford. "Wait, I see what you bastards are doing. You've started already. Good work. Try your best to get them in there. Don't stop believing you can do it. If you sense an opportunity, just think it's now or never and go for it. Right, Justin?”

“Right.”

“That goes for everything in life. When love is in the air, you have to reach out and grab that too. I imagine someone like you is tired of being alone, am I right?”

“Yeah. I'm, er, I'm sitting on the dock of a bay.”

“What? What's that supposed to mean?”

“I don't know. I couldn't think of anything quick enough and I didn't want to miss my window.”

“It would've been better to say nothing.”

“Yeah, in fact, you say it best when you say nothing at all,” said Chip.

“Okay, time to get started. Good luck. By the way, Jolene, are your parents big fans of Dolly Parton?”

“What? Dolly Parton? What are you talking about?”

“You know. Jolene.”

“I have no idea what you're talking about.”

“The Dolly Parton song. Jolene. Don't tell me no one has ever said that to you before.”

“Never.”

“You're not serious.”

“No. Of course I've heard it before. I hear it all the time. I'm sick of hearing it.”

“Well?”

“Well what?”

“Are they Dolly Parton fans?”

“No.”

“Where did they get the name from then?”

“If you must know, my dad is called Joel. So I'm named after him.”

“I prefer the Dolly Parton thing. I'm going to go with that.”

“You shouldn't. It's wrong.”

“Well, I like Dolly. Big tits.”

Jolene shook her head and turned back to her computer. Ford suspected he saw the hint of a smile on her face though. That went well. A bit of team-building plus a spot of casual flirting. If Justin wasn't going to nail Jolene, someone should. A girl that fit was begging for a banging. Anyway, now the team had something fun to do while on their calls and they had Ford to thank for it. He should probably have a little drink to celebrate that win. Things were going pretty well today.

#

This could be quite fun, thought Jolene. She had enjoyed Linda's word of the day but it had been more reactive than proactive. There wasn't much that could be done about a caller's choice of words. Sure, a little bit of prompting here and there, but you were mostly relying on them. This was a competition that you could really take by the scruff of the neck and run with!

She considered her song title knowledge to be average at best. Better than some but not nearly as comprehensive as it could be. Well, she would have plenty of time to brush up now that her detox had started. It was supposed to be a full break from everything: drink, social media, men, but she'd already checked Facebook twice today, so it wasn't really going all that well.

"You ain't seen nothing yet," she overheard Justin saying. Nice! He was getting stuck in already. She smiled. They hadn't talked about the kiss and Jolene wasn't sure if she wanted to or not. She wasn't sure how she felt about it and hadn't really processed it yet. The whole situation had caught her off guard and she'd been too hungover to think it through. They had their afternoon break at the same time, so she would just play it by ear. Now it was time to get some song titles in!

Just before three o'clock, Ford told them all to come off the phones. "The breaks are going to be starting soon, so let's see what we've been able to get so far."

"We didn't have enough time," said Jolene. "We only had a couple of hours and I didn't get a chance. The only one I managed was my name."

"That doesn't count," said Ford, "otherwise you'd get it on every call."

"Not every call."

"You're supposed to give your name on every call."

213

"Oh yeah."

"Anyone else get anything?"

"Nothing from me," said Chip. Poor guy. He looked distraught.

"I said to a caller if you think our current phone is good, you ain't seen nothing yet," said Justin.

"That's not bad. Did you get anything, Tanya?" asked Ford.

"Not really. I managed to get in 'Changes' and 'Help', of course, but not much more than that."

"You can get one word into anything though," said Justin. "We should ban one-word answers."

"I agree," said Ford.

"You do?"

"Yeah. No one-word answers. Anyway, no points today, that was a trial run. It starts properly tomorrow."

"What do you mean no points today?" asked Justin. "I should get a point. Mine was perfectly valid."

"It was a trial run."

"You didn't say that beforehand. That's not fair. Now I've lost a great one. I can't use that again now."

It really wasn't fair. Poor Justin had done great to get that song in there and now Ford wasn't allowing it. That wasn't on. "No way, Ford," said Jolene. "It's perfectly valid. You never said that today was a trial, even though it was only a couple of hours. You should give him a point."

"All right, then. One point to Justin."

"Thanks, Jolene," said Justin and smiled at her.

"No problem. See you at break time?"

"Yeah. See you in ten."

Only ten minutes to break time. This day has flown in, thought Jolene, and it has actually been pretty good.

#

Justin joined Jolene in the break room. There were a few others there from another team, but they ignored them and sat in the corner. He wasn't quite sure what to say. They hadn't talked much yesterday, and only a little today. This was the first time they were alone since Saturday night. He looked at her lips. He really wanted to just lean over and kiss her there and then. Maybe he should. What's the worst that could happen?

He turned away from her. It was difficult to meet her eyes for too long without thinking too much. There was a magazine on the table. Cosmopolitan. There were always women's magazines in the break room but never anything for men. Not that Justin wanted to read some shit about cars or gadgets anyway, but still. The headline read '8 Ways To Improve Your Orgasm'. Fantastic.

"Have you seen this?" asked Jolene, pointing directly at it.

"No, what is it?"

"The usual shit that's in these magazines. Improve your orgasm."

"Need to have one before you can improve it," said Justin. What the fuck? Why had he said that? He felt the blood rushing to his face. God damn it.

"Yeah." At least she looked a little embarrassed too.

"What's up with that eight?" asked Justin. He could still save this.

"What eight?"

"That eight on the magazine. Look. The two circles are both the same size. That's not an eight. That's an infinity symbol sideways. When I was at school, I was taught that the top circle should be slightly smaller than the bottom circle."

"Me too, actually. Why is that? That's a bit strange when you think about it."

"Right? I don't know why. And sometimes, they're not even circles. More like ovals. Two ovals on top of each other."

"It's not on, Justin."

"It's not on at all. Fucking eight. Hate the eight. I've never liked it, to be honest. I never really knew why until now."

"Me neither. I never cared for the eight. In fact, not only have I never cared for it, I would actively say it's my least favourite number."

"What's your favourite?"

"Probably a seven."

"Oh. You like the seven? Don't you think it's a bit too pointy? Sharp, I mean."

"I like sharp."

"Fair enough. I like nine. I like the way it's all round. Not sharp at all, really."

"Nine's okay."

"It's great. But I'm not overly fond of six. Isn't that weird? I mean it's the same shape just the other way around."

"It's a little weird."

They laughed and Justin felt better. He really wanted a cigarette but didn't want to leave Jolene. They were having fun. After the nightmare that was yesterday, Justin hadn't been sure whether they would ever have fun again. It had seemed like the kiss had changed their friendship but now they were laughing again. It was still an elephant in the room though. Neither of them mentioned it but it lingered. Justin didn't want to make things awkward between them like they had been yesterday. He was just happy that they were friends again. Things were going better. Even work hadn't been too bad. In fact, it had been a pretty good day.

Chapter 21

"It's more than a feeling. I'm certain of it."

"How certain?"

"Let me check my records. Hold on a moment please. Where is that? I'm sorry but I still haven't found what I'm looking for. Where is it? I can't find the file. You can't always get what you want, I suppose. Anyway, I can't find the official date here but I'm a believer in our engineers and I'm sure the software update will be released within the month."

"I've been told that before. This software update was supposed to be rolled out two weeks ago. I didn't believe it then and I don't believe it now."

"Have a little faith in me."

"Well, you, I do. You guys in the call centre always do your best. It's just that your company is full of lies. The phone is lagging behind the competition. If I don't see this upgrade by the end of the month, I'm going to switch to another brand."

"Well, that is your consumer right and I can't tell you what to do. You can go your own way. But if you're asking yourself should I stay or should I go, then consider our great battery life."

"There is that, I suppose."

"Yes, and there's a light that never goes out in the phone, even when the battery is drained. Something to do with a liquid screen."

"Well, you're convincing me, I have to say. I'll wait a while longer before making my decision."

"Okay. Is there anything else?"

"No, that's all."

"Well, thank you for calling. It's been my pleasure to help you today."

"That's very nice of you. I don't often get thanked for calling."

"We pride ourselves on exceptional customer service here. Every time we say goodbye, we thank our callers."

"Wonderful. Goodbye."

Justin hung up and started to wrap the call. He could write that one off as a 'General Enquiry' and spend the next eighty-five seconds looking around the room and at Jolene. He saw Ford walking out of his office and straight towards him.

"Mate, go on 'Not Ready' there and come into the office," said Ford.

"What's this about? It's not another bullshit warning like on Monday, is it?"

"I don't want to discuss it here. Come into the office."

Justin followed Ford into the office. Ford shut the door behind them and indicated for Justin to sit down. "What's going on?"

"I'm afraid I do actually have to give you a warning. A real one this time."

"What for?"

"Well, I've been listening to some of your calls."

"Again? You listened to some last week. Why are you picking on me?"

"I'm not. I've been listening to everyone's calls. It's just that I noticed something in one of yours that I can't let slide."

"I know I haven't been following the greeting prompt."

"Never mind that. It's something else. Do you want to hear the call in question?"

"No. I don't want to hear myself."

"Okay. Well, I have to ask. Rules and what not. Anyway, on Monday at 13.41 hours, you told a caller to fuck off. At first I thought you said 'I've a cough' but when the caller asks you what you said, I can distinctly make out 'fuck off'."

"Wasn't it the other way around?"

"So, you're admitting it?"

“I suppose so.”

“Can you explain it?”

“Not really.”

“I'm going to have to give you a warning.”

“Fair enough,” said Justin.

“It's going to have to be a written warning, I'm afraid. This offence constitutes a written warning.”

“I suppose it does.”

“But don't worry, I'm not going to write it down.”

“What?”

“If I write it down and Phil sees it, you could get in real trouble. So, I'm going to give it to you verbally. If Phil sees the warning in your file and asks for more information, I'll just tell him you had a small disagreement with a caller.”

“Well, it wasn't really a disagreement.”

“Whatever, Justin. Let's do this. That's an official written warning for you.”

“A verbal written warning? That almost makes sense for this place,” said Justin.

Ford nodded.

#

He watched Justin leave the office. He'd gotten away with it, his explanation worked. A verbal written warning. The truth was he was an idle bastard and couldn't be bothered with the paperwork. That would have to change though. From tomorrow.

He sighed. Too much was changing and too quickly. He had already severely cut down on his drinking during working hours and the drugs had gone entirely. He'd been on time every day since becoming team leader, too. Ford wondered what he was turning into. He took the job in the first place because it was more money for less work, a great deal in anyone's book, or so he thought. It was true that there was less phone work but he had more to do in other areas. Like discipline. He'd given Justin a pass here, even if it was for selfish reasons. He hoped Justin would appreciate it.

The two of them hadn't really clicked yet and Ford forced himself to admit that was partly his fault. Not everyone understood his sense of humour. A lot of what he said was just world class banter but if you didn't know that, he supposed it was possible that someone might take him the wrong way. Hopefully his relationship with Justin would improve now after this. In fact, he needed to work on things with the whole team. He'd been with them for over two weeks now but they still hadn't really accepted him. They seemed to be enjoying his new song title game, he'd heard quite a few this morning already, but they still weren't talking to him when they weren't on calls. Maybe they were just an anti-social bunch. It hadn't been like this on the Robin Hood team. Could it be possible that they just didn't like him? No. Absolutely not. It was just a matter of finding a connection and he was off to a good start with the song game. He had to try to separate his new, team leader self from the old Ford without losing what made him great in the first place. He could do that. He liked being an authority figure. He liked that Phil now valued his opinion and leadership skills. He wanted people to look up to him.

He looked at his watch and decided it was lunch time. He opened the bag that he kept locked in his office and looked at the bottle of rum that was in there. He decided he'd leave it in there today. He'd also just take the designated forty-five minutes for lunch.

After the break, he threw himself into his work. He had some stats to crunch and see how his team was performing at the mid-week point. From there, he would figure out a plan to improve their efficiency for the rest of the week.

Then the door opened and he looked around. It was Donna from HR. She didn't normally come up here, so it must be something serious. All eyes were on her as she walked the length of the call floor to Phil's office. She was tall and her five-inch heels made her even more statuesque. She was wearing a white blouse with the two top buttons undone and her black bra was clearly visible through the thin material. A pencil skirt to just below the knee showed off her shapely nylon-clad calves as she sashayed across the room. Her hair was tied up in a bun and her horn-rimmed glasses were slightly down her nose. She was the living embodiment of the sexy secretary, almost as if she'd deliberately patterned herself on every male's fantasy. Ford's eyes nearly bulged out of their sockets and he simply could not tear them away from her round, swaying arse. It may have taken twenty seconds for her to reach Phil's office but it felt like time itself had slowed down as she walked. Ford thought he heard saxophone music from somewhere. He imagined her turning to him, licking her lips and winking, before letting her hair out and shaking it slowly. She then climbed onto one of the desks, ripped her blouse open and tore her skirt to reveal stockings and suspenders. Phil's door slammed and brought him back to reality. Wow. That was one for the bank.

#

Justin was desperately pretending not to notice her. He was glad that Jolene was still on her lunch break, not that he supposed she would care who he looked at. Chip also looked a little hot under the collar and didn't quite know where to put his eyes. Justin looked over at Tanya.

"Would," she said.

Justin smiled and went back to work. Every ten minutes or so, Phil would come out of the office and call someone else in. Vik had just come out and was looking a little shell-shocked. What the hell were they doing in there? He took another call and as he was wrapping up, he heard a voice.

"A word please, Justin."

He hadn't noticed Phil approaching. "Just a minute," he said.

"Now, Justin."

He sat down at Phil's desk. Phil sat opposite and Donna was off to one side. He could smell her perfume and lipstick. It was intoxicating. He felt guilty about feeling this way but he couldn't help it. He looked at her cleavage and felt dizzy. She crossed her legs and Justin quickly had to cross his too to hide his arousal. She definitely had the upper hand.

"Donna is here because we're legally required to have a

representative from Human Resources any time we have a disciplinary issue to deal with."

"Since when? I've been in here before and there was no one else here."

"Er, yes, that was an oversight that has since been corrected. Anyway, Justin, do you know why we've called you in here?"

"No."

"There's nothing you can think of?"

"Nothing. I'm a model employee."

"Well, I'm not so sure about that. We've been listening to random calls and you took one on Monday that requires a little explanation."

First Ford and now Phil. Why was everyone listening to calls all of a sudden? Months had passed without anyone so much as entertaining the notion of listening to a call and now suddenly everyone was at it.

"I've already had a written warning about this."

"Oh, where is it? I don't see it in your file."

"That's because I just got it this morning and it wasn't written down."

"Excuse me? Did you say it wasn't written down?"

"Yeah."

"Your written warning wasn't written?"

"No."

"Well, I don't know what's going on here but it seems I'll have to keep a closer eye on these things. Who's your team leader? Ah, it's Jim Jefferson. Well, he's just new, so we can't expect everything to be perfect just yet. Nonetheless, it should have been a full written warning. Anyway, would you mind explaining what happened?"

"Well, I wasn't having a great day and a caller demanded compensation for something stupid, so I told him to fuck off. I didn't really mean to, it just slipped out."

"So, you did tell him to 'f off'. We weren't sure if that's what you said. It sounded to me like you had a cough, so I wasn't sure. That's why I wanted you to clarify. But if that's what you said, then

I will have to give you a proper written warning."

"Actually, Phil," said Donna from HR, "swearing at a customer is gross misconduct. Justin, you've admitted that you swore at this man, you do realise what that means?"

"Er..."

"It means we have motive, evidence and a confession of your misdemeanour."

"Oh, come on. I just told an arsehole to fuck off. Have you never told an arsehole to fuck off?"

"Not at work."

"Hang on a second," said Phil. "Surely we don't have to take this any further than this room. We can deal with it here, give a second warning or whatever and that'll be the end of the matter."

"I'm afraid not, Phil," said Donna from HR. "I couldn't in good conscience overlook this incident. I'm left with no choice but to terminate your employment, Justin. You'll be paid for the days you've worked this month, plus any holiday allowance remaining."

"What?"

"Now hold on, Donna, this is a bit much," said Phil.

"Sorry, Phil. A line has been crossed. I'm going to make it official. Justin Bramble, this is hereby an official verbal termination of your employment. A written confirmation will follow."

"You can't fire me, I quit."

"You can't quit, you don't work here any more. I just terminated your employment, so you don't have a job to quit."

"But, but... I quit!?" said Justin.

"I'm afraid not. I think you'll find you were terminated first."

"You are such a bitch, Donna."

"You see, Justin. It's a mouth like that that got you in trouble in the first place."

Justin left the office in disbelief. He couldn't fathom what had just happened. He knew he shouldn't have sworn at that caller but he'd been having a bad day. He was perfectly prepared to accept a warning, had accepted a warning, in fact, from Ford. He thought that would be the end of it. But no, he had to go and put his stupid fucking foot in his mouth and admit to swearing. Shit. Now he'd been fired. God damn it. How did that happen?

He walked back to his desk in a daze and sat down quietly. All the others were on calls, so he just logged off without saying a word to anyone. Jolene looked around and shrugged questioningly at him. He just shrugged back.

Chip finished his call and turned to Justin. "Is is your break time already?" he asked.

"No."

"Why are you logging off then?"

"I've been fired."

"Fuck off."

"Seriously. I've just been fired. I swore at a caller the other day and they found out. They fucking fired me."

"No fucking way, man. That's unbelievable. That's not a sackable offence. Warning, maybe, but not the sack."

"Seems like it is."

"You're not fucking around, are you?"

"No. I've really been fired."

"What the fuck?" said Jolene, who had just came off her call. "Fired? No."

"Yeah."

"No. That's... not... that's... really?"

"Yeah. Really."

"What did you do?"

"Swore at a caller."

"Is that all? They can't fire you for that."

"They have, Jolene. I'm done."

Ford came bouncing up the stairs from a cigarette break. "What's going on here? Why aren't you lot on the phones?"

"I've been fired," said Justin.

"Fuck off."

"Seriously."

"Why?"

Justin explained the situation to Ford.

"I'll take care of this," Ford said. "Wait here and I'll speak to Phil."

Tanya had finished her call now too and they all sat around on 'Not Ready' waiting for Ford. No one said much, they were all still a little shocked. After ten minutes, Ford came back. "Sorry, mate," he said, "there's nothing I can do. Phil said it's a done deal. And actually, you have to go. You're not allowed to be here anymore. He's letting you say goodbye, but if you're not out in five more minutes, he's going to call security."

"Twat."

"Yeah, mate."

"Okay, I'll go. But can we all meet up in the pub?"

"Tonight?"

"I can't tonight," said Jolene. "I'm really sorry, Justin."

"What about Friday?" suggested Tanya. "That way we can all get really pissed and don't have to worry about work the next day."

"Friday, then," agreed Justin.

"Mate, you better go," said Ford.

Justin nodded and waved goodbye to the Brian Clough team and walked through the doors of the call centre for the last time.

Chapter 22

Justin had been standing outside the pub for the last fifteen minutes, chain smoking. He could see Chip, Jolene, Tanya and Ford sitting inside but they couldn't see him. He didn't know why but he was nervous about seeing them, even though it had only been two days. He was a little embarrassed and was hesitant to go in. He knew he'd have to soon, because it was only a matter of time before someone came out for a smoke and caught him standing there.

He finally decided it was time. He took a deep breath and opened the door. As he made his way to the table, Chip caught sight of him and stood up. He said something to the others and they all stood up too.

"For he's a jolly good fellow, for he's a jolly good fellow, for he's a jolly good fellow and so say all of us," he chanted. Everyone cheered and burst into a round of applause. Justin felt incredibly moved but also kind of wanted the ground to swallow him up.

"Thanks. There was no need for that, though," he said as he sat down.

"There was every need for that," said Chip.

"Well, thanks."

"How have you been the last couple of days?" asked Tanya.

"I've been okay. Not really too sure what to do with myself. I still can't believe what happened."

"None of us can," said Tanya.

"Well mate, at least you got fired and weren't tempted to quit in a blaze of glory first. You know you can't claim benefits for at least three months if you quit a job of your own accord," said Ford.

"I tried to quit but Donna from HR got in first and fired me."

"Donna fired you? Phil never told me that. He just told me your contract had been terminated. Donna, eh? Can she do that?"

"Apparently."

"Naughty girl."

"She's a real bitch. I bet she's kicked a few cats in her time."

Jolene smiled at him and put her hand on his arm. She didn't say anything but she didn't have to.

"Good thing you arrived when you did, mate. We're all starving. I'm on my second pint already and I need to get something in me. I'm here for the long haul," said Ford.

"We all are," said Chip.

"We're definitely going to need some food, then," said Jolene.

"I'm buying," said Ford.

"What? For all of us?" asked Tanya.

"It's the least I can do. One of my team lost his job and we're giving him a send-off tonight, so yes, I'm buying for all of us. Except Alex. Let's get it ordered before he arrives and starts fucking going on about ethical food and farm sourcing and shit like that."

They ordered food and made some small talk for a while. Justin was happy to sit and listen, contributing a little occasionally. He wanted to talk more about what happened to him but thought it was better to wait until he'd had a few drinks. They talked about the weather, football, buckets and why door frames are the size they are. It was fun but Justin felt like some of the lustre had gone from the banter already. He was an outsider already. Fucking Ford was more part of the group than he was. He was glad when the food arrived as he was able to focus on that. Then, as people who work together invariably do, they started talking about work.

"So, Tanya, did you apply for the team leader job?" asked Ford. "I told Phil you'd be perfect for it."

"He didn't think I'd be perfect for it a few weeks ago, did he? Nothing's changed since then. So, no, I didn't actually go for it this time. I spoke to Jeff about it and it turns out that not only was he a team leader but he was also the union rep."

"We have a union?"

"Yeah, but Jeff didn't give a shit about it. He never tried to get people signed up or anything. He just did it for the pay rise. I'm going to be taking over and encouraging everyone to join up. That way we can have our rights protected. We should be getting overtime when the calls run past finishing time, for example. Do we? Do we fuck, but that's going to change when I take over. I've got lots more ideas too."

"Could've done with that when I was on the phones but that's great. Didn't you have to apply for that though?"

"No one else wanted it. I don't think they knew about the pay rise."

"What about you, Chip and Jolene? Did you apply for team leader?"

"Not me," said Jolene.

"I did," said Chip, "but let's not talk about work. This is Justin's night."

They were just finishing their food when Alex walked in and looked around. He saw them and walked over to the table. "You ordered food?" he asked. "I haven't eaten."

"You can order your own, mate," said Ford. "Just be aware that they're all out of pistachio tacos and the only chicken they have wasn't raised free-roaming in a field of rye. I already asked. Gutted."

"What about the beef?"

"I didn't ask about that."

"Well, it's probably unethical. I'll just have a packet of crisps or something. I'll grab something better later on." He turned to Justin. "What happened?"

"Well, I got fired."

"I heard. I called in to let Ford know my doctor's line was extended by two weeks and he told me. It was him that told me to come out here tonight. Fuck. I'm sorry."

"Thanks Alex, but it is what it is."

"Lex."

"What?"

"It's Lex. Anyway, I'll miss you."

"Thanks."

"Give me a hug."

"What?"

"Give me a hug."

"Okay then."

Alex pulled Justin into a big hug. He wrapped his arms fully round him and held tight for longer than Justin thought was socially acceptable. Justin held his arms out and patted Alex twice on the back, as was the standard for men, but Alex kept holding. He made a little sighing or humming sound. He then started rubbing Justin's back. That was enough of that! Justin broke the hug. "I'm just going to go to the bar," he said. "What does everyone want?"

"You don't have to buy the drinks tonight," said Chip. "I mean, you don't have a job, after all."

"Funny. I want to. I've only been unemployed for two days. I'm okay for money."

"I'll help you carry the drinks," said Jolene.

Justin took everyone's drink order and walked to the bar with Jolene. He ordered and waited for the drinks to be prepared.

"So, I guess you're leaving, then," said Jolene.

"I guess I am."

"It's what you wanted."

"Not like this. I wanted to save a bit more money, leave on my own terms, you know."

"Yeah, but who knows how long that would have taken. Now, you have to go and do something else. You're free."

"Yeah, and actually, you know, by the time I get my last pay check, plus holidays and savings, I actually have quite a bit more than I thought."

"What are you going to do with it?"

"You know I've always wanted to travel. We've talked about it a lot and now it might finally be time to do it."

"Do it."

"Yeah."

"So, it's been different without you at work these last couple of days."

"I've been off before."

"Yeah, but it didn't feel like you were just taking time off. There was an atmosphere. It just feels so different already. Tanya is going to be the union rep and Chip might be team leader for another team. It feels like the team is breaking up. I don't like it. I think I need a change in my life."

"You could come travelling with me."

"Yeah, I guess I could. Where are you thinking of going?"

"I don't know. Southeast Asia, maybe."

"Cool."

"Yeah. I mean, I know that's where everyone goes but it seems amazing."

The drinks arrived and they carried then back to the table. Justin set the drinks down and sat down.

"Fancy a smoke, mate?" asked Ford.

"Sure."

"I'll come too," said Chip.

"No, you stay. I want a quick word with Justin in private."

The two of them walked outside. Ford gave Justin a cigarette and lit it for him. He was still using that ridiculous lighter with the dancer engraved on the side.

"Listen, mate, I'm really sorry about what happened," said Ford.

"Don't be. It happened. I was the one who swore at the caller."

"Yeah, but you were having a bad day. I saw that. It might even have been my fault or at least I made it worse for you, so I'm sorry for that."

"I appreciate that."

"I don't want to make this about me and I know it's too late but you've taught me a lesson. One of my team getting fired on my third day as team leader and it was my fault. I have to change, Justin. I've been treating this thing like it was a joke and acting like

I was still a call agent but I have to face up to my responsibilities a bit more."

"See how that goes."

"Yeah. I know we weren't exactly the best of friends but I really am sorry to see you go."

"Thanks. Mate."

"Shake on that?"

"Sure."

They clasped hands and held firm for a couple of seconds, before nodding to each other, putting out their cigarettes and going back into the bar without saying another word. They had only just sat down again when Nicola walked in. She looked around the pub until she spotted them, waved and walked over.

"Hi guys," she said. "Listen, I can only stay for one drink, then I have to go, but I had to come and see you, Justin."

"Thanks, Nicola."

"I can't believe it. Chip called me yesterday and told me what happened. What the fuck is wrong with them? They're losing a great worker over something so small. Talk about making a mountain out of a molehill."

"Heh. I don't know about great worker but I did think it was a bit harsh. I could have just taken a warning or something. I'm not the only one who's ever sworn at a caller and most of them are still there. Some of them are even team leaders."

"Yeah, it's ridiculous. Can't you go to a tribunal or something?"

"I wouldn't have a leg to stand on, to be honest. It's fine. I hated the job anyway."

"We all hate it, Justin, but we have to pay the bills."

"Yeah, I suppose so."

"I just can't believe I'll be going back on Monday and you and Chip won't be talking about the price of fish in Honolulu or what if hedgehogs could actually run as fast as Sonic or some nonsense like that. The place just won't be the same without you."

"Thanks, Nicola. I appreciate it."

"What will you do now?"

"I don't know. Maybe go travelling or something."

"You've been talking about that for years. Good idea. Go and do that. I wish I could go travelling but with Rob and the mortgage and the cars and everything, I can only afford two weeks in Spain and I'm just back from that."

"Spain's nice."

"It is, but I'd like to see a bit more of the world. Do it, Justin. You'll regret it if you don't."

"Yeah."

Ford was struggling to carry all the drinks he'd bought back to the table, so Justin went to give him a hand. He took his beer and sat beside Chip.

"Thanks for organising this," said Justin.

"Well, it was your idea. I just got in touch with Nicola and Ford told Alex, so it wasn't much."

"Thanks anyway. It sort of feels like it's a leaving do."

"It sort of is."

"Yeah, I suppose it is."

"Have you decided what to do yet?"

"Well, I'm probably going to go travelling. I've been talking about it with people and it seems like I'm finally going to do it. Feels strange, I've been talking about it and thinking about it for years but now that it's a proper option, I'm shitting myself."

"That's normal. It's fear of the unknown and all that."

"Yeah, but still. You've been to Thailand, right? Do you want to come over to my place on Sunday? There's a few things I want to run by you."

"It was a two-week package holiday in Phuket. I'm not exactly a globe-trotting vagabond who goes where the wind blows him."

"It's more than I've done. Come over and we'll order in pizza."

"Sure, sounds good."

"I'll crack open that bottle of single malt at last."

"Do you even know what single malt is?"

"No, but it sounds good. Do you?"

"No, but maybe it's not such a good idea on a Sunday."

"Just a glass or two."

"Okay then. I'm going to miss you, man. I know we'll still see each other when you get back from travelling or whatever but that call centre is going to be a lot duller from now on."

"It was always dull. We just made some fun out of it, that's all."

"We did. So, what about Jolene?"

"What about her?"

"Nothing more happened after last week?"

"We didn't even talk about it."

"Are you going to say anything now? I mean, you don't work together anymore, so maybe something can happen now? Well, maybe not if you're going travelling."

"I don't know. I spoke to her a bit earlier and I said she could come with me. We'll see. I haven't committed to anything yet. I'll talk to her later. Maybe let her have a bit more to drink. She's supposed to be on a detox but that doesn't seem to be going too well. We'll see. She was drunk last week when we kissed, so maybe she needs to be drunk again."

"Don't talk like that."

"I'm serious, though. I just don't know if we've already had our moment or if we've missed it or what."

"I hope not."

"Me too. Don't miss yours. You know what I'm talking about."

#

Chip had lost count of how many drinks he'd had. They just kept coming. Even Alex was getting his round in without having to be told. It felt like they were sending Justin off in the right way. Nicola had stayed for a lot more than the one drink she said she'd have and only left ten minutes ago at eleven o'clock when her husband Rob arrived in the pub looking furious and practically carried her out of the place.

He looked over at Tanya. He could do this. He'd definitely had enough to drink to build up his courage. And if things went wrong, he could always blame the booze and say he didn't remember much.

"Tanya," he said.

"Yes, Chip?"

"Listen, I know this might be a bit out of the blue, but I was just wondering if you would...?"

"If I would...?"

"If you would, er..."

"Yes, Chip, I would."

"You would?"

"Sure, I mean, you're a bit short but why not? Tomorrow night?"

"Yes! I mean, yeah, tomorrow works for me."

"I think you should tell me your real name though. If we're going on a date, I should know that, at least."

"Fair enough. It's Graham."

"Just like that? I thought I'd have to prise it out of you."

"A couple of weeks ago, you would have. And it doesn't go any further than us, okay? But you're right, if we're going to go out, you should know."

"Why don't you want people to know? There's nothing wrong with Graham."

"Really? You don't think of Golden Grahams? The cereal?"

"Does anyone still eat those? God, you really are a retro guy. Anyway, you'd prefer to be named after deep fried potatoes?"

"How do you know about that? Weren't you off the day I told everyone about that?"

"Jolene told me."

"Ah. Well, let's just stick to Chip."

"Really?"

"Don't you like Chip?"

"It's okay for a dog, I suppose."

"A dog?"

"Yeah."

"That's not a good name for a dog. I know a dog called Sergeant Shinynose."

"I know one called Paw McCartney."

"Shit. I can't beat that."

"You don't have to. You don't have to try too hard. You're all right the way you are."

#

"Elephant."

"Tiger."

"Rabbit."

"Turtle."

"Lemur."

"No, Ford. Turtle ends with e, not l," said Alex. "You need to think of an animal that starts with the last letter of the animal before."

"I know how to play the game, Alex. I fucking invented it. I've just had a few drinks is all. Couldn't think fast enough."

"You just wanted to say lemur, didn't you?"

"No, Chip, I'm not obsessed with lemurs. I only like them a little bit. Right, what's next? Items of clothing?"

"Actually, they're just about to call last orders," said Justin. "What does everyone want?"

"I'll get this one in," said Ford. "My last gift to you, Justin. Shots all round?"

"I'll take a pint, actually."

"Pints and shots then."

Ford and Chip went to the bar and Tanya to the bathroom, leaving Justin with Jolene and Alex. He really wished Alex had gone to the bar too but Alex and bars didn't meet very often. He looked at Jolene. She was stunning despite that glazed over look in her eyes. They were both pretty wasted by now and Justin had been trying to get her on her own for the last two hours but every time he tried to take her aside, someone would buy him another leaving drink. What might happen when they were finally alone? There were no restrictions now, they didn't work together anymore.

The boys could barely carry the drinks back to the table, in spite of the tray that Ford had procured. It only held the shots, while Chip was delicately balancing four pints, stacked two by two. He also had a glass of vodka in the front pocket of his shirt.

Luckily he had a low centre of balance and was able to manage just fine.

"To Justin," said Chip when everyone had their shots.

"To Justin," said everyone else.

"It's been said already tonight by everyone but I just want to say one more time that the place won't be the same without you. I can't believe you're not there anymore. I'm going to miss you so much. After all, you're my wonderwall."

Everyone broke out in song at this. Justin felt his face flush. It was funny, he had hated his job and couldn't wait to leave. Now that he couldn't go back, all he wanted was to go to work on Monday and give callers the best technical support for their mobile phones that anyone had ever given.

"You all right there, mate?" asked Ford.

"Yeah."

"You sure? Looks like you have a tear in your eye."

"No, no. It's just a bit of dust or something."

"Sure. Here, get that down your neck." He passed Justin a hip flask. Justin opened it and took a swig. It was some aniseed and cinnamon concoction. It felt like his entire body was set on fire but he liked it. He took another swig, then joined in the singing.

The bar called last orders and everyone finished up their drinks and continued singing outside the pub. They had worked their way through most of the standard repertoire of drunken songs: Delilah, Livin' On A Prayer, Come On Eileen, 500 Miles, Bohemian Rhapsody and were now finishing up Hey Jude while having a group hug.

"Right, that's me," Ford announced. "I'm starving, I'm going for something to eat."

"I'll come too," said Alex. "I didn't have dinner. I need to eat before the last of that alcohol hits my blood or my chi is done for."

"I'm going for a kebab."

"Sounds good."

"Mate, it's not ethically sourced. It's a fucking kebab. No one really knows how it's sourced, or from which animal."

"I don't care. I could eat a fucking lemur, I'm so hungry."

"All right, then. Let's go. Justin, all the best. I'm sure I'll hear from Chip how you're getting on. Maybe we'll see each other some time." He shook Justin's hand and left with Alex.

"I'm going to go too," said Chip. "I'll see you on Sunday, though."

"Yeah. See you then."

"I'm off too," said Tanya. She gave Justin a big hug and a kiss on the cheek, then took Chip's hand and the two of them left together.

Justin turned and looked at Jolene. She was standing with her shoulders and arms squeezed tight to her body, even though it wasn't a cold night. She looked beautiful and drunk. Justin smiled at her and she smiled back.

"So..." he said.

"So."

They kissed. Justin pulled back and looked in Jolene's eyes then kissed her again. It felt like goodbye.

Epilogue

Two Months Later

It had been more than two months since she'd been back and Linda
was looking forward to visiting her old colleagues in the call
centre. She had meant to call in before but never got around to it.
She hadn't been so good with keeping in touch with people either.
Still, it was the same from them too. Everyone says they'll stay in
touch but they never do.

She still had her old pass card and even though she knew it
had been deactivated, she touched it against the panel anyway. It
didn't work. She had to buzz through to reception. The security
guard recognised her voice and let her in straight away. The stairs
leading up to the call floor were still the same as always. She
wasn't sure what she had been expecting but nothing had changed
at all. The call board was still on the wall, along with the same
faded posters that were always there. Rows of people were sitting
with headsets dealing with calls. Still, there was that buzz that she
missed. That feeling that life was going on around her.

She looked over to her old team section. Jim Jefferson, or
Ford, was still there. This was both a surprise and not. He had a
headset on, so must be taking an escalated call. She couldn't hear
him from here. Poor Jim. She wondered where his avoidance
streak had been before he had to take that one. Chip was also there
and taking calls, along with Alex and Nicola, both back at work
since she'd left. There were two new people there too. There was

no sign of Tanya, Jolene or Justin. She hoped that they weren't on their lunch break. She wouldn't want to miss them.

As she walked towards the Brian Clough team section, she waved at a few agents she knew. When she got there, Nicola gave her a wave and a big smile and motioned for her to wait until she finished her call. Ford also smiled at her and asked her to wait. She sat down at an empty spot. Ford was the first to finish.

"Sorry about that, Linda. Escalated call. I'm taking quite a few of them these days."

"You're taking them? You don't try to fob them off?"

"Sometimes, when it sounds like something silly, but most of the time I take them. Why?"

"No reason. Anyway, it's good to see you. I had a day off so I thought I'd pop in and catch up with everyone."

"That's nice of you. How's the new job treating you?"

"Oh, it's wonderful, thanks. I still miss this place, though."

"No, you fucking don't."

"I do. A little bit, anyway."

"It's the same as always. Staff come and go. Callers have the same problems. You know."

Alex and Nicola both finished their calls at roughly the same time and turned round to greet Linda.

"Listen, guys. As you can see, Linda has popped in to see us. I'll let you all take your break early today if you want to have a quick chat. Take twenty minutes instead of fifteen. I'll swing it with management," said Ford.

They all huddled around and asked Linda about her new job. She told them all about it and they seemed genuinely happy for her. Chip appeared to be listening to both her and a caller he couldn't get rid of. After five minutes, Ford went to the office to alter the break schedule. "Nice to see you again, Linda," he said. "All the best."

"What's going on with him?" she asked as he walked away. "He seems to have stepped up."

"Yeah, he has," said Nicola. "He's really taking things a lot more seriously. He's taking responsibility and is doing a pretty good job actually. Doesn't seem to be drinking as much either."

"He's still full of shit though!" said Jolene, who had just returned from the break room with coffee.

"Jolene, there you are. I didn't see you or Justin or Tanya when I came in. I was worried about missing you."

"Yeah, things have changed a bit already since you left. You didn't hear about Justin?"

"No. What about him?"

"He got fired for swearing at a caller."

"Really? Justin did that? I know he didn't like the job but I didn't think he'd do that."

"I think he just had a bad day."

"When was that?"

"Like, three days after you left."

"Really? Have you heard from him? What's he doing?"

"He's travelling," said Chip, who had finally managed to finish his call. "I heard from him last week. He's in Thailand."

"Nice. Haven't you heard from him, Jolene? I thought you two were... well, I don't know what, but don't you two keep in touch?"

"Yeah, we've exchanged a couple of emails."

"That's not all that's changed though," said Alex. "Tanya's not in the team any more. She took over as the union rep."

"Good for her," said Linda. "She should have had the team leader job."

"She should," said Chip. "Another one came up but she went for the union job instead."

"Another one? Who left?"

"That guy from Derby with the French name. I can't remember it. Voldemort or something."

"Voldemort? You mean Moreau? Jeff?"

"Yeah, that guy."

"You went for his job, Chip. Don't you remember his name?" asked Nicola.

"I didn't get it, so I don't care about his name."

"Who got it?" asked Linda.

"Kerry," replied Alex.

"Fair enough, she's good. So are you, Chip, don't get me

wrong."

"That's okay. It was good to apply and do the interview. It was good experience and it's made me sort of think that it's time to start thinking about progressing in life."

"You're progressing with Tanya!" said Jolene.

"Really?" asked Linda. "You and Tanya? That's... interesting."

"Yeah, well, we've been seeing a bit of each other outside of work, yeah."

"That's great, Chip. I'm happy for you. Where is she, by the way?"

"She has a new office downstairs."

"Okay. I might call in and see her on my way out." She knew she wouldn't. "It really is all change."

"There's more too," said Jolene. "I handed in my notice a couple of weeks ago. I'm leaving."

"Where are you going?" asked Linda.

"I don't know."

"You don't have another job lined up?"

"No, I'm just going to see what happens. I realised I needed a change and with all the changes happening round here, it seemed like a good time to do it, so I did."

"Will you go travelling with Justin?"

"I don't know. He said I could, of course, but I'm not sure what I want to do. Travelling is his thing. I'm not sure what mine is yet, but I want to try different things, places, jobs, people, you know. Until I find the one that fits. Then I'm going to keep doing that."

Linda spent another few minutes chatting before it was time for the team to go back on the phones. It had been really nice to come back and catch up with everyone. So much had changed already and so much was the same as always. Yes, it was nice to catch up. She probably wouldn't be back there again.

#

Justin held the straw to his lips and took a big sip from the coconut. He had always thought that coconuts were brown, he hadn't known they were actually green before he came here. There was a lot he hadn't known before he came here. Three years of university and three in a call centre didn't exactly prepare you for the real world. He'd been as green as the coconut when he arrived, and yes, he'd been ripped off, and yes, he'd been mugged, and okay, there was that thing with the rice wine and the public nudity, but he'd learned. A month on the road and he was wiser and more worldly already.

He looked out across the sea. It was exactly what he'd dreamed about. Blue and warm and beautiful. The beach was lined with palm trees and he had a little hut right on the waterfront. It was paradise and yet there was something missing.

Hindsight was an absolute fucker. When he worked in the call centre, he was convinced he hated every minute of it. Now that he was gone, it didn't seem so bad. He got paid to talk shit with his friends after all. He missed Chip and Jolene. He wondered what they were doing now. Probably sleeping, what with the time difference and all. He'd see them again for sure when he got back, whenever that might be. He had emailed them both a few times but hadn't checked his email for over a week now, so who knew what they were up to?

After he left the call centre, he hung around for a couple of weeks to see out the month's rent he'd paid on his flat and to see if anything more would happen with Jolene. They had texted each other about meeting up for a drink. It seemed that they just kept missing each other and were never both available at the same time. It was like fate was telling him something. At the end of the month, he moved back to his parents' house and booked his flight to Thailand the very next day. One week later, he arrived in Bangkok.

That had been strange and difficult. He hadn't been prepared for the full-on assault to the senses of that city. He went straight to the backpacker ghetto at Khao San Road and spend the first two days adjusting to the climate and the time difference. He spent the next two days drunk after underestimating the strength of 6.4% Thai beer and the two after that hungover. He got a tattoo and fake dreadlocks. Prostitutes of three genders offered to let him do whatever he wanted to them, and for a very reasonable price. He took the dreadlocks out again. On day seven, he got high with some Aussie lads, then drunk, then high again. An old German man with an impressive moustache told him he wanted to suck the shit out of his arse. It had been quite the experience but after a week in the city, he decided to try the islands.

After finding similar places to Khao San Road all over the islands, he'd considered moving to another country. Thailand was nice and all but he didn't really feel like he'd gone halfway around the world. There were so many Brits here that it felt like he'd just found a place in England with better weather.

He lucked out when he found this final island. It had been his last roll of the dice in Thailand but he'd found it and it was wonderful. There were a few other tourists around his beach but for the most part it was peaceful and the nearest town was half an hour's walk away. He rented a motorbike on the first day to get into town and explore the nearby waterfall but he fell off and ripped his leg open, so decided that walking was a better option. It made getting booze back to the hut a little tricky but it was worth the effort. Besides, there were several little bars and restaurants along the beach where he liked to sit and have a beer or a coconut shake in the afternoon.

He finished his drink and went for a swim in the warm water, then went back to his cabin and took a shower and a short nap. After waking up, he decided it was time for a drink. On his way past the reception area, he saw a girl at the desk with her back to him. That was one huge backpack she had with her. Maybe it was her first time travelling too? Justin had been ridiculed by a Canadian vagabond on Koh Samui for the size of his backpack. Apparently all novices brought way too much on their first trip.

Justin stood and looked her up and down. Her legs looked fantastic in a pair of shorts that covered enough to keep the locals happy and showed enough to get Justin excited. She ran her hand through her long hair and shook her head. That was hot. She picked a key up off the desk and struggled to pick up her backpack. Should he do something?

Suddenly she turned and looked straight at him. Her eyes

sparkled in the sun. They held each others' gaze for what felt like quite a while, before she smiled brightly.

"Hi," she said.

"Hi."

"Sorry to bother you, but do you have a minute?"

"Er, yeah. Sure." Justin gulped. "How can I help?"

#